The Enigmatic Girl

Agnes Moya

Contents

Chapter 1

Today in the corridor, he disregarded me. Again.

It shouldn't have stung as much as it did, but as I turned to look at all the engaged seniors making plans to enrol in college together after the current academic year is finished, kissing, embracing, and engaging in PDA everywhere, I realised that I wanted that, too.

That was mine, but not here. Never at school, never in public.

He would pull me to his side and caress the skin of my arms while I vented about the things my foster parents had done that day and he shared his football worries with me in the comforting silence of his bedroom as the steam from our bodies began to cool.

In spite of the fact that we weren't dating, we were quite explicit about the fact that we weren't seeing anyone else during the two months that I spent every night of the week with him.

Why then, after clearly ignoring me, would he have his arm carelessly on Leah Maren's shoulder in the hallway?

"Hello? "Earth to Cami" Is anyone present?

My best friend's hand waved abruptly back and forth between herself and my eyes, and I winced.

I'm sorry, Mo. I was merely sidetracked. What exactly said you?

"I questioned you about the optional field trip to the museum. You promised to let me know on Friday if David or Nina signed the document, but you never did.

My best friend mentioned my foster parents, and I cringed when I heard their names because I hadn't told her how horrible things had gotten at "home."

I told her with pride, jutting my chin and plastering a smile on my face that I really tried not to let slip as the person I couldn't take my eyes off of took his arm off Leah's shoulder and instead started pretend-wrestling with his best friend.

Mo's dark, charcoal-lined eyes twitched and wrinkled at the edges, almost as if she didn't believe me, but when her crush started strolling towards us in step with the rest of their friend group, her uncertainty vanished in a cloud of male testosterone and Axe Body Spray.

My lungs' air suddenly became frozen, and the oxygen became covered in ice crystals, preventing me from taking even a single breath to keep my brain functioning normally.

I could see Colton, my Colton, looking at me.

I will say it again: THIS IS NOT A DRILL!

Colton walked down the hallways of Hartingrove Academy as if he owned the entire place, and I hardly had time to notice the cacophony of students blathering on with gossip or even pretend that I was busy with something at my natural mahogany wood locker (because of course the fancy rich prep school had to have wooden lockers).

He was almost in charge of the entire campus since the son of the dean, who was also his best friend and the reigning home-coming king (as well as the captain of the football team, where he played quarterback, and the shoo-in for prom king).

Although it was technically incorrect to give preferential treatment based on friendship with the dean's son, nepotism was evidently still prevalent despite their denial.

Why is Colton Wright looking at you, Cam?

I had absolutely no idea.

At school, he often pursued his own path, and I did the same.

We never discussed it when the dim light from the orange streetlamps peaked through his dark grey window treatments.

We chatted about his football games, his resentment of teammates and coaches, the stress he was under due to his ACL injury, which kept him in the ice bath for longer than required, and briefly about my foster home and how I wanted I could just go away.

However, as the talk started to drift towards the sinister, I always changed the subject to something amusing, odd, or even sexual. Anything to avoid discussing the situation at home.

He served as both my diversion and my refuge.

What we had was also good.

Even though we avoided each other at school and in public and I wasn't in love with him, I couldn't pretend to myself that I wouldn't desire anything similar for myself.

particularly with him.

His lovely brown eyes were framed by brows of chestnut brown hair that swept over his forehead in a sweeping cut.

Colton Wright always appeared perfectly put together and yet effortless at the same time, as if he had just stumbled out of bed. However, after waking up with him numerous mornings, I realised that there had been a lot of thought put into that artistic sweep of hair and his choice of clothing.

Colton represented every student athlete at Hartingrove. He was dressed in grey sweatpants, trendy sneakers, a game-day t-shirt with a matching sweatshirt thrown over top, and game-day sneakers.

On game days, the football players were permitted to "dress out," but the rest of us had to wear the traditional white button-up, black pleated skirt or slacks, black tie, and black blazer.

I cautiously ran my fingers through the dark strands of my hair and regretted not accepting Colton's invitation to have a shower with him this morning rather than using the rest of my dry shampoo.

I had little choice in the matter; my hair was never glossy and silky, but rather a cheap imitation from items from the dollar store that did more harm than good.

I was forced to steal Colton's high-end hair products in the shower when he wasn't looking because I didn't have a car, a job, or a foster family that wanted me. Sadly, this didn't happen very often because even after two months of essentially living together, Colton still used every possible method to see me naked.

However, not a single time over those two months had he looked me in the eye in public without turning away.

"Scholarship pussy,"

As the "golden boys" slid past the two females who were rendered speechless in the middle of the hallway by Carter Jennings, I shivered out of my daydream.

You probably already know the two girls he was referring about.

Mori Catawnee, better known as Mo, was the first Native American student at Hartingrove as part of the school's 'inclusivity and diversity' initiatives, which essentially meant that the institution needed a certain number of students from a particular national or cultural group.

Me? I spoke for the population of vulnerable foster children. There were several options, but my academic performance was what made the choice.

In other words, there weren't enough low-income students going and the school was simply too white.

My objective was to graduate from high school, which I thought of as "hell," with a 4.0 GPA and a scholarship to another prominent university that would cover my tuition, room and board, as well as other costs, leaving me with only extras to pay. I could endure just about anything if I had a place to live and food to eat.

I at least got this far with a lot less.

Yes, we could be considered "scholarship pussies," but Carter Jennings was never going to know that.

I turned to look at Colton to see how he was reacting, but all he did was smack his friend on the shoulder and continue walking while laughing loudly, which he usually saved for our private tickle fights or when I was acting particularly strange to him one night.

Not when he openly made fun of my best buddy and I in front of the rest of the students.

Other than Colton's best friend, Parker Hartingrove (yes, the school was named after his ancestors), who had his eyes trained on the scene his friends were making with something resembling disgust in his dark brown eyes, his other friends paid us no mind. Parker was the dean's son and an all-around perfect golden student who was apparently the only one standing in my way of earning that coveted valedictorian spot.

The boys had every sport covered, with the exception of perhaps the group's swoon-worthy bad boy. The lads included football gods, the basketball team captain, the school's leading pitcher in baseball, and a lone lacrosse star.

No, he was the "outcast"; there was nothing alluring about a silent, alcoholic bad kid who routinely vandalised school property yet was nonetheless allowed to remain a student.

Why? Considering that he belonged to the elite group of "privileged." Grey Hartingrove was the brother of Parker Hartingrove, and everyone I knew avoided him, including myself.

But they were all evil—each in their own way—and the group probably didn't even need a "bad boy" for their ranks.

Colton Wright, Carter Jennings, Alec Reed, Nate Covington, and Parker Hartingrove pushed stragglers up against their lockers to make room for them as I turned my hot, humiliated face away from the males who took up much too much space in the corridor.

Just as Colton passed me, Leah Maren unexpectedly caught up with them and put her arms around his shoulders from behind.

She murmured something to him inaudibly that caused me to deflate like an ill-fated balloon as I turned and met his eyes once more.

Guess who received the supply closet key?

I pulled my belongings out of my locker, slammed it shut, and shoulder checked the boy who was meant to have saved me from my destroyed existence. My face was a flawless blank mask at this point.

Now? I was completely unsure about my next move. Although he wasn't technically cheating on me, I needed to have more self-respect than to allow him to manipulate my thoughts.

When Mo caught up to me, she had a startled and half-frightened expression on her face. I managed to suppress my discomfort for long enough for her to think I was fine when I was anything but.

"What was that all about?"

Why is that? It annoys me so much when those asses believe they can block the corridors.

Aside from the occasions my foster family had me return because they anticipated a social services house visit, Mori was unaware of my relationship with Colton and the fact that I was essentially homeless.

It seemed like the house visits were blood in the sea and they were sharks. How well they could plan for such visits and present the ideal front of a caring foster family alarmed me.

I didn't want to see the pity in Mo's eyes when she realised that I wasn't as happy as she thought I was. Even though her family couldn't take me in because they didn't have space, I occasionally prayed that Mo would see through the façade and understand that I wasn't okay and that I was staying with a boy who made fun of me in public so that I would have a safe place to sleep at night.

Prior to our class excursion to the National Museum for the Arts, homeroom was the last class we would be attending, and I was going to switch off my phone when Colton texted me.

Colton: It wasn't as it appeared. Before the trip, we're all gathering in the supply closet to get buzzed.

Cami: I assumed you wouldn't give a fig about what I thought. I'm just a pussy for a scholarship, right?

Before he could respond, I turned off my phone, stifled the nausea that was about to explode from my stomach, and linked arms with Mo before going into homeroom. I avoided making eye contact with the other students who would be going on the class trip.

In contrast to the rest of his buddies who, if Colton was to be believed, were probably getting smashed in the supply closet, Parker, the major instigator of his group, was in the spotlight.

Before that brief encounter in the corridor, I would have wondered why Parker wasn't partaking in the fun, but I was suddenly too exhausted to care.

Parker's pale blonde hair was in direct opposition to his angular cheekbones, cold eyes, and slightly darker eyebrows.

The last thing I saw of Colton before he entered the room was the back of his head. Leah was giggling and hanging off Colton's arm.

If I had felt that this class trip wouldn't already do the trick for me, I would have thought, "Kill me now."

Chapter 2

The only thing Colton could fucking speak about was his new bootycall.

The jerk wouldn't stop gushing about her 'beautiful tits,' her hair, or her ass. Sincerably, it was becoming a nuisance.

Since I'd only ever been with one person before in my life, I didn't particularly enjoy the "locker room talk" like the other guys did, and I didn't want to discuss how attractive or desirable she was with anyone, least of all a room full of thirty guys who would drool at her the moment she walked by.

But on the good side, he hadn't revealed her name to us.

I remained curious about the person who had done so, if only to warn her and shield her from Colton, who I knew to be the person.

This would only hurt the girl in the long run because the guy couldn't even keep it in his pants for five seconds, much less long enough to be faithful to anyone.

Unless Leah Maren was involved. She was identical to Colton in all respects but the fact that she lacked a dick between her legs.

How did I find out?

because it was her who had stolen my virginity after homecoming my sophomore year.

She was the first and only female who had ever broken my heart, and what she had done was sufficient to make me never go near a woman again.

At least until I was in my twenties, if not forever.

So she was laying on me, correct, and her tongue was making these fucking perfect circles around the end of my diaphragm.

"Colton! Put a stop to that. How you got your dick wet last night is not something anyone wants to hear.

The senior class could hear every single thing the jerk said on the school bus that was taking us to our field trip to the National Museum of the Arts, so I didn't care that my friend's eyes widened in astonishment at my angry outburst.

Others were doing their damnedest to ignore every word coming out of the dirty asshole's mouth while some were craned their necks to see who was telling the lewd story.

I was firmly in the group of those who were attempting to ignore him, but it was getting increasingly difficult due to the sheer intensity of his voice.

Colton's neighbour Leah spoke up next, saying, "I wanted to hear what happened next."

She trailed her hands over him as if he hadn't just had sex with someone else the previous night, and I tried to hold back my shudder of revulsion.

Multiple sex partners were acceptable, but damn, at least wait until the sweat stops before moving on to the next one.

The funniest (worst?) thing of it all, considering I had been the one to break up with her after she cheated on me after our first (and only) time, was that Leah was trying to make me jealous.

I still have nightmares about her fiery red hair sticking out from under the covers in my brother's bed.

Stop being so pessimistic, Parker. What, you're no longer sex positive?

"Colton, be quiet."

I ignored them all and focused on my phone in their place.

Since Colton was aware of what Leah had done to me and to my brother, who was presently missing the class trip to either go high with his pals or something worse that I didn't want to think about at the time, I was growing increasingly irritated with our friendship.

My thoughts continued to stray until the bus abruptly came to a stop in the parking lot of the art gallery we were touring.

We had to travel to Sacramento, a major metropolis, from our small town in northern coastal California to see a museum like this one. Despite being surrounded by massive structures and concrete, however, I realised how much I missed Redding's solitude and natural surroundings.

I had to keep my eyes on my phone the entire time to avoid Leah trying to catch my eye and ignore Colton's repulsive sexual play-by-plays that only seemed to make Leah more attracted to him (because, sure, why not). This made the two and a half hour drive from our well kept secret from the rest of the country town feel longer than it actually was.

Before I could get off, Nate, Colton, Carter, and Leah pushed their way through everyone sitting in front of us. They all got off before me. Typical. Despite wanting to exit before everyone else, they preferred to sit at the very back.

The two scholarship students, I believe their names were Mori and Camille, gave my friends a stern look and started packing their belongings while I was taking my time to let everyone get off before me.

I couldn't blame them because Carter and Colton were often making jokes about them because they were students there.

This morning, after yelling something equally unsettling at them in the hallways, Carter leaned over to Colton, and I overheard a sample of something racist. I wanted to slam my fist through his face.

He pretended he didn't understand what I was saying when I quickly asked to know what he had said.

I could have ignored it, but I knew there would be consequences if I ever heard him say anything similar again. They would all have been excommunicated if it weren't for Alec, but I couldn't do that to my closest buddy. I was barely hanging on with this gang. He required my help, and leaving his friends would also mean leaving him.

I only needed one more justification, and I would be free. Alec would eventually forgive me if he understood that I didn't want to compromise my morals for him, but I had my doubts about that. I doubt he would accept my apology, but I wouldn't give up on him.

Perhaps we could form our own clique so that he wouldn't have to rely on these other jerks to make him happy at school.

"Are you going to leave, um?"

I managed to get myself out of my thoughts long enough to notice that I had been blocking one of the scholarship girls' route.

Her long, dark brown lashes framed her olive-colored face, and her dark brown hair was naturally curled around it. Her deep-brown eyes caused my chest to thud in reaction.

She appeared to be wearing a size too small uniform that was closely fitted to her body because she didn't have an additional to wear. It seemed more likely that she couldn't afford one because our uniforms were prohibitively expensive and weren't covered by the scholarship.

I made a mental note to speak with my father and request that the uniform expenses be added to the scholarship packages for forward. When they outgrew their old outfit, not everyone had the extra $100 every other season.

Sorry, you may proceed.

She gave me a sceptical look as I put a composed grin on my face, as if she believed that my politeness was a trap.

My stomach churned with guilt at the fact that she spent so much time with jerks like Colton and Carter at the school that my dad ran. I felt compelled to speak up and set the record straight.

"You're Camille, am I right?"

I could hardly breathe when she inserted the bottom half of a pink pouty lip into her lips as those dark eyes flickered back up to meet mine.

"Yeah. Why?"

She appeared to be scared of someone finding out who she was because there was a flash of anxiety on her face. That wasn't right, no. Why would she be afraid if I called her by name?

The question "And you're Mori?"

With her wide, doe-like dark brown eyes, the girl standing behind Camille nodded without saying a word. She looked at me intently, her eyes flitting between me and Camille as if attempting to answer a challenging maths problem.

Welcome to you both. Even though I am aware that we had attended school together the entire semester, I never truly introduced myself. Parker Hartingrove here.

When I introduced myself, Camille made a noise like to a snort and her big lips twitched in an amusing manner to the side.

Oh, we recognise you. Greetings to you as well.

She wasn't quite impolite, but neither was her voice. Given the company I maintained, I figured I deserved that. She presumably thought I was the same as them.

From behind Camille, Mori squeaked, "Yeah, great to meet you. When Camille didn't break my gaze and her almost too huge for her face eyes issued a challenge, it was clear who was the more assertive of the two.

Her brown eyes turned a gorgeous shade of amber as the sun slanting over the top of the bus in an arcing spear. My chest breathed a little shakily. She was near to me, so close that I could have reached out and curled a strand of her jet-black cheek-framing hair.

Her adorable tiny button nose, the arched tips of her cheekbones, and the faultless expanse of silky skin were all highlighted by the light, which was also bathing her in the bronze hue of the early afternoon sun.

I only realised that I had been gazing at Camille for much too long once Mori cleared her throat behind us. How much time had passed?

If what I saw from the window of my 'friends' loitering and playing around was to be believed, they were waiting for me outside the bus.

I moved to the side, not in front of them, saying "Sorry, I'll just move out of your way."

I had to make a tiny room for Camille to exit her bus seat, and then she was abruptly wedged between me and the stale, worn-out leather seats, which had to rub against mine.

Her little frame reached as low as my lower chest, and as she walked by, she cocked her head back and craned her neck to look directly into my eyes.

"I don't know what you're attempting, but don't come near us. None of you should cause us any trouble.

Mori's head whipped back to me as if she were ready to say something, but Camille was a lady on a mission, and suddenly they were gone, leaving me standing alone on the bus and appearing to be a complete moron. She had pulled her friend's hand, and then she disappeared down the rows.

She would naturally want to avoid me.

Even if I had been interested in her, the fact that I had been friends with her bullies—not to mention the fact that I didn't do relationships, girlfriends, or anything romantic at all—was enough to turn her off of me permanently.

But the moment I saw her sweet face and innocent eyes again, I began to doubt that way of thinking for the first time in almost two years.

Chapter 3

S crew boys.

Screw them and their beautiful faces.

Their sculpted bodies, staggering height, drool-inducing cologne smell, swirling pools of icy blue eyes...

No!

Screw them and their infuriating asshole friends.

Screw them and their need to call me and my best friend 'scholarship pussy' just because we weren't rich.

Screw them and their need to be racist assholes to the only friend that I'd made at the cesspool that was Hartingrove Academy.

And most importantly--SCREW Parker Hartingrove and his annoying way to make my heart skip in my chest like no other boy has ever been able to do before--not even in bed.

You're just full of surprises, aren't you?

I shoved his voice out of my head.

One past memory with Parker notwithstanding, the boy was a complete stranger.

Ugh.

I was pissed off.

I hated this new school.

I only had one friend, and even that was tenuous at best considering the fact that I'd known her for a total of one-and-a-half-months.

We'd been thrown together the first day of senior year at Hartingrove, and while we each had our own reasons for starting a brand new school for our last year of high school there, we had just clicked instantly.

It helped that the rest of the school kept a wide berth around the both of us, unwilling to make new friends so late in the game.

So it was Cami and Mori against the world.

Or, more accurately, against Carter and sometimes even Colton.

I'd never asked him about it, about how he seemed like a completely different person at home than he did in school.

At his house, he was courteous, polite, quiet, shy, funny, and even sweet sometimes.

At school? He was a typical overgrown playground bully, following every word from Carter's mouth as if he were the one who was the dean's son and not Parker.

It was only early October and even I could discern the social hierarchy structure in the school.

Parker and his little group of athletes and assholes were at the very top, then of course you've got the girls who are always at their side--Leah Maren (the only senior girl in the group), Kennedy Mercer and Victoria Vanderberg, the three of them lighting the halls with their various styles of uniform that somehow didn't get them in trouble for being in violation of the dress code.

They weren't all terrible--Victoria had once helped pick up my books for me when I'd dropped them on the ground in front of everyone, giving me a smile and introducing herself in the process.

She was the sweetest person I think I'd ever met, constantly helping others, tutoring students that needed help, always keeping a smile on her beautiful face and even keeping the rest of them from slinging insults toward me or Mori in her presence.

I couldn't say the same for the other two girls, however.

Leah Maren had stayed out of my way and I stayed out of hers, same with Kennedy who was the unofficial ringleader of the girls, but that didn't mean they liked me.

None of them liked me, in public, anyway.

Which was why I was completely mystified at the fact that not only had Colton actually held eye contact with me today in the halls, but his friend Parker had spoken to me on the bus to the class trip.

Was this his idea of integrating our relationship into the public? If so, he was doing a real shit job at it, especially considering his best friend Carter had insulted us and put us down right in front of him and all his friends.

What I would've given for Victoria to have been there, or at least on the class trip.

Their behavior was always worse when the nice girl of the school wasn't with them.

Which was why, as I grabbed Mori's dark hand in mine and twined our fingers together, I kept us far, far away from the group that had, at least before today, virtually ignored our presence.

The presentation at the museum beckoned us forth, and I silenced my mind as I took in the lecture from the tour guide.

Art from all corners of the world had been displayed in this museum, starting from the earliest found cave paintings in North

America to the modern interpretations portrayed on large can-vasses to abstract statues and sculptures.

There was a giant ball of cotton dribbling red paint that was supposed to be a metaphor for the female struggles women had to endure that men would never experience.

I rolled my eyes as the guys behind us snickered and laughed, asking girls if they could shove a tampon that big inside them.

We ambled back to the beginning, to the first cave paintings, and finally my interest was piqued.

My major in college was already laid out and ready for me when I finally graduated, archaeology with a minor in anthropology.

Art was a part of history, as it was influenced by the experiences and situations of the times, and the art museum, while not one filled with historical artifacts, was almost better at capturing the state of the times.

People created and painted out of creativity and the need to ex-press themselves, to escape and to state their message, whether explicitly or not.

I had been obsessed with history, with ancient humans and their social mannerisms and how they compared to humans today, ever since I was younger.

I didn't know what spurred it on in me, but learning about others was a way to throw myself into work and books, art, and literature and to hide away from the prying eyes of the rest of the world.

It was easier to slink into the stacks in the library than it was to escape my foster family of the month and the leering gazes of the men in those homes.

I would always run away, and I would always get moved.

Until now.

I was determined to stay in this home, as my scholarship and spot in the school was predicated on the location of my home. If I was re-homed again like a stray dog that bites or growls at babies, then I could be put anywhere in the entire state of California, or worse, a group home.

I would always wonder what happened to the children no one wanted in the times of the Neanderthal during Pleistocene Epoch. Were they left outside to freeze to death or be eaten by a stray saber-tooth? Or were they found and put in their own kind of foster care program before they could become some prehistoric animal's snack?

"Now, not many people would immediately think of North Amer-ica when they hear about ancient cave art. The pictures you're seeing here are from the Tennessee Mud Glyph Cave. Does any-one know where the first modern discovery of cave art was made?"

No one spoke up, but I knew the answer. I had been fascinated with the discovery in northern Spain.

"It was in Altamira, in Spain."

My head whipped to Parker, who had been paying closer atten-tion to the lecture than I had realized.

Since when was he interested in ancient cave art?

"That is correct. They first didn't authenticate the site, not be-lieving it to be genuine, but multiple more discoveries proved its validity. The Mud Glyph Caves discovery led to surveys of caves in the southeastern states in the U.S. which..."

I tuned him out until we moved on, the tour guide asking more questions that Parker answered effortlessly.

Parker was top of his class in math, which I struggled the most in, and excelled in science and english, when english and history were my best subjects, somehow he still beat me.

Granted, he had a stable home life and his family was well off, so on the surface, I didn't see any stressors that would keep him from being the top of his class.

Me? I was practically homeless and had to work my ass off for anything I wanted in my life.

My journey to attending a top tier college required that valedictorian spot.

Applications to my big three--Harvard, Princeton, and Yale--had already gone out in the end of the summer, but I still had multiple more to send out.

Columbia, Brown, Stanford, Vanderbilt, Cornell, UCLA, UPenn, and Dartmouth were all strong contenders as well, but I'd spent the most time on Harvard, Princeton and Yale so far.

The SAT's had gone well, at least.

I had taken the test the first time for free courtesy of the school's scholarship program, but the second time I'd had to pay the fee since I hadn't gotten the score I wanted.

1450 wasn't a good enough score to get into the Ivy's, so I'd enrolled in the elective prep classes, stayed after school everyday until they locked up, then took the bus to Colton's house where I'd spend half the night reading and the other half tangled up in the sheets and his arms, only to repeat it all over again the next day and find some time in the day to eat.

I was finally rewarded with a 1490 score after everything I'd done to improve from August when I'd taken the test first to last week when I'd finally achieved a score I wanted.

Math was the subject I'd struggled the most in, but there was no surprise there.

The rest of the tour dragged on and on as we got closer to modern times, and I forced myself to stay awake despite the lack of sleep Colton had allowed me to get the night before.

I could still feel the imprint of his fingers on my skin as the memory of him trailing them slowly and sweetly up and down my arms to wake me up for a middle-of-the-night romp and while our time wasn't unpleasant--quite the opposite--that didn't meant I wanted to be woken up during the short time of sleep I was actually able to get.

"Well, that was dull, wasn't it?"

I couldn't help but laugh at Mori's facial expression.

Despite being in the archaeology club (because I forced her to so we could spend more time together) and on the track team with me (because, extracurriculars = ivy league school crack), Mori still hadn't taken well to my interests, which was completely fine.

I had joined her modern feminists club no questions asked, and though we were two of the club's paltry five members, it was still my favorite club I'd ever been apart of.

"Yeah, towards the end when he wouldn't shut up about the 'transcendent nature of using art to make a sociopolitical state-ment', I felt like I could've typed it in Google and it would be his dissertation in his Intro to Art I class."

We were laughing and following the last stragglers on the large yellow bus when I spotted Colton and his friends already occupy-ing the last row. Of course, they'd raced to the bus as soon as the presentation was over.

I ignored him and his piercing dark eyes while I picked an empty seat in the middle for me and my best friend, when suddenly the entire bus stopped talking.

My head swiveled, but there was no one else there besides Mori.

The guy walking in front of me had thrown his bag down in the floorboard of the seat I was aiming for.

That said guy was Parker Hartingrove, and he was waiting pa-tiently beside the seat, his hand motioning for me to slide in first.

My eyes flicked between him and his friends, who were watching the scene with curiosity and Colton with barely veiled jealousy.

"Um, excuse me?"

I hated that my voice squeaked out weakly, that Parker was making my stomach churn with anxiety and...excitement?

"Sit with me. I'd like to ask you some questions on the history test for tomorrow."

He remembered that we shared that class together?

I turned my head to look at Mori but she was already pushing me with her hands into the seat, hard enough that I stumbled right into Mr. Dreamy Eyed Hartingrove and his suspiciously awaiting hands.

"I'll just sit over here," Mori said sweetly, motioning to an empty seat a few rows up.

I only nodded mutely, because I was pathetically awkward, and noticed that the seat we were taking was the one with our bags marking them.

Had Parker gone to the back, grabbed his own bag where he'd left it, and then brought it here specifically to sit with me?

Why?

I shook off his warm hands off my shoulders where he'd captured me to keep me from falling face first onto the sticky and wet bus floor and got comfortable by the window.

He sat and affixed me with a blindingly optimistic smile that made my stomach churn again, but this time I knew there was no anxiety there, only attraction, and I wanted to punch myself in the face for that as I felt the laser glare of Colton's gaze into the back of my head.

This was sure to make for an interesting bus ride.

Chapter 4

"**S**o did you make it to the Mongols yet and the Golden Horde?"

I hoped she didn't notice the way my voice shook just being this close to her.

I had no idea what prompted me to grab my things and stride to their seat they had been previously sitting in, but I couldn't take another second being around Colton and those assholes.

Alec made things tolerable, usually, but lately had taken to putting his headphones in and ignoring everyone else like the plague, and so that left me suffering while my ex girlfriend flirted with Alec's friend right in front of me.

I would've called Colton a friend, too, but it was more like we were acquaintances. I didn't want to be friends with anyone who treated people the way he did, least of all women.

I felt terrible for anyone being shackled to that asshat. The woman he eventually married was going to be doomed.

The least I could do was spend some time with Camille, who'd looked at me as if I'd grown a second head just to even attempt to sit with her on the bus, though her friend had been all for it.

I couldn't help the magnetic pull that drew me to her.

Yes, I felt terrible that I allowed the guys to say horrible things about her and sometimes her friend, but there wasn't much I could do besides tell them to knock their shit off and remind them they'd beat the hell out of anyone who spoke about their sister or mother that way.

The reprimands only went so far, though, and they usually picked up right where they left off once I was out of earshot, anyway, if their never changing behavior was any clue.

Only for Alec. If it weren't for him...

Camille shifted uncomfortably in her seat, eyes flicking from me to the confused 'friends' seated at the back of the bus.

I had no problems ignoring what they thought was 'appropriate' for me. Who I hung out with outside of their toxic group was none of their business, especially since once Nate came to his senses about their true nature we'd be out of there faster than Usain Bolt crushing another world record.

There was a sense of rebellion that came with sitting with Camille, but it wasn't just that about her that made me want to sit with her.

I couldn't help but feel that there was some strange familiarity that called me to her, like I'd met her before but had no recollection of it whatsoever.

A flash of the sunlight scorched into my retinas and I was suddenly brought back to a football game in August, our first of the season.

The weather had been unseasonably hot and by the time the sun set, the stadium lights blinded me just as effectively as the daylight had.

A gorgeous silhouette cast in a dark shadow laughed in a twinkling cacophony of brightness that flooded the dark night around us.

Her hand fit perfectly in mine, soft and smooth and sweet as her scent that floated into my nose as I bent down to push her silky strands of long brown hair behind her ear until--

--shit, she'd said something and I completely zoned out, fantasizing about how familiar she was to me and a memory I didn't know I'd forgotten, courtesy of a concussion at the start of the season, which I also didn't remember receiving.

"I'm sorry, what did you say?"

She was giving me 'the look'. The one decorated with her light brown eyebrows raised over impeccable doe wide eyes and suspicion and confusion laced together in an intricate weave braided together on her face.

"I said...nevermind. You're top of the class in every single subject, why are you asking me about content we won't cover until after the Chinese Dynasty module we're on right now?"

"Because you're already three modules ahead, and I wanted to know if you think Gallagher is going to play that Lady Gaga parody video about fleas on rats for the plague module."

Camille half snorted, half laughed, and at first I was expecting her to grow mortified from the sound that just came out of her mouth like Leah or Kennedy would've done, but she merely brushed it off as if she did it all the time, and I found it so damn refreshing.

She wasn't fake or preening or attempting to make herself seem like something she wasn't in front of me.

"God I hope not. My last history teacher was obsessed with it and it was stuck in my head for at least three weeks."

"Your last history teacher, at the school you were at before?"

"Yeah... at Ridesdale, remember?"

Remember? Why would I remember that?

But she was looking at me expectantly, like it was definitely something I should've known, so of course I went along with it.

"Right, right. Why did you come here from Ridesdale? That's a pretty long ways to transfer from."

And a much less expensive school to attend, but I didn't add that on. She would've been better off in public school with the amount of bullies and assholes she was interacting with on a daily basis.

"Um...are you, like, Dory or something?"

"What? Dory the fish, from Finding Nemo?"

"Yeah, are you like Dory? You either have really good short-term memory for school, or you can't remember personal details for shit, but I can't tell which one it is yet."

"Why do you think I'm like Dory?"

"Because, you obviously know why I moved from Ridesdale to Hartingrove."

"I do?"

"Yeah," she said, with the air of 'duh' hanging in the space between us, space so small that it hadn't occurred to either of us in our conversation that we were moving precariously closer to the other, but upon noticing it, neither of us were willing to shrink back to our respective sides of the leather bus seat.

If anyone happened to walk by or peer behind them, they'd see our faces inches apart, heads ducked down low and so intrinsically together that I could only imagine the things they'd assume about us, but their opinions or thoughts were the last thing on my mind.

"Right, yeah, sorry. Stupid question I guess."

My hand flew to my neck and I pulled back as I realized that I was definitely missing something here, but what that was, I had no idea.

"Uh, do you have your notes from the textbook readings for the next three modules, though?"

"Are you intentionally trying to insult me?"

"What?"

Her words were accusatory, but her tone and the small smile on her mouth was a clear indicator that she was, in fact, joking.

Sometimes it was hard for me to read social cues, so watching for small tells like smiles when there shouldn't be where clear indicators for sarcasm.

"Of course I have the notes. Are you trying to tell me you haven't read the next three modules and taken extensive notes yet? *The* Parker Hartingrove?"

My face heated to an almost unbearable level.

"Oh shit. Sorry, have you really not done the readings yet?"

"No, football has taken up more of my time than usual, so I haven't been able to get ahead in any classes except AP Physics and AP Lit. What about you?"

"I'm ahead in everything *except* AP Physics and AP Lit."

"Well, I think you know what that means?"

Suddenly, Mori turned her head sharply towards us, obviously having been spying on every word out of our mouths.

"Has anyone told you that you two are the nerdiest hot people on the planet? Seriously, you're getting excited over-"

"Note swap!"

Camille was already digging through a hot pink three-ring binder covered in Sharpie song lyrics and flower doodles.

"I have absolutely no patience for Physics. I'll give you literally everything I have, even my calc homework even though I know you're better at that than I am."

"I don't think I'm better at Calculus, you're probably just more left brained."

And that sent Camille on a fifteen minute tirade about the pitfalls of trusting the pseudo-science of right and left brained personality dominant traits. I couldn't stop the smile from blooming on my face the entire explanation.

Her fingers brushed over mine in her frenzy of handing over a thin, pink notebook with perfectly scrawled penmanship and amazingly organized notes inside once her rant was over.

I followed suit with my plain navy blue colored notebook with tabs determining which section was for which subject.

"You'd better not lose this, it's worth more than the crystals I found with my dad in the diamond mines in Arkansas when I was five."

"You've been to the diamond mines? I've always wanted to go there."

"Well, it wasn't *that* great. It was hot and crowded and there was no way you'd actually find a real diamond, but it's still any hopeful archaeologist's dream."

"Again, I say--nerds!"

Mori butted in once more and I couldn't hold back the laugh from her interruption this time.

"Says the girl with a bird feather collection categorized alphabetically by breed."

Mori stuck her tongue out at Camille then went back to scrolling aimlessly on her phone, but began packing her things up when she realized we were stopping.

My gut churned in anticipation.

The bus came to a screeching halt, and I realized that we'd been talking for far longer than I'd imagined.

"Camille, I--"

"Oh, just Cami, remember?"

My heart began pounding way too fast in my chest to be normal. Was it normal to feel this way?

"Cami, right, sorry. Look, I wanted to ask you if you were doing anything this Saturday? Maybe we could grab something to eat together?"

She looked stunned into silence for a moment, like she couldn't believe what had just come out of my mouth. I almost hadn't, either.

"Like...as a date?"

Her furrowed eyebrows surrounded a crease in the middle of her forehead that I wanted to smooth out with my thumb, push her hair behind her ear like I had done in that strange flash-back-that-wasn't-a-flashback.

Shaking my head to clear the image, I focused again on the upturned half smile adorning her pouty full lips and swallowed once, twice, three times, attempting to answer, but just as the word came out...

"Yes, like a date--"

"Sorry bro, Cami's got plans with me all weekend, just like always. Isn't that right babe?"

Colton appeared in the aisle, and did the very last thing I ever expected him to do.

He grabbed a stunned Camille by the arm and pulled her into a very deliberate, very passionate kiss, one that displayed his role quite clearly.

My heart sank down to the soles of my feet watching the show in front of me, and that vision that I'd had in the back of my head of a gilded silhouette flooded in the after-lights of the stadium turned into a wispy shadow and disappeared from my mind completely.

Chapter 5

The sun drenched bleachers were hot to the touch, and I had just lost my only reason to stay at this football game--Mori had already gone home.

I'd only come because she had asked and I was terrified of falling into shaky ground territory with a tenuous new friend, so of course I'd immediately jumped on her offer of attending the first practice game of the season, and hadn't even protested when she told me she had to leave early per her strict grandparents.

Pastels and neons splayed across a watercolor sky broken up by a blinding orange sun, and my book became saturated in honeyed beams of light refracting off the metal bleachers beside me.

A glance at the clock revealed that the game would be coming to a close soon after the sun finished its final waning descent below the horizon line.

The clanging of helmets and stiff plastic padding slamming to-gether on the field below grew distracting enough that I decided to pack up early, but a scuffle on the scrimmage line had me perking up and shielding my sensitive eyes from the blazing ball of fire in the sky to view the action occurring in front of a gasping audience.

Two players were involved in a heated standoff, both from opposing teams. The initial school team had split into two for this scrimmage, much like shirts vs. skins, though they were both very much clothed in this situation.

Spittle was flying, their rage burning hotter than the sunset warm at their backs.

Helmets thrown off, the shorter of the two was the first to shove, and then the ref was there, backing a hand into the shorter one with the red jersey while the one with the blue jersey only shook his head, dark brown curls flying as he stalked away shaking his head as if disappointed in the other's behavior.

I had only been at Hartingrove for a week, so names weren't sticking in my brain, but I was positive they were two of the popular guys, the sporty ones who everyone fell all over in the halls and the cafeteria, two places I tried my best to remain invisible, especially considering the last name that was almost infamous in these rich people circles.

I was just Cami now, no need to announce my last name unless a teacher called out names to check attendance, and if anyone got curious I could always feign indifference. There were millions of people in the country, and Astor could be a popular surname.

The crowd around me let out a collective sigh of relief when the tension receded, but my interest was piqued enough to stick around a few minutes longer to watch the next play unfold, see if the two guys actually came to blows in front of the practice field filled with students, teachers and parents.

The blue jerseys won in the end, and I hadn't taken my eyes off the taller guy the whole time. He was the quarterback for his blue team, but I could tell from his skill that he was most likely the main quarterback for the actual team when they weren't split in half and playing against each other.

Every snap was perfect, each play executed to perfection, every throw a delicate yet powerhouse spiral that landed effortlessly into the hands of an awaiting running-back to sprint it through the end zone.

Grassy clumps of flying dirt pelted the players during the last play, the spotlights shining down hot upon them as their knees quaked from the exertion of holding one another back, but the ball was snuck through the line of players by the blue jersey guy with the gorgeous hair and by the shock on the red jersey's faces, it was a damn good play.

They'd won the scrimmage by three touchdowns, but the last score was clearly an F-You to the player who had instigated the fight.

But as the tall blue jersey guy walked off the field during the extra point kick, red jersey trailed him.

My heart fell to my feet. I knew what was going to happen just as Red Jersey grabbed Blue Jersey by the shiny, reflective material of his shirt and sent him careening into the beverage table, Gatorade spitting everywhere, and then suddenly they were a tumbling fighting messy tangle of limbs and fists and--

And then a sickening crack sounded across the field. Even from my seat, I heard it.

Had his neck snapped somehow? A broken bone?

The game officially over, coaches and parents stormed the field, demanding to know what was going on just as a medic rushed over, the fight broken up quickly as a golf cart drove by on squeaking wheels.

The good thing about this happening on the practice field was that it was so close to the action, which also coincidentally turned out to be a very bad thing, as well, as all the cheerleaders and play-ers had a front row seat to the audience and the faces watching them.

I was so tired of being watched. I wanted to be invisible, live out the rest of my time in Care quietly, no more drama.

I never seemed to get what I wanted, though.

Tucking my books back into my bag, I dialed the number for my new foster mother. She'd been nice enough this week, driving me to school and even bringing me to the game.

Their house was modest, middle class and comfortable and felt like a home--just not mine.

Her phone went directly to voicemail.

Well, there went my ride...

I huffed out a breath as I scrolled through my options.

There was a bus stop a few blocks down, and I could ride it to the street closest to the foster home, then walk from there.

I had no money, so taxi was out of the question, same as any ride share apps--I'd have needed a debit or credit card to link to those in order to even get a driver out here.

I decided sitting out alone on the bleachers, however, in direct line of anyone walking by was not the best course of action.

Maybe I'd just walk to the exit and see about calling my foster mom back then.

I wasn't going to call the foster dad. He was an asshole through and through. Mean, rude, but not abusive. Still an asshole.

If all else failed, it was warm enough, and the neighborhood park seemed relatively safe--it even had a gazebo with a seating area inside. I had my hidden knife in my thigh sheath, courtesy of my favorite foster sister I'd ever had at the last house, so defending myself wasn't an issue, and it would hardly be the first time I'd slept on a park bench.

Care hadn't been all that kind to me in the five years I'd been inside.

Fingers trembling slightly, I zipped the hand-me-down backpack I'd managed to snag from the last home and stood while trying to ignore the ice shooting down my legs.

My heart raced as I took step after step down the metallic steps that rattled like the breath in my lungs, desperate to get away from the strangers with their ever-watchful eyes.

There was the girl who'd knocked into me on accident and hadn't even stopped to apologize the first day, then beside her was the girl who'd knelt down and scooped them up with a what-can-you-do smile and shrug at her friend's behavior and lopped off behind her to catch up.

And then there by the exit, the Red Jersey, speaking animatedly with a coach in official garb, i.e. a black baseball cap, black Nike shirt, Khaki pants and thick looking white tennis shoes completing the look.

Red Jersey was...well, hot. There was no other way to describe him. Sweat slicked the side of his face, his words showing off the pure white of his teeth, and his skin had tanned from the summer sun pounding down on him all season long, but his attitude...

Apparently, the coach wasn't happy, so that made Red Jersey furious.

My stomach seized at the violence displayed on his face, a face so cut and beautiful, he would've been better off with an easygoing smile, a disgusted grimace, a joking grin--anything besides the rage filled sneer that encompassed his features.

"Hartingrove!"

The group of men all turned to the approaching player, Blue Jersey, who apparently had the same last name as the school we attended. Okay, so this was definitely Parker Hartingrove, the

Dean's son, and apparently had a family connection to the owners of the school.

Mori had told me as much, at least.

Parker approached Red Jersey and the coach with another official by his side, most likely a medical professional.

There was a white bandage across his head, but he wasn't limping and didn't have any marks on his face.

"Hey, sorry it took so long. Sheila here gave me the all-clear."

I couldn't help but stay hidden in the alcove behind a beam that held up the bleachers--I couldn't risk stepping away and have all of them see me and know that I'd been spying on their conversation the entire time, so I'd wait out their confrontation.

"You boys done with this shit? I can't have this come our first game. We need to get this settled. What's the issue?"

"No issue coach, we're totally fine."

Parker's words seemed to shock everyone in the group.

"Really? Because you were just--"

"Coach Anderson, if I can cut in here...Parker needs to follow up with his primary care physician on Monday morning. He says he has no memory of the fight, or what started it in the first place."

"Really?" Red Jersey guy speaks up, sounding skeptical.

"Yeah. Did I start it? If I did, sorry I guess."

"Wow. If you're apologizing then you *really* don't know what started it."

"Colton," the coach barked at Red Jersey, letting me know his name so I could stop calling him 'Red Jersey' in my head.

"Don't make this worse than it already is. Parker's willing to get over it, so I expect you to do the same."

"Hey, I wasn't the one who started it! He just got mad at me."

"I don't give two shits who started it! You'll both be on your best behavior next game, next practice, in front of everyone. Are we understood?"

"Yes Coach," the both of them parroted back at the middle aged man who looked, for all the world, a glorified gym teacher who thought too highly of himself.

"Good. Now Parker, head home. Colton, with me for now."

I was just backing away into the shadows as both of them strode their separate ways, but I didn't calculate how visible I'd be once they turned the opposite way--the exact same way that Parker Hartingrove was turning toward me now.

His eyebrows rose as he noticed me, trying to adopt the powers of a chameleon to no avail. I was not, in fact, the silver of the bleacher pole beside me. Damn.

"You know, spying isn't considered very polite."

Oh, so he was talking to me, now.

"So is fighting your teammate in front of a whole crowd, but hey, I'm not one to judge."

The golden, blinding smile he sent me was sure to make me delirious. I needed to pinch myself to make sure this was real.

My arms were crossed around my body and sure enough when my fingers pressed too hard into the skin of my arm, it hurt like hell. *So* not a dream.

He cocked his head, examining me like I were his prey underneath a microscope, but then his smile turned warm and amused.

"Glad you're not the judgmental type, otherwise I wouldn't ask you for your number."

"Oh, you think you're going to ask me for my number, is that it?"

"I mean, I was going to...but if you don't want me to I can just--"

"Yes?"

He was sweating a little, but it wasn't from the after-effects of the game. Maybe it was from the harsh lights beating down upon us in the practice stadium.

"I'm Parker by the way. You don't go to Hartingrove, do you?"

So he changed tactics. Damn, and I was having fun watching him squirm.

"Just transferred this year. I'm brand new."

"Thought so. Well, what'd you think of the game, mystery new girl?"

I shot him a wink that I didn't use often, only to throw the flirtatious boys off their game.

"Maybe try keeping the fight for the other team? I don't know much about football, just a suggestion, ya know?"

His face grew redder from my words, a sheepish grin appearing on his boyish face.

"I know, I know. To be fair, I totally have no idea why we fought, no one will tell me."

"Ah, standard male testosterone fueled bullshit, huh?"

"Exactly," he said, looking me over more intently as it was my turn to squirm beneath his gaze.

"Wait. You're in my Ethics of History class, aren't you? I knew you looked a little familiar!"

"Maybe? I'm really bad with faces, but I do have Ethics of History third period."

I was rewarded with another blinding grin.

"I knew it! Well, if you have any questions in that course, feel free to find me after class. I'd be happy to help."

I was extremely tempted to roll my eyes.

"Thanks, but history is my best subject, plus I took an elective ethics course online through my old school's free concurrent course program, so I technically already have my freshman year completed depending on if the school I go to will accept the classes as college credit."

A glimmer of something pleasant and wonder flickered across his features as he ran a hand through hair slightly damp with sweat.

"You're just full of surprises, aren't you?"

"What's that supposed to mean?"

Shit. Had he guessed already who I was?

"Nothing, it's just--you're beautiful, funny, *and* smart. Isn't it illegal to be all three at one time?"

I barked out a surprised laugh myself, then shook my head.

"Apparently not, otherwise Zendaya would be in jail right now."

He was about to respond when Red Jersey--Colton--shouted his name and jogged over to where we were talking.

"Hey man, let me give you a ride home. I don't want you injuring your head any more than you already have."

"Nah, it's fine, my brother is already waiting to drive me back."

The two exchanged wary glances.

"Your brother? Aren't you like, ready to kill him for what he did?"

Colton seemed nervous and fidgeted with his hands, but above all else was the telltale signal of someone feeling extremely guilty and secretive. I knew that look all too well.

"Not enough to remember what even happened. I'll figure it all out once my head stops pounding. Oh, hey, this is my friend Colton. Colton, this is...actually, I never got your name."

"Camille, but I go by Cami."

"Cami. Well, it's nice to meet you. I'll see you third period then?"

"You will," I told Parker, watching as he waved and sauntered off toward a lanky and dark featured person in the shadows, flicking a glowing cigarette butt onto the ground and squishing it beneath a booted foot.

The figure turned, and sharp angular features and black as midnight hair caught a snare of the moonlight and it shone almost as bright as the memory of the flickering cigarette fire in the dusky night.

Parker slapped a hand on his brother's shoulder and they turned as one out of the stadium and I was suddenly left with the realization that Colton was still standing before me and had asked me a question.

"I'm sorry, what'd you say?"

"Nothing. Just wondering why you're still standing around after the game's been over for at least thirty minutes now."

To emphasize his point, the stadium lights flicked off as one, the loud sounds of the massive lights powering down filling the night air with the buzz of quieting electricity and crickets chirping obnoxiously.

Elsewhere, a locust's song bleated into the air, chilling my bones.

"My ride forgot about me."

"Lucky for you I have an opening. Where do you live?"

Absently, I replied, "I don't even know anymore," but he took my strange answer with a shake of his head.

"Lucky for you again, I *also* have a futon that pulls out into a bed. If you're interested, that is?"

Was I? Who was this person standing before me but a fellow student who I probably shouldn't put my trust in, but it beat going back to that house with people who didn't care about me any more than I cared about them.

"Really? And what about *your* bed? Is that available, too?"

The wolfish grin that spread across his face was gorgeous, even if I knew the person behind it wasn't so beautiful.

It didn't matter. I'd hardly cared about virginity, so why not a stranger to start me down that path? Why not let go of my childhood and innocence now, rather than let someone take it by force later in life? It was inevitable for someone like me, anyway.

"Seems like I'm the one about to get lucky."

I followed him out to his car, only sparing a glance at the sleek black motorcycle that rumbled out of the parking lot with Parker and his brother on it before sliding into Colton's red Jeep and closed my eyes before sending up a prayer that it wouldn't always be like this, that I'd stop feeling so alone.

Colton's warm hand wrapped itself around mine as he asked me questions about who I was and where I came from, asked about my friends, hobbies, interests, parents, relatives, and I was too heartbroken to tell him the truth, so I lied.

I made up an entire fantastical family, but I was in foster care because they'd died loving me, not because they'd betrayed everyone they'd ever known, including their own twelve-year-old daughter.

I'd had a multitude of friends. I enjoyed makeup and action movies, loved sports and soapy teen shows.

I became a completely different person for Colton, and as I soaked up his story that night, the both of us staying up until the sun rose talking our ears off, I enjoyed this new persona I'd created, the person I wanted to be rather than who I was.

And then the next day I came back, and we sealed the deal with my first kiss.

He didn't know I cried myself to sleep that night in his arms when I gave him my virginity.

Mo never noticed a change in my behavior, and Parker forgot I existed come Monday morning.

It was better this way. With Colton, I was someone else, and to the rest of the world, I was just me, alone, by myself.

Lonely.

Chapter 6

My life could be described in a series of words in a run-on sentence with no punctuation marks to document the passing of time: monotonous, sad, cliche, predictable, tragic, and borderline traumatic.

These words were just that--words, something consisting of the same twenty-six letters of the alphabet combined in countless ways to describe something that was so tedious and exhausting that sometimes I hardly opened my mouth to form them.

Granted, that was when I was actually able to make words, when the scratchiness and almost unbearable pain coating my throat and vocal cords wasn't absolutely paralyzing to attempt to speak.

Sure, there were surgeries, and they sometimes helped, but the truth was that this was what I would have to deal with for the rest of my life.

Flicking another barely smoked cigarette to the ground and stomping it out, I grunted my distaste for the fact that I could hardly take a single puff without the pain becoming excruciating.

My doctors hated me--that was a definite--but that didn't mean I had to stop trying to smoke, no matter how much it hurt.

Parker's voice rang through the air and I braced myself for his scathing looks or insults, but none came.

Instead, he flung open the front door to the house and stormed inside. I followed, naturally, to find out what the hell had crawled up his asshole. Again.

"Fucking asshole! I can't believe he did that right there in front of everyone, in front of Leah, too! What did I ever do to him, anyway?"

I rolled my eyes, realizing that he was probably talking about Colton, the shit-stain on the boxers of the world that was his 'friend'. In reality, I knew he only kept him around for Alec's sake.

After what had happened with me, I didn't blame him for sticking close to his best friend for the warning signs he'd already been showing.

"And she just stood there and stared at him like he was crazy, but she still said yes! Since when were they a thing? Was she the booty call that he'd been bragging about the entire fucking time, and I had no idea?"

I wanted to interject and ask something--anything--but my vocal cords were shredded and my throat burned from the one puff I'd inhaled of the cigarette, so there was no way I'd get a single word out without coughing a lung up, shredding everything up again.

So, I stayed silent, like always, while Parker went on and on about some girl who was fucking his friend that he clearly wanted to fuck instead.

Damn. What I wouldn't give for *that* problem instead of--

Nope. Feeling sorry for myself was more cliche than wanting your friend's girl, and I wasn't going to do it.

"And then her best friend stood there all excited and happy while Carter--fucking *Carter*--asked her out too, like he hadn't just called them scholarship pussy that day! It was like he wanted to show me that it didn't matter who I wanted, he would get her first! It doesn't matter who I want or who I like, someone else just gets there first, or ruins what I already have with them."

He threw that last bit toward me but I kept my mouth shut, unwilling to speak the truth about what really happened with his shitty girlfriend from tenth grade that wound up in my bed.

It wasn't worth it, because it wasn't like he would believe me anyway. That didn't mean it didn't hurt, though.

"And even if I wanted to go out with her, how could I now? She's clearly been fucking him for a while, he's been talking about this girl for like, two months now, and I haven't put two and two together. I mean, I always thought she was cute, but I didn't notice her until today, and isn't that how it goes though? But still...I really liked her. Is that crazy, that I just met her today, but I already liked her so much? It was like I'd already met her before but couldn't remember..."

I hadn't a clue who the fuck he was talking about, but still I nodded empathetically, eyebrows raised to seem as if I were interested, when in reality I was just looking forward to using this as source material for a short story.

In the story, Parker would be a giant worm--no, centipede--and the girl would be a fly buzzing around his head. Colton would be the spider that caught her in his web, and Parker was forever attempting to climb the silk that this mystery girl was caught in only to slide down it and fall into a pit of mud with each attempt.

I'd name the story after the girl who had my little brother so out of it, if he'd ever tell me her name.

"I mean, am I the asshole here? I just can't stand Colton and how much of a dick he is to women, and the one time I find someone I think is smart and beautiful and funny, and he got there before me. But it's not like he has a claim on her--they're not dating, and he never even used her name before today! It's like...I get she's on scholarship, but that's nothing to be ashamed about and he was acting like she was beneath him at school, laughing with Carter about her and her friend. Carter was being a fucking racist about her friend, too, and Colton didn't do anything, he just laughed with him! I'm not the asshole, right?"

I just quirked up an eyebrow as if to say, 'Well, what did you do to make you the asshole?' and he seemed to understand my silent question, like he always did when I didn't talk.

"Nothing. I mean, not *nothing*, I just...I asked her why she'd be with Colton and he told me that they'd been together for a while, every single night. Like she fucking lived with him or something, and nobody knew about it? Like, why would you hide it if you weren't ashamed of it? And why wouldn't she put a stop to it if she knew that he was ashamed of her, right? Like, doesn't she have respect for herself or--"

He stopped his tirade after I slammed my hand down on the quartz countertop beside us, the sound reverberating through the large all white kitchen.

It was my signal for him to shut the fuck up and take a breath or something. Jesus, what did this girl have, a magical pussy? She had my brother whipped and had hardly spoken to him once.

"Fuck, okay, sorry. Yeah, that was me thinking asshole thoughts. I'm not trying to judge her or her choices or anything, but...*Colton*? Seriously? She could do so much better."

I leaned my head forward and my eyebrows rose up into my hairline as if to say, 'like you?' and he rolled his eyes, striding to the stainless steel refrigerator to pull himself out a pre-packaged meal our mother had meal prepped that week since she'd be out of town again.

"I mean, yeah, I'd be a much better boyfriend, or whatever the hell they are, to her than he is. Come on, tell me I wouldn't?"

He did this sometimes, baiting me in conversations to see if I'd try to communicate past the usual eyebrow raise or sweeping gesture, but Parker knew when he was being a jealous psycho over some chick he'd only met once, so I didn't need to respond. He knew, and just wanted to see what I'd do, which in the end was stare at him without blinking.

We engaged in the epic brother stare-down for about a minute before his eyes watered and he blinked hard.

"Fuck. Why are you so good at that?"

Years and years of practice with shitty therapists.

It was like those jackasses thought they could see straight to my fucked up brain through my eyes.

There was a reason the word 'rapist' was in their name. A therapist basically forced you to tell them your 'feelings' but I'd yet to crack.

Shit. That was another fucking cliche, wasn't it?

Damaged guy who doesn't want to get better refuses to talk to therapist and wallows in self pity instead.

Well, at least I was aware that I was a sad, walking cliche with no friends except my brother who was basically forced to speak to me. At least I didn't have to talk back, medical exemption and all.

With the therapy, they'd given me this portable keyboard so I could type my words to the therapist or psychiatrist depending on which day it was, but my fingers never moved across the keys.

One time, I'd written out the plot for a short story where the therapist in front of me was really a sex worker and the therapy was a front for her actual business.

Needless to say, I wasn't invited back to that office.

"Anyway, I'm not gonna let Colton win, not this time. I'm so fucking sick of the girls I want slipping through my fingers. I'm going to ask Cami if Colton is her boyfriend, and if he's not then I'm getting her number and I'll ask her out. I'll just have to remember never to bring her here, unless I want you to steal another one of the girls I like."

My face scrunched up in disgust at the fact that he still thought I'd slept with his little tenth grade girlfriend, but he'd already turned around to the food dismissing me completely, the tension stiffening his body.

I obviously wasn't going to say anything against what he'd just accused me of, because I physically couldn't, but also because if he knew the truth about that day then he'd just be even more pissed at that asshole Colton.

I'd thought he found out the truth at the game at the start of the season and that was why they'd fought hard enough for him to sustain a fucking concussion, but the damage must've screwed with his memories, because he still had no recollection of the fight or why it had even started in the first place, and Colton sure as shit wasn't about to come forward with the information, the pathetic twat.

I ambled out of the kitchen and to the driveway, slipped the helmet on and swung a jean-clad leg over the black motorcycle my father had given me as his parting gift and final fuck-you to his wife and kicked the stand up before the thing roared to life beneath my hands and body.

One of the girls next door who'd been washing her car stopped and gawked as I flipped the visor down over my eyes, ignoring her stare pointed stare at me that resembled everyone else's: half fear and half lust,(at least from the girls).

I rocketed out of the driveway to get myself into some real trouble where the pain from the idea of a real relationship with my only brother and my demons would finally leave me alone--at least, for a little while.

Chapter 7

I couldn't feel my shoulder.

That could've been because my entire arm was pressed against Colton's, and the entire bus was staring at us as if they were watching a zoo exhibit.

"You're going on a date with Colton? Since when are you two a thing?"

Mori's shock was palpable as I opened my mouth to explain but Colton beat me to the punch.

"Since I asked her out for this weekend. My boy Carter needs someone too."

"Yeah, come on Mo-mo. Not gonna leave a guy hanging like that, are you?" Carter asked my best friend who I was sure had immediately gone silent and beet red underneath that deep colored skin of hers.

Mo-mo? What did he think she was, a flying fucking lemur?

Before I could say anything to keep her from accepting the offer from the bully who often made our lives hell, Mori agreed to his offer for a date this weekend.

Was I in the Twilight Zone?

All of this occurred whilst Parker was staring dumbfounded at the scene unfolding in front of him.

What, he didn't think I would already be involved with someone? Was I just the poor, smart orphan to him who he would be doing a favor by paying some attention to?

All of a sudden, the landscape changed and the actual events of the day before morphed into something gruesome and grotesque, something out of a horror movie as Colton became deformed and dangerous.

His smile deepened until it resembled a circus clown's.

His teeth sharpened into knife points, serrated and jagged and dripping with blood, my blood, as he sunk his fangs into the skin of my neck.

I jolted awake with a harsh scream that jostled Colton who had been laying underneath my arm, hence why it had fallen asleep and was filled with pins and needles.

"Are you okay? What's wrong?"

His sleep-filled voice filled the silent air around us, gruff and groggy and something that I usually found to be sexy, but in the aftermath of the terrifying dream I'd had of him, it only made me shiver with disgust.

"Fine. Go back to sleep."

"I would but I can't go back to sleep once I wake up. You know why?"

I groaned internally, because yes, I did know exactly why.

Every single time Colton woke up, whether it was from a ten minute nap or full eight hour sleep, he always had a boner. Every time. And he always expected me to do something about it.

"Yes, I know why. Can't you just ignore it?"

"And get blue balls? I don't think so. Come on, you're the one who woke me up, so it's your job to fix it."

"Fix it? You want me to 'fix' it?"

He wasn't usually this much of an asshole.

I didn't know what he would do if I refused him, but he'd basically gone public with us earlier that day, so maybe saying no when I'd never said it before wouldn't screw me over.

"Well, yeah. Come on babe. I'm dying over here."

To make his point, he found my hand that was still tingling and half numb and placed it on said boner.

And while, yes, it was a very average and nice member he had in his boxers, I didn't necessarily want anything to do with it.

Especially not after we'd had sex earlier in the night before going to sleep.

"Colton," I groaned, trying to pull my hand away but he held firm, rubbing himself against my hand like a dog in heat humping anything it could get its hands on.

"You see what you do to me, baby? Please, I promise I'll be quick."

He wouldn't be quick, not unless we had sex, which I didn't want to do considering I was still sore from the first time.

If I didn't want sex, he'd demand a blow job, because 'hand jobs are for pussies' according to him.

"I'm tired, Colton," I said, trying to pull my hand away yet again, but he brought his other hand around and locked his fingers around my wrist in an iron grip, subduing me as effectively as if he had handcuffed me to his dick.

"Colton."

I could practically hear him rolling his eyes.

"Cami."

"Let go of my hand."

"Come on babe, you're the one who woke me up with your bad dream. Why don't I help you forget about it for a little bit?"

It was my turn to roll my eyes.

"Because I'm tired and I have so much work to do tomorrow it's not even funny. I'm sorry I woke you up, I couldn't really help my bad dream."

The sheets rustled, and suddenly I was rolled onto my stomach as soon as his hands left me.

"What are you doing?"

"I'll give you a massage, help you calm down from your bad dream."

His hands started rolling smooth circles into my skin, and I huffed out a conceding breath.

"That's--you don't have to do that," I tried to get out but it sounded choppy with the karate chop motions he was performing against my back.

"Yes, I do. Gotta keep my baby happy."

I rolled my eyes into the pillow even as a small smile overtook my lips. That was kind of cute.

His hands trailed down further along my lower back until he reached my ass, and then it became more about that than the actual massage.

I could feel when it turned inherently sexual immediately.

His hands pushed away the material of my sleep shorts and my underwear beneath, his fingers teasing along the line of my panties.

My body immediately seized up.

"Colton, what are you doing?"

"Come on, it'll be good for you. You need a good massage--in here," he said as soon as he slipped a finger inside me.

It felt good, but I didn't want it to. I really was tired, and I didn't want Colton to keep acting like my boundaries were unimportant and that my protests were valid.

I didn't want to be convinced to have sex, I wanted to want it with my very being and beg for it, not endure it and just wait for it to be over, which was usually how it went with us.

I was tired of it. Tired of him...but how could I tell him that without him kicking me out on the streets, and then where would that leave me?

I'd have my dignity, my pride, but I wouldn't have a warm bed to sleep in, food in my belly, a hot shower ready for me whenever I needed it, a washer and dryer for my clothes, and so much more.

It was the little things that made the homelessness feel so pitiful. It was having no clean underwear or having to free bleed on your period because you couldn't afford tampons or pads.

It was washing your hair with hand soap in public bathrooms and using the super sonic air dryers which created a myriad of tangles.

It was worrying about that small cut on your finger and if it got infected and not knowing where you'd go or how you'd pay for the medical attention to make sure you didn't die from it.

It was a hell of a lot worse than someone coercing you to have sex that you kind of didn't want at the moment.

Still, the feel of his hot breath against my shoulder made me shudder, even as the dual pulse of pleasure from his fingers stirred something deep inside me.

His thumb circled the spot at the apex of my thighs and I trembled.

I didn't want to. I really didn't want to, but I orgasmed right on his hand, against my brain telling me that it was wrong and that I should've held out. Should've pushed him right off me and told him the hell with what he wanted, but still I let it happen.

Did that make me weak? Pathetic?

I felt dirty.

His hand retracted, and I felt him pulling the waistband of my sleep shorts down, along with my underwear.

I started squirming beneath his considerable weight.

I had let him push past enough of my boundaries for the night.

"Colton, no."

"What? You weren't saying no a second ago."

I felt him at my entrance, hard and ready, and panic shot through my blood.

"I said no! I'm tired, I don't want to have sex right now. I'm still sore from earlier. *No!*"

"It'll only hurt at first. Calm down," he said, gripping my hips tightly to keep me from moving out of his grasp.

I bucked and writhed against him, my hands flying up to slap his out of the way, but before I could get him to stop, he entered me in one quick thrust, and my resolve faded completely.

He was already there, doing what he wanted, taking what he wanted, and a little piece of me withered and died right there on the bed with me.

Sweat dripped off his body onto mine as he relentlessly took and took and took and I laid there and took it, silent tears streaming from my eyes.

His cry of ecstasy mingled with mine of despair, and he kissed the center of my back before rolling over and falling asleep.

I shivered in my nakedness until dawn painted the sky an alabaster blue.

My brother was being uncharacteristically talkative.

Granted, he hadn't actually said a single word, but he'd actually been following along with my conversation, grunting occasionally and nodding his head, his eyes glittering like he was actually paying attention to what I was saying which was a miracle in and of itself.

"Anyway, so they were supposed to go out last night with the whole group, but since she hadn't been at school most of the week I figured she was just sick or something and would come since her friend was going with Carter, but nope. She never showed up, and even her friend Mori hasn't heard from her."

Grey nodded his head, seemingly intrigued with our conversation.

"And Colton was so pissed. I don't think I've ever seen that guy so mad. I asked him where she was and he almost hit me. Hit me! Can you fucking believe that? It's some bullshit, is what it is. I wonder where she is."

I hadn't been able to take my mind off of Cami all week, especially not since she'd pulled her great disappearing act.

She'd become the talk of the school after Colton's show he'd put on at the museum trip, and she had just blown school off for the rest of the week like she wasn't suddenly the school's newest shiny toy to talk about.

It was wrong, the things they were saying about her.

Camille Astor wasn't well known in social circles. She'd been best friends with Mori since coming to school at the start of the semester, but before that she was a complete mystery.

I'd even broken down to googling her name, but the internet was either scrubbed clean of anything mentioning her, or she never had anything noteworthy ever reported about her.

Of course, the Astor name had pulled up tons and tons of search results, being the prominent family name that it was, but ever since the scandal a few years ago that wiped most of them off the map, they'd gone silent.

Scarlett Astor hadn't gone silent, though. No, she'd been murdered by her husband, who was sitting pretty at San Quentin State Prison carrying out a life sentence for that one.

The articles wouldn't shut up about the money laundering, the cheating wife who'd stepped out on her husband with his work partner, and their twelve year old daughter caught in the crossfire who'd gone into foster care with a massive trust fund hanging over her head, being lorded over by the state of California, per her parent's will.

Who knew where that poor girl was now. The articles had never named her for her privacy.

Grey rubbed his eyes with the back of his hand and I realized the time, wondering why my big brother had let me ramble on about some random girl for fifteen minutes straight without walking away.

"Hey, so, are you doing okay?"

Grey became deathly still. He always hated the 'how are you doing' question.

Partly because he physically couldn't answer, and partly because he didn't want to.

He settled on a gentle shrugging of his shoulders that I translated into meaning 'fine, I guess', but I could tell there was more to it.

The faraway look in his eyes told me a different story. There was a dimness in the blue of his irises that were normally bright and emotive.

Tonight, they were dark and stormy, like he was waging war in his own mind.

"You sure?"

I had no idea why I asked him that. He always shut down when someone pried, and I was no different.

There was a time that I hated my brother.

The time I found my ex-girlfriend in his bed.

The time he stole my Power Rangers two-in-one transforming action figure.

The time he scratched my car with his bike.

It all changed and became something else, something resembling resentment and less full of rage.

Everything changed when I found him hanging by his belt in the closet of his bedroom.

I shook the images out of my head of my once blue-faced brother and faced him, already knowing what I'd find.

There was the scowl that I'd grown so accustomed to.

I almost smiled at the familiarity of it all.

"What? You can't blame a brother for caring. I mean, well, you can, but you shouldn't."

Grey's eye roll felt like a warm hug.

The smile that he couldn't fight but hid behind his hand was like him telling me he loved me.

My priorities shifted when my brother did what he did. Our whole family changed, but my outlook changed more than anything else.

It was my life's goal to be there for him, even if he didn't want to be there for himself.

I wouldn't let him down again. Never again.

He let me drive him to school that morning instead of taking his motorcycle.

My little brother was scared for me.

Worried.

Anxious.

I couldn't blame him, either.

Trying to kill yourself would make any decent brother concerned, so it was no surprise that Parker had tried to go above and beyond with watching me and trying to take care of me after recovery and even now, three years later.

My medication had been regulated, I used my writing as a form of coping from my daily anxiety and my depression had subsided, at least for the moment, so I felt like I was in a good place aside from the constant annoyance that was therapy.

I absolutely hated that shit, and no amount of pleading from my mom would get me to interact with their psycho babble bullshit.

So I let the kid drive me to school, just to make him happier.

I should've been in college by now, halfway through my freshman year, but my attempt three years ago and the subsequent recovery I'd gone through pushed me back a grade year.

It wasn't that I was stupid, but I would've had to work day and night to make up every missed test, quiz, assignment, project, and whatever the fuck else they assigned us.

It was Monday morning, a brand new week, and we were starting fresh, so naturally I was wearing all black.

My clothing choices were mainly to keep people the fuck away from me, and partly because I enjoyed my style.

Black jeans and black combat boots, black shirt and a black leather jacket. The only thing with a little bit of color on me was the silver chain hanging from my belt loop with my wallet attached to it.

I gave no shits about the 'dress code'. My dad was the Dean. It was the one use of nepotism that I actually enjoyed.

No matter how hard I tried to fade into the background with the stoner kids and the 'emo' kids, it didn't matter--there were always eyes on me.

One of the drawbacks of having the famous 'Hartingrove' name meant that I was constantly on the radar, especially for girls who had the idea in their mind that they could 'fix' me.

There was no fixing depression, only working through it with time and day by day treatment that worked best for me and my own mind.

I stalked past row after row of lockers until I reached my destination, the metallic monster refusing to accept the combination on the lock three times until I finally got the damn thing right.

My new medication caused my hands to shake uncontrollably at the most inopportune times. For example: when lighting a cigarette. When typing a new story. When taking a test. When trying to open my locker.

I had just deposited my books when I noticed the hallway growing quiet around me.

A quick look around showed Colton, Parker, Carter, Victoria, Kennedy and Leah (or the shit-stains as I liked to call them) staring at a girl walking alone through the aisle lined with rows and rows of lockers.

She was beautifully tragic, in that 'I've seen too much of this world' kind of way.

She was beautiful in a way that felt desperate and unhinged, as if to look upon her was to stare too closely into the sun. Gaze too long and you were likely to end up with crispy retinas and a seeing-eye dog prescription for the rest of your life.

Red made a ring around dark doe eyes, puffing them out and making it seem like she'd been crying or hadn't had enough good sleep.

Her clothes hung limply on her frame, her long hair in loose waves that cascaded down her shoulders.

She reminded me of...well, me. The me from three years ago. The me who'd been a shell of a person and had viewed the world as my enemy rather than my salvation.

And this girl...she had that same distant and cold look in her eye, the same look that told me she didn't give a shit what happened to her.

What scared me even more than that, though, was the way that my brother was looking at her.

I'd just spotted the girl he couldn't stop obsessing over, and I could tell the instant his eyes registered what I'd seen seconds earlier.

Colton tried to stop her. He called her name and even reached for her arm but she flinched and yanked it back quickly, like his hand on her arm had burned her.

Parker tried next, saying her name gently, but her eyes were unseeing, unfeeling, unblinking.

I knew all too well how it felt.

I had been numb to everything. Numb, until the pain filled in the cracks at night where I'd rock myself over and over until I fell asleep sitting up for a few minutes, only to wake again and have a panic attack at the state of my body and my life.

I knew a broken shell of a person when I saw it for myself.

Jesus. Was this what my parents and my brother had to go through? Watching me live half-alive, a walking corpse?

My blood turned to disappointment in my body as I watched her duck her head from the leering states and blatant laughter at her expense while Parker did absolutely nothing to quiet their mocking.

He listened to their jokes about her, stood there with his asshole friends and just let it happen.

Even as a lone tear slid down her cheek, he stood silent and did nothing.

No one followed her as she ran down the hall to an empty classroom and shut the door behind her.

No one followed her. No one except for me.

Chapter 8

Social services had dumped me at my brand new house the day after I was released from the police station after being declared a run-away by the previous family who hadn't give two shits about me.

Thankfully, the family's children, (two boys, from what the mother had said) were already gone to school.

I didn't have time to shower, only to say hello to my temporary foster mother who was sheltering me until they could find a more permanent solution for me and put on my school uniform and get out the door.

The woman was in her mid-forties and stunningly beautiful. It was her work with the social services division as a family lawyer that gave her access to more...high profile kids like me.

Then again, hardly anyone batted an eye at my file as it slid across the desk anymore. The Astor name was infamous, but Camille Astor was not.

My belongings had all fit into one giant duffle bag (not counting my school back pack) that I'd brought with me to Colton's house. I'd filled it up after he left for school that morning exactly one week ago, pretending to be sick so he'd leave without me, and packed up everything that belonged to me.

I didn't care if I had to sleep on the park bench. I wasn't going to go back to him.

My feet took me to the police station, where I reported him.

It didn't do anything, of course. It never did. But at least I put his name on a statement, even if the cops didn't believe anything I said.

Once I called my case worker and my last name got thrown around, as well as my inheritance money tied up in my trust with the state that would eventually belong to me, however, the police started changing their tune.

I got an exclusive trip to the hospital for a rape kit, and even the nurses smiled at me.

Why couldn't I get this kind of treatment in the homes I was placed in? Oh yeah, because my money would never affect them.

But the trust overseen by lawyers to take care of every medical and legal bill, however? The trust that would pay handsomely once billed? *That* got people to sit up and take proper notice.

Maybe when I came into my millions, I'd donate a wing to the hospital who treated me so gently. Maybe I'd donate to the officer's campaign for Sheriff if he handled my case correctly.

I was nothing but a walking dollar sign to these people, but if it got me the justice I needed, then I wouldn't care.

Colton was brought in for questioning the next day while I was sat in a cushy conference room in the same building, and I was so dissociated from my own emotions that when someone asked me for a banana, I started laughing hysterically.

They looked at me like I was crazy.

The room smelled like moth balls and molding walls, but when the female detective assigned to my case came in with gourmet coffee and a pitying smile on her face, I knew it was the end.

"It's a he-said, she-said situation. There's no evidence of foul play, no restraining marks on your skin, and all the evidence points to consensual sex, as well as the fact that you two were practically living together. No jury is going to convict without substantial proof."

"I said no."

"The jury will be sympathetic to him because he's a young man with his whole life ahead of him."

"I said no."

"If you'd fought back, punched, kicked, done something--"

"I said NO!"

The memories washed over me like a slithering oily snake.

At least they hadn't booked me for running away, like my old foster parents had wanted.

Instead, and god bless her, my case worker had found me a family amenable to a run away foster, and I ended up on their doorstep.

I hadn't prepared enough to come back to school, though, and even if this new foster mom--Maria--had known about the circumstances surrounding what had happened with me, my case worker made it apparent that skipping school would make me truant, and any adult in my care would get in trouble if I didn't get my ass to school.

As if I could survive falling behind in my classes anymore than I already had.

"Alright Cami. I'm only a phone call away if you need me, and I haven't told my boys what's going on, but I can give you their numbers if you want to text them the situation if you need anything at all."

She was sweet. Kind. She'd even packed me a lunch with specialty kale salad and vegan chips. I sometimes wondered about my mom, if she would've turned out to be someone like her.

Maria squeezed my shoulder but I reared back as if she'd hit me.

She didn't flinch, but an old sadness swallowed up her features.

"Right. I forgot about the after effects. I'm sorry, no more touching. Got it."

"No it's--" I started, wanting to be more than just a shell of a girl that she'd drop at a moment's notice for being such a burden.

"No, it's not okay, and it won't be for a while. It'll never be okay. But while he might've taken a few moments of you, a few seconds or minutes of your dignity and your pride and your soul, he can't take anything more than what you keep giving him. So let him keep those moments, that fear and pain, but don't give him anything else. He's not worth it."

Oh, from the old anguish swimming in tearful blue eyes, it was clear to me what she'd been through, maybe why she'd agreed to take me in.

I'd heard her fighting with another social worker through my case worker's door, arguing about me not being allowed in a home with two teenaged boys, but she'd shut them down instantly. How, I had no idea, but she wanted me in her home, and someone wanting me was a big change, so I went with it.

Wasn't like I had anywhere else to go, anyway.

"Thank you," I whispered to her, voice thick with unshed tears that I refused to let fall.

She reached out a hand like she wanted to grasp my cheek but thought better of it.

Who was this woman and where had she come from? Surely I couldn't have gotten this lucky...

To have someone who actually cared.

Someone who saw behind the dollar signs and glimpsed the damaged, fragile girl beneath my hardened walls that I portrayed to the outside world.

Someone who'd scaled walls even rougher and sharp spiked than mine and won, cresting over the top to view the sensitive insides of a traumatized soul.

"Here's your pass to the counselor. You don't even have to go to the office; it's like a get-out-of-jail-free card whenever you need it. Just show it to your teacher and you're good to go."

I nodded and swallowed over the lump cresting in my throat, then stared at the imposing walls of the school I'd come to loathe.

Maria's car didn't leave until I was inside the school, and by then it was too late to run. Everyone had already seen me.

Colton and his friends were there--the girls and Parker, Carter, Alec...

I didn't need superhuman hearing to know what they were joking about.

Did Colton tell all his friends?

We'd managed a restraining order, but still, having to see him everyday at school meant parts of it were inevitable.

He couldn't keep five hundred feet away from me at all times if the hallways were this thin, this narrow, closing in on me like blood vessels constricting with each thump of my racing heart.

Panic shot through me like an arrow from a taut bowstring.

Sweat rolled down my back like a bead of poison.

My legs shook like the branches of a tree in a windstorm.

I didn't think twice before darting past the group of laughing friends into an awaiting classroom where I broke down, body and soul erupting in a silent sob that tore through my body like a weapon of mass destruction.

A malestrom of fear and shame wiggled its way into my mind, shoving rational thought out through crevices in my nose and ears.

Could I have fought back harder, done more? Shrieked and yelled and bucked him off and punched and kicked and scratched and fought and fought and fought until he knew--

but what would the point have been?

Could I could I could I could I could i why would i try why even try at all why why why why why

let him keep those moments, that fear and pain, but don't give him anything else

Could I have fought harder? Yes. Why didn't I? Did I think I wasn't worth it?

The next time someone tried to hurt me, to pressure me into something I didn't want, I would fight.

I'd fight like goddamn hell, because I was worth it, even if I didn't feel like it sometimes.

I was worth it.

I had just plugged the hole in my emotions and began collecting myself when a chair in the corner squeaked and I whirled, heart a raging inferno inside my chest as I came face to face with the most beautiful person I'd ever seen.

Hair as black as night, matching the jacket and boots he wore, he was familiar and unfamiliar all at once, like I'd seen him in passing, but hadn't given him enough of my attention to fully admire him in person.

"Who are you?"

He didn't answer, only tilted his head to the side.

He filled up the entire doorway, his height staggering as I realized that I was shut inside a room with a man who had the potential to hurt me.

I had to get out of this.

Sharp, angled cheekbones adorned his face, accentuating the light brown eyes that stood out amongst his tan skin.

"Okay, well, I'm gonna go."

I stood, straightening my skirt and grabbing my bag from where it had fallen on the floor, thanking whatever holy gods above that I'd grabbed every school book I'd needed from Colton's house before the mass exodus.

He didn't move. Like a still frame from a 1950's photo given colorization, he blocked the exit.

Wait. His name suddenly surfaced to my mind. This was Parker's older brother, Grey Hartingrove. The 'outcast'. Seemed to me like he gave himself that nickname, dressing and acting how he did.

Seriously, didn't this guy ever talk? It was freaking me out.

I rolled my eyes and spoke while I used sign language at the same time, "What, are you deaf?"

His eyes jolted in surprise, like he hadn't known that I could use sign language, before using his hands to sign back to me.

No, but I don't speak.

It was my turn to be shocked.

I had lived with a deaf foster sister for a year, spending all that time learning the language in and out before they'd found her somewhere else to go, and I had left soon after that. I still texted her from time to time.

She'd found a forever home. I was happy for her.

I didn't sign anymore since his hearing was fine.

"So, you're mute?"

He nodded, not giving anything else away.

"Well, this has been interesting, but I really need to get to class."

Still he didn't move.

"Okay, I know you're not deaf. Please move."

His mouth quirked up on one side, apparently amused at my annoyance.

"So you can use sign language to speak, but you'd rather just not say anything at all to be an asshole, is that it?"

He merely shrugged his shoulders, light brown eyes alight with a humor that danced in his irises like something akin to happiness.

"Excuse me," I said, moving as close to him as I could bare, but then I was swallowed up in his scent.

His cologne wrapped around me and threatened to bring me to my knees. Fuck, why did he have to smell so damn good?

I came up to his shoulders, and he only looked down on me as his body silently shook with restrained laughter.

I wondered briefly why he was mute, but then cast the thought away immediately.

I brushed up against his body as I edged past him through the doorway, and the slight touch was thrilling--and terrifying--enough that I walked as fast as I could (more like ran) down the hallway as the tardy bell rang.

Maria texted me before I walked in my first class.

Chapter 9

M om was acting weird today.

The scent of blueberry muffins permeated the large white pristine kitchen decorated with stainless steel appliances that didn't show even a single smudge or fingerprint, thanks to the housekeeper employed weekly by my parents.

Mom *never* baked.

I would've written it off as store-bought, but the proof was on the steaming cooking sheet left out on top of the barely ever used oven.

She flitted back and forth between the living room and laundry room with baskets and baskets of laundry piled up.

"Umm...what's up?"

"Oh, good, you're home. Can you get your brother to come down soon? I have a surprise for the two of you, and I need to make sure that he'll be on board."

"Uhh...sure. Let's see if he'll actually listen to me."

Trudging up the stairs to Grey's room had me questioning...lots of things. Mainly the fact that Grey hardly listened to anything I had to say, least of all requests made by our mouther.

"Hey, you in there?"

My fist pounded on his door twice. Three times. Four. Nothing.

Would he absolutely kill me if I went in his room without asking? It wasn't like he could yell for me to come in.

I slowly nudged the door open a crack, then a few inches.

The scent of weed and cologne sprayed over it thickly hit my nose and my eyes watered at the strong combination.

"Dude. You really think that's going to work? Just hop in the shower or throw on some different clothes and wash your hair over the sink real quick. Mom wants you downstairs now. A surprise or something."

I got a guttural grunt from the corner of the room where his bed was hidden underneath piles of fantasy novels (my brother was a closeted romance freak, but he liked people to think he was a Tolkien fan, which was just as worse in my opinion) and grew momentarily surprised.

A grunt was the equivalent of a "be right there", and he gave those out about as often as hundred dollar bills.

So, not frequently.

The scent of fresh baked cookies tore me away from the hallway and running straight back into the kitchen where I found our mom hunched over a piping hot tray of cookies that looked burned around the edges.

"Mom. What are you doing? Maria Hartingrove does not bake. Ever."

"I know, I know. I just want to make a good first impression, that we're a good, normal and stable family."

"And why would you need to do that? Did someone call child services on you? Are they coming to check on Grey? Because if they're coming you might want to deep clean his room before..."

"Why?"

There was a suspicious gleam in my mother's eye that I definitely did not like. I also didn't want to rat out Grey, but if child services really were called...

"No reason."

"Mhm. Well, it's a surprise, but no, child services were not called. I work closely with them and would know about it, but my home is very safe and clean and stable. Which is why we're going to be having a guest staying with us for a bit of time. How much time depends on a few things."

Grey chose that moment to slide onto the barstool at the end of the counter, and at the word 'guest' immediately perked up and paid rapt attention to the words coming out of our mom's mouth.

"A guest? Like...a foster kid, coming to live with us? Haven't we tried this before? That little boy a few years ago that took all our kitchen knives and hid them under his pillows in case someone tried to get him in the night?"

I shivered at what a nightmare that had been.

"Yes, a foster is coming to live with us, but she is nothing like that little boy. He actually found a loving home after staying with us, and she hasn't had any luck on that front, so we thought we could give it a shot, to see if we might be her--"

"I swear to god if you say 'forever home' I'm gonna puke."

"...forever home. Look, I know it's not ideal to introduce another person to our dynamic right now, but she needs this. She needs us. I need you to all be on board in helping acclimate her to our house. Understood?"

"She? Well, how old is she?"

Visions of a half naked woman in my shower was a definite plus in having a new house mate.

"She's a year younger than Grey, seventeen. Don't get any ideas, this girl's been through the wringer. I expect you to all be on your best behavior. I want her to feel comfortable around here, like this is her house too. I want to be that stable, loving home for her, and I don't want you two to mess it up by being inappropriate with her. And if you do happen to make her feel uncomfortable in any way, if she comes to me with any issues?"

I waited in the uncomfortable silence for her to finish, to tell us what our punishments would be.

"No phones, no television, no car or motorcycle privileges. Our housekeeper won't be cleaning your rooms, doing your laundry, nor doing your dishes. I won't be making your lunches. It will be school and home and staying in on the weekends. And I will be home to enforce these punishments, because I will be home for the next two months to make sure her transition is seamless. Do we all understand each other?"

"So, if we do anything to make her uncomfortable, or hurt her feelings, or make her feel unwelcome, we're basically in jail? Yep. Pretty much covers it."

Grey's eyebrows rose in silent question. I could translate it immediately.

"What does Dad think about this?"

Mom put a hand on her hip at my question.

"Your dad agrees wholeheartedly with me. This is a young girl in need of help and a loving home, and we have all the resources available to us to give that to her."

"No. There's something else here. There's gotta be a reason you're bringing her in like this, especially with our fucked up situation," I said.

"There is something else, but that's on her to decide when and if she wants to tell you. Now, she should be here soon back from the library. I told her to be back by five for dinner. Go get ready, I want you to meet her as soon as she walks through the door."

"Aye aye captain."

Grey started dancing, very badly, to some song that he was signing to so I whacked him on the back of his head and turned around to head back up the stairs after seeing the silent shake of his laughter moving his shoulders up and down.

I turned back around at the last second and rummaged through the cupboards to grab him a bag of hot Cheetos and a Honey Bun.

I assumed he was thanking me profusely in sign language but I couldn't make out the words.

Shame washed over me, but I let it become doused in amusement as he kept signing words to me that I assumed were as follows:

"Best brother ever," "So hungry," and *"How did you know?"*

The red lining his eyes and the scent of weed was more than enough to know, not to mention his easygoing attitude that usually only followed a few good hits of his bong upstairs.

It was better than his angry alcohol phase, and his nearly catatonic Xanax phase. I'd prefer him to not do drugs on medication at all, but with Grey, you take what you can get.

We're all a little fucked up inside.

My eyes stung with tears as dust from the books floated into them after slamming them shut.

I couldn't believe she'd given me a car.

A. Car.

An actual vehicle with four wheels that ran on gasoline and took you from point A to point B.

The school day had been nerve wracking waiting for Colton or any of his friends from his posse to corner me and taunt me about what had happened...but it never did. No one said a thing.

I was still reeling from meeting Grey, reliving the experience over and over in my head that I hadn't noticed the text messages until school let out.

The dean of the school himself had met me outside my last class and hand delivered the keys to me with a little note.

Figured you might need this. Meet back at home for dinner at 5 to meet the boys! -Maria

The shock coalesced with giddiness mixed with utter amazement.

Walking out to discover a silver Mercedes Benz convertible, however...

That was pure and clear disbelief written on my face.

Something slick and oily wrestled its way into my veins as I questioned why in the hell this woman was doing this for me, what she might've wanted from me...

She knew that I could take care of myself the moment I came into my inheritance that had been frozen by the state, so was she only buttering me up until the time came?

What was her ulterior motive?

She'd seemed so genuine and sweet, but now...

Now, I didn't know anything anymore.

I tossed my book bag into the back and cranked the car on.

The controls were high tech and hard to figure out. My phone connected to the monitor without me even hooking it up.

The steering wheel decal glimmered in the afternoon light, and the dashboard glowed as if lit from within, the whole thing feeling like one big joke on me.

Like any minute, the camera crew would pop out and laugh at me for ever thinking anyone could ever be this kind without something in it for them.

So, I drove the car to the library and studied until my brain hurt. I studied until I forgot.

I even forgot Mo, the plans that we'd made to meet up at her house to study. A quick text remedied that.

Me: Can't come over, foster parent drama. Tell you later.

Mo: Oh no! Keep me updated! Let me know if there's anything you need.

Sometimes it felt like I didn't deserve a friend as good as Mo.

The drive back to Maria's home was stilted, and it felt like I was driving on the water, each bump or pothole I hit feeling like it would jostle me and send me flying overboard into the churning seas of the life I shouldn't have been living.

I should've been in a life where I didn't have to question someone's kindness and put their motives into light.

Should've been living in a home where I felt loved and safe, not one where my parents cheated and murdered and went to prison.

But this was real life, not some fantasy I'd concocted in my head while staring at the ceiling of a foster home I hated.

This was real life, even as I pulled up to an astute two story home, glistening white in the afternoon sun. A home that resembled my old one, the one where I was supposed to be loved and cared for.

I pulled into the large circular driveway and parked beside a sparkling black motorcycle I'd seen at the school a few times.

Great. So I went to school with these people, too?

Maria was there, then, arms swathed in a basket filled to the brim with baked goods.

Was this real? This happiness to see me, this eagerness to make me feel welcome? Or was it a ploy to somehow get control of my inheritance?

Considering her job, I wouldn't be surprised if she could afford a lawyer who could petition the courts for her to become my Power of Attorney and get access to my money that was supposed to be mine when I turned eighteen.

Slinging my heavy backpack over my shoulder, I steeled myself to approach the front wraparound porch that reminded me of warm summer days and family barbecues.

"You made it just in time! The boys are setting places for dinner. I baked these for you."

I reached out to grab a cookie that was hard as a hockey puck and blackened on the bottom.

"Thanks."

Walking into the lavish home with my teeth trying to break the barrier on the cookie, the crumbles dropped out of my mouth and onto the floor when I noticed the two boys standing in the dining room, staring at me like they'd seen a ghost instead of an actual human being.

"You wouldn't happen to have two intruders setting the table right now, would you?"

Maria laughed. It was a sweet, twinkling laugh that fell on my ears like warm spring rain.

"Of course not. Camille, meet Parker and Grey, your new family for however long you want. We want you to feel as welcome as possible, but we will understand if in time you don't feel this is a great fit. We only ask that you give us a chance."

I nodded my head, because, yeah--what else could I say to that?

"Boys, come on. Introduce yourselves."

"Oh, that's okay. We've met once or twice at school."

Well, that was an understatement.

I locked eyes with Grey and the laughter in them was enough to make him sign something to me discreetly enough when Parker and Maria turned toward the kitchen island at the exact same time.

Needless to say the awkward tension in the room was...palpable.

Grey signed one sentence to me that about summed up everything that I was feeling.

"Well, this should be fun."

Chapter 10

The kitchen was painted in foggy grey fading sunlight coming in through designer accent curtains covering the large floor to ceiling windows of the dining room.

Mom was passing around the salad bowl before she spoke.

"So, why don't we all take our seats? Richard should be here soon and then you'll have met the entire family!"

I highly doubted dear old dad would be joining us, but I didn't want to ruin my mom's optimism.

It had been far too long since she'd smiled like this.

Maybe despite my earlier confusion and questioning of this little arrangement would prove to be wrong.

Maybe this Camille would be good for us, for all of us.

I couldn't help but notice the look gleaming in Parker's eyes though, the kind that portrayed his actual feelings about Camille. He was looking at her like she was a piece of mouthwatering meat and she was his dinner.

I definitely didn't appreciate that look.

"Uh...I might have to dip out a little early after dinner if that's okay mom?"

Mom was not one for a change of plans, so when she stared at Parker and practically seared him through to his soul with the devil glare she pinned on him, it was hard not to feel the flames myself.

"And what's so important that you can't have a good family meal with our newest member? What if I had a special dessert prepared?"

I highly doubted it would be any good, but since she was trying, I would gladly eat whatever burned concoction she'd whipped up in the kitchen.

"I had plans with Colton and Carter."

Cami visibly tensed in her seat where she'd shrunk her posture down low enough to try and make herself invisible.

I knew that feeling all too well; the desperate desire to make sure no one saw you and what was going on behind your eyes, down to the turmoil roiling in the depths beneath.

Her dark brown eyes fell down to her plate filled with uneaten food, not similar to my own considering my stomach begging for food.

Without the help of a certain green herb I'd been smoking earlier, however, and my plate would've looked exactly like hers: untouched.

Mom sighed, clearly fed up with Parker.

There'd been a change in him ever since he'd started hanging out with those guys. I knew it was all because of Alec, but that didn't mean that he had to change or start acting like those assholes, either, it was just how it happened.

You reflect those you spend time with.

I wondered what that said about me--considering the only person I hung around was myself.

"Alright Parker. But be back by eleven, it is a school night after all."

"Awesome. I'll text him to pick me up, since my car is on loan and my amazing older bro won't let me touch his motorcycle with a ten foot pole."

"Wait. On loan? Please don't tell me you're letting me use his car? I can walk or ride a bike to school, it's really not a problem."

Mom had told Parker she was taking his car in for an oil change and ended up loaning it to our new house mate. Not the best way to instill respect between all of us, but I was glad my father had gifted me my motorcycle instead of the flashy Benz out front.

"Nonsense, Parker is happy to let you borrow his car, and you can even give him rides until we can find you a more permanent car. Or we could even give you his and get Parker an upgrade, he's been talking about the new SL Class."

She pushed her eyebrows up into her hairline as she spoke, the words she didn't say all too clear: *don't make a fuss about her using your car and you'll get a brand new one even better than the old one.*

Parker was anything but stupid and rightfully kept his mouth shut.

Too bad Cami wasn't having any of it.

"No really, I'm perfectly fine to walk or ride a bike, I could even catch a ride with my friend Mori. This is too much, I was going to respectfully decline the car anyway."

I rolled my eyes before signing something to her.

"*Just shut up and take the car. Parker wants the newer one enough to let you take his old one.*"

It was comedic watching my brother stare open mouthed at my first attempts at real communication in front of him, but mom only smirked, having read the sign language and understanding what I was saying.

Parker, who hadn't learned because I refused to sign anything to or around him, was just...shocked. I didn't pay him any attention.

Cami rolled her eyes. She didn't bother speaking aloud back to me, instead deciding to sign back what she had to say.

"*No. It's the principle of the thing, it's too much and I'm brand new here, I don't deserve it. Plus I'll probably gone in a few months anyway.*"

I rolled my eyes. Again. They were going to get stuck back there if what my parents used to tell me as a kid was actually true.

"*Even if you're gonna be gone in a few months, why not make the best of it and take the damn car?*"

She huffed and crossed her arms over her chest.

"*Thank you for the car. It would be great to not feel unsafe walking back and forth to school or the library. I appreciate your hospitality.*"

Parker watched the whole thing in complete disbelief. He knew that I could communicate if I wanted to. The fact that I didn't want to with him must've hurt, but I couldn't bring it in me to...care. At all.

But for some reason, I wanted to with her. For her. For someone who actually, finally, understood.

Even if it wasn't exactly what I had gone through, it was still something.

Maybe with her in the house I wouldn't feel so damn lonely.

"What, so you can talk to her but you can't talk to me?!"

Parker stood, pushing back his plate from the table as he did so.

Cami's eyes grew wide as saucers, the color immediately draining from her face as she sunk lower in her chair, like she couldn't stand to see someone so upset, or more like she were...afraid of the confrontation itself.

I could only shrug my shoulders in response. There wasn't really anything else I could say to him. Why would I want to?

I knew it wasn't his fault what had happened in the past.

But that didn't make it hurt any less.

It didn't make the memory of it disappear.

It didn't make it any less true.

So I tried my best to stay away, to stay distant, to remain closed off to everyone, because the truth?

That was the hardest of all to bear.

"Are you seriously mad at me? After everything *you've* done to me? And all this time, I didn't learn sign language because I thought you barely ever used it, but you just refused to sign a word to me even though you're obviously fluent in it? You're...you're something else, man."

"Parker. Why don't you sit down and finish your meal?"

"Nah, I'm headed up to my room to get ready. Welcome to the family Cami, with all your damage I'm sure you'll fit right in."

"Parker! That's enough. Do you remember what I told you before this dinner?"

"Yeah, yeah. I'll just invite the guys over then, no going out remember? Didn't say anything about staying in."

And then he disappeared while the rest of us were left to pick up the pieces, just like always.

Because Parker always did whatever he wanted, no matter the consequences.

The last time I tried to do that, I ended up in the psych ward.

Funny how the golden child never had to deal with any actual responsibility in his life.

"Camille, I am so--"

Cami shook silently in her chair, and my heart sunk as she covered her face with her hands.

What kind of pain must she have been going through in that moment? What must've been going through her head?

I was going to wring Parker's fucking neck for making her cry--

"I'm sorry, it's just so funny," she said, lifting up her head as a wide smile played out on her face.

She wiped a tear from her eye--a tear that came from her laughter--and shook her head before laughing some more.

"It's just been so long since I've been with a real family that obviously actually love each other. It's refreshing."

It was like music to my ears, like some long forgotten song that my memory decided to conjure up in my worst moments--something to remind me of what I could've had, just to torture me with the reality that it would never be mine.

I saw the way Parker looked at her.

It was just the way things were, even when we were little.

He got all the shiny new toys, whereas I got his throw-aways, like I was a kid from another marriage or something. We had the same parents, but I never understood why I was always treated like I was second-class.

"Well, on that note--Grey honey, would you mind helping me clean up Parker's plate? Looks like all of us are finished after that."

"*Eat your food first*," I signed to Cami, who hadn't touched the food since it had been plopped onto her plate.

"*I'm not hungry*," she signed back, sulking down lower into her seat.

"*I'm not cleaning your plate unless you eat something on it*."

She rolled her eyes but still picked up her fork and shoveled some mashed potatoes into her mouth, brown eyes glaring defiantly at me all the while.

"*Good*," I signed back, sure that a wolfish smile was planted on my face, fully ignoring the fact that my mother watched our back and forth like a spectator at a tennis match.

I didn't know why Cami signed back to me instead of speaking--it wasn't like there was anything wrong with my ears, but it made something in my chest grow warm when it had been dormant and cold for so long.

After a few bites, Cami started to lose some of the fiery defiance and graced me with a small smile of her own.

A smile that only grew when she noticed me staring, like she couldn't help but to smile even as the shyness began to kick in.

I started to stand and pick up the plates without the two of us taking our eyes off each other, but that smile--beautiful and inviting as it was warm--fell from her face as the front door slammed open and in walked Carter Jennings and Colton Wright, along with Alec and Nate Covington and the girls, Victoria, Kennedy and Leah.

Jesus. He invited the whole crew over, on the first night that Cami was staying with us? I must've really pissed him off by speaking to Cami and not bothering to do the same with anyone else, but it wasn't like I could help it.

I couldn't physically stop myself from talking to her, even if my vocal cords wouldn't allow it.

"Hi Mrs. Hartingrove!"

"Hey Maria!"

"Hi girls, hey boys. I hope you'll be hanging out either in the attic or the bonus room; we have--"

"Hey, follow me."

My mom was interrupted from telling the 'whole gang' about our new house guest by Parker's entrance to the party.

Everyone filed out with him. Everyone, that is, except Carter, Leah and Colton, who were staring suspiciously at Cami who was trying her best not to cry.

Something had happened there. I had no idea what, but it wasn't going to happen in my own house.

"Hey Cami, missed you at school last week. I was surprised when I didn't see you last Saturday too. Thought we had a date."

Colton's words roared in my ears.

Cami stood and flung her shoulders back while pasting an indifferent look on her face.

"Then I guess you got stood up. Safe to say there won't be anymore 'dates' between the two of us ever again."

My mom took the chance to stand up and link her arm with Cami's.

She whispered something into her ear that made her stiffen up, and even my enhanced listening skills couldn't help me figure out what was being said.

"Something wrong? Regret your choice already? It's obvious you chose the cripple over me."

I couldn't punch this asshole in front of my mom, but I could get Cami away from him.

"*Come on*," I signed to her before grabbing her arm in mine, relishing the feel of her skin on mine and the fact that she didn't pull away until we were in the entry way.

"*Where are we going*?"

I stared into her deep brown eyes and beautiful heart shaped face sprinkled with tiny freckles.

"*Anywhere but here.*"

"*I love that idea.*"

I couldn't help the smile that pulled my face up.

"*Glad to hear it.*"

I had just opened the front door before I heard my mom telling Colton that it was time for him to leave, and that no one insulted her son in her home.

He had just walked out onto the front porch when I handed Cami the spare helmet to my bike.

"Really?" she said aloud.

"*Come on. What, you scared*?"

"Never."

But when she looked back toward Colton, she shivered.

I couldn't help but think there might be one thing she was afraid of.

Chapter 11

T he pavement whirred by in a whorl of different colors and textures, but they were the only thing I could focus on at the moment.

Not the warmth from the legs I'd wrapped my own around.

Not the roar of the thunderous engine of the motorcycle I was currently riding on the back of.

Definitely not the feel of a stomach cut from steel my arms were banded around, grasping for dear life.

If it were up to me, I wouldn't have been touching Grey so intimately, but I would've found myself splattered on the solid yellow lines had I not been using him as my own personal seatbelt.

I had started to ask him where we were going until I remembered he couldn't yell the answer back to me.

More than once I'd wondered what had caused him to be mute; was it a birth defect? An injury? A personal choice?

From the way he refused to sign to communicate with his own brother showed me that that part was definitely the choice, but I wasn't about to pry.

He had saved me from Colton. Not literally, not in the way that I'd needed saving a week ago, but he'd been there to get me away from him.

Had he seen it in my eyes? Did the quickening of my heart give away everything? Or was it the look on my face?

I was positive Maria knew. She'd asked me as much during dinner when Parker's entire friend group had shown up at the dinner out of nowhere.

She even asked me if I wanted her to kick all of them out, to which I'd declined.

It wasn't my house, no matter how hard she would most likely try to make it seem that way in the coming weeks or months or however long I was going to stay.

Probably until graduation.

My birthday couldn't come soon enough. June 10th had never seemed so far away. It was only November, and I was already dreading each and every school day until the end.

Until I turned that coveted age of eighteen.

I'd sometimes questioned my social worker, about the status of my inheritance and why the trust had failed me.

Why I was bounced around to shitty foster home to shittier foster home instead of placed in the care of a trusted adult from my family's estate and sent to some uppity boarding school where at least I'd be taken care of.

She always told me that the funds were still tied up in probate, and that the beneficiary of the trust (a person I still didn't know the name of) wasn't able to access the money left for me.

I didn't question it at such a young age but now, in my research into trusts and estates and probate...it didn't seem right.

None of it did.

But I didn't have a voice of my own, a poor, sad teenager at the whims of the system, a troublemaker, a runaway...

The motorcycle hit a bump and I instinctively wrapped myself even tighter around Grey's body, feeling the tensing of his muscles as I did so.

The scent of burnt rubber and asphalt became overwhelmed by the splash of cologne that clung to his skin, and the faint aroma of weed had me rolling my eyes. Of course the troubled rich kid could get high whenever he wanted.

I still got periodically drug tested by the school and my social worker as part of the stipulations set forth after my first runaway attempt.

Someone really didn't want me getting away from the state, but at that point in my life, waiting for the money to hit wasn't worth staying in the homes I'd been placed in.

No amount of money was worth that.

Grey's motorcycle headlights illuminated a trailhead, and I suddenly wished I'd have thought more about hopping onto the back of a glorified stranger's bike.

Sure, we were suddenly housemates by some random twist of fate, but what did I really know about this person?

"Um, Grey? Can we turn back around? I'm kind of cold."

He held up one finger as if to say 'give me a second' and I held on tight as the bike careened down a dirt road trail that went on for about two miles.

With the bike going so slowly, I could make out the symphony of crickets and frogs chirping in the night, the winter not having truly taken over the greenery of northern California.

Soon, we'd see snow. Maybe.

The cold from winter didn't catch until late January to early February, the temps toward the end of the year fluctuating day by day like the weather couldn't be bothered to make up its mind.

But once the cold snap stuck? It would be ice and snow and frigid air that burned your lungs upon the first intake of breath outside.

Grey pulled the bike over at what seemed to be an overlook that rose above the entire town, lights glimmering in a shining cascade of incandescence that shadowed the light of the moon.

"Wow. This is beautiful."

Grey leaned the bike up on one side and gave me his hand to help me off.

I ditched the helmet on the handlebars, not really caring about my messy hair since it was mostly dark and unless Grey had night vision, he definitely wouldn't be able to see it.

His hand led me closer to the edge of the lookout, to the railing where the drop-off would definitely kill someone if they went over.

I pulled my hand free of his despite the comfort it gave and placed both of mine on the railing, the cold metal grounding me in a way that I desperately needed in that moment.

Grey watched my side profile and then the view, constantly looking back and forth between the two until he noticed my shiver and placed his leather jacket across my shoulders.

"Thanks. Not just for the jacket but the escape too."

I didn't know why I'd just said that. He'd clearly wanted to get out of there too after they'd been insulting him. Maybe I was just a convenient way to get away without his mom wanting him to stay for my sake.

He gave a noncommittal shrug that I felt as his arm was pressed up against mine.

A sigh fell from my lips unbidden as I leaned forward to catch more of the view.

The sun had faded beyond the skyline about an hour ago, but you could still see the fiery outline of where it had been sinking, a foggy afterglow painting the dusky sky deep purple and navy blue where the overhead sky bled into a charcoal black.

I didn't want to enjoy his company this much.

It was wrong, wasn't it?

To have gone through something so traumatic and yet still feel at peace with another guy right beside me who could do the very same or worse to me when I wasn't looking?

But it wasn't like that somehow with Grey.

I'd only just met him, and he'd barely said two words to me, and for some reason his presence calmed me, his aura soothed my frayed nerves.

Flashes of cars the size of ants whirled by street after street. A spotlight rotated in a circle over and over and over. A building in the center of town was already lit red and green for Christmas.

Maybe I let myself lean a little bit into Grey's shoulder--the feeling a forbidden touch that sent sparkling nerves dancing along my skin.

And maybe he angled his body towards mine slightly, just enough for me to feel the heat of him through his long sleeved tee, the brush of his dark hair against my forehead.

There was a certain peace to the moment in the fact that I didn't have to make idle conversation if I didn't want to, but for some reason, I wanted to talk to him.

I got the feeling that a lot of people spoke about him to his face, spoke at him, but I wanted to speak to him, to engage him in a conversation even if he didn't want to reciprocate. It might've helped that he couldn't repeat out loud what I told him.

Maybe that's why I told him.

Or maybe it was because it felt like he already knew, but he was just waiting for me to put it into words.

"My last name is Astor, my family used to be the famous Astors. Now they're famous for a whole other reason. I don't know if you already knew that; if Maria told you the background of the person living in your house. You probably deserve to know because of that anyway."

His sharp intake of breath was the only indication that told me he didn't know who I was--or who I came from. Still, I continued. Might as well get his preconceived ideas about me out of the way first and then see what was left in the rubble.

"My dad murdered my mom when I was twelve. Shot her right there in the living room and I was the one that found her. Ready to drive me back to your house and pack all my stuff up yet?"

He kept silent. Of course, he did. He couldn't sign out here in the dark. He could've grunted or breathed in deeply, butt here was absolutely no change in him; no response to what I'd just dropped in his lap.

"He went to prison for life and I was put in foster care since I had no living relatives willing to take me in. The state got control of my inheritance that I get when I turn eighteen. Apparently it's a lot; I wouldn't know. I've never seen a dime of it."

I flinched as his arm came around my waist underneath the warmth of his jacket that smelled like his cologne and mint--a mouthwatering combination that was no match for the real thing.

His fingers hooked around my hip, pulling me in tight to his body.

How could I have felt so comfortable with him, a stranger I'd hardly known before that day?

And how could I tell him things I hadn't even told Mori?

"Anyway, I've been in foster care ever since. Back and forth to a bunch of homes. So maybe yours is my last stop before graduation and turning eighteen. Who knows? I honestly don't know how Maria did it. I mean, a foster home for a seventeen year old girl with two teenaged guys living there, too? She must have some connections."

A slight grunt from Grey told me that he didn't disagree with my last point.

And then I told him about foster care. About how it felt being shuffled from home to home. About the creeps I was faced with there. About the rude siblings and the ones I missed to this day. About the sister I'd had who taught me sign language so we could communicate behind the parent's backs because they didn't bother learning it for her.

I told him about as much as I could before finally getting to present day, and then I shut it all down. I couldn't tell him anything about here. Not now, not ever.

Not after what had happened in that police station, in that hospital room.

Maybe the only one who'd ever know would be Maria. And maybe that would be for the best.

I shut down and cast a look to Grey.

What I'd hoped to find--contented indifference or thoughtful-ness--was not there. In it's place was a mask of anger and rage and a glare I'd never seen from him in the short time since we'd first met.

I tried to pull out of his embrace but he held firm, and I didn't fight him. I didn't actually want him to let me go, but I also wanted him to be able to explain why he was so angry. Had I said some-thing wrong?

"What's wrong? Are you mad at me?"

Grey had me turned directly toward him and staring into his midnight eyes in a flash of a moment.

Both his hands gripped my hips and I couldn't stop the stutter in my heart as he stared down at me in a tumultuous wonder.

His mouth began to move, as if he wanted to speak aloud but his vocal cords just couldn't produce the sound.

"N-n-"

"No?"

Grey shook his head as if in repeating what he meant. He wasn't mad at me.

"Then why...?"

Without warning, he let go of me and the cold was immediate, the shivers left in his wake...almost unbearable.

He loped off to the side of the overlook, towards a light pole with a small picnic table underneath.

The dim yellow halo of light that surrounded Grey made him look absolutely gilded; like some Greek apparition from the pantheon of Olympus gods.

I didn't know what overcame me, but I had to know.

His voice had sounded so scratchy yet so deep...I had to understand why. He would tell me if he wanted to; I had told him practically my entire life story.

That meant I had a right to ask...right?

"Grey...how did you lose your voice? Were you born without it, or...?"

I meandered closer to where he sat atop the picnic table, legs resting on the bench as he leaned back on his elbows to stare up at the sky.

He leveled me with a heated stare before bringing his hands up to sign, his hands illuminated in the foggy yellow glow from the pole lamp beside him.

"You sure you wanna know? I don't think you'll like it."

"Of course I won't like it; it's how you lost your voice. I was pretty sure it wasn't going to be pretty. You don't have to tell me if you don't want to...forget it, I shouldn't have asked."

His mouth quirked up on one side as if to say, 'no, you really shouldn't have', but he answered anyway, and his response nearly knocked me over with it's enormous weight.

"I lost my voice because I wrapped a rope around my neck and kicked the stool. It severed my vocal cords."

Chapter 12

T he crickets and frogs and trilling insects created a symphony of sound that drowned out the pounding of my heart in the night air.

A cool breeze wound by me and stirred underneath the hem of my shirt, bringing chills to the surface of my flushed skin.

The rough wood from the planks on the bench bit into my palms.

Camille was standing in front of me with a shared look of horror and confusion on her face.

Of course she was horrified.

I'd just told her how I'd tried to off myself.

She had no idea when or why, just the how...and after her story of her family's fucked up history, I could understand the distress at how gruesome my attempt had been.

I immediately followed up by signing everything everyone always asked after they found out.

"No, I didn't think about my family and how it would've felt to find me. I didn't really think about anything except the escape. It was a few years ago, so I don't feel that way anymore. Therapy and all that, right? Parker found me. It messed him up. I've had a few surgeries, but I destroyed my vocal cords basically. They want to do a surgery

where they do a structural implant and see if that will work since the repositioning and replacing the damaged nerves haven't worked. We'll see, but I'm not planning on being able to speak again."

"Wow. So we're about equally matched in our fucked up-ness, huh?"

I laughed. I couldn't help it, but the ugliest sounding half grunt squealing gasp sound came out of my throat, and at first it was dead silent, like even the frogs and crickets had stopped their singing to cover their tiny ears in protest of the sound.

And then Cami opened her mouth and let out the dorkiest sounding snort laugh I'd ever heard, and somehow, it made every-thing so much better.

I could read the short story in my head in that very moment.

'The Laugh That Changed the World'.

Parker and his friends would be the animals and insects watch-ing this moment between us in jealousy that they couldn't ever match up to the beauty and intrigue that was Camille Astor.

She was like a filament of translucent gold, impossible to catch and hold like a tangible thing between your fingers, but free and wild somehow, even with all this pain and fear blanketing her glow.

She seemed to shine through even the darkest of clouds.

She came to sit down beside me, close enough for our thighs to touch.

So, she was brave, too.

I guessed she had to be feeling pretty good around me. I hadn't shown her the bad side yet.

She'd need all the help she could get when that side of me came out.

"Hey, so now that I'm living in your house, you need to show me all the best hiding spots. Maria is great, but sometimes I definitely need my own space."

"She can be overwhelming at first, but she means well. I think she likes to fix. Things, people, animals, situations in her client's court cases. She thought she could fix me, too. Still trying to with all these surgeries and speech therapy and regular therapy and...yeah. She can be a bit much. But that's just who she is. She loves too hard."

"I know someone who's like that. He loved too hard, and then he snapped. Now he's in prison. Maybe it's the 'loving' part that's the problem."

"What do you mean?"

"Maybe if people didn't become so wrapped up in someone else and actually focused on themselves, there wouldn't be crimes of passion like what my dad did to my mom. I don't think love is the root of all evil, but if people just stopped caring so much...I don't know. Maybe I just have warped views on love because of everything that's happened to me."

"Have you ever been in love, Cami?"

Her cheeks turned pink in the glowing yellow lamplight above us.

The world seemed to stop spinning as it waited for her answer.

"No. I don't think it'll ever happen for me. I just feel so...disco nnected to people, everyone I meet I keep them at a distance. I don't want to let anyone in."

"Because you're scared they'll hurt you?"

"No. Because I'm scared I'll hurt them."

"Like your father hurt your mother?"

Her body jerked in a flinch that made me wince.

I waved my hand in front of her face to get her to look at me once more before I signed again to her.

"I'm sorry, I didn't mean--"

"What about you? You ever been in love?"

I had no idea what to do with my hands.

Lately, my mind had been so connected with my hands that signing was becoming second nature.

I had only taken it up to keep up with school and classes because I was failing everything, and because I refused to communicate in any way, I was bound to fail out completely of high school.

What a cliche. *Another* cliche.

So I'd spent hours and hours and *hours* on the internet learning ASL and testing it out at a local club at school filled with deaf students I'd never met.

I'd practiced and signed until my arms were sore, until the words I wanted to communicate started coming from my hands until trying to come from my mouth, like my body knew it was out of commission, for good.

But now? Now, my hands faltered for the first time.

Because...

"No. No, I've never been in love."

I'd had plenty of girls who'd wanted to try that route with me.

Sweet, nice girls who'd come over for studying and end up with their hand on my thigh preaching to me about how they could save me from my trauma, about how they could *fix* me just like my damn mother thought she could.

Talk about a turn-off.

"Why not? Scared you're gonna leave and they'll be left heart-broken?"

I didn't miss the slight venom in her tone, nor the glare she threw my way at what she'd said.

"No, because like I said before, I don't feel that way anymore, so I'm not going to have another attempt and leave someone like that in the first place."

I didn't add that if I tried again, it wouldn't be considered an attempt. It would be successful.

Isn't that fucked up, though? When you try it, you're just another attempt if you fail. But if you really go through with it, if your soul crosses over the threshold of the dead and the alive, it's considered *successful*.

Like you're some damn thing to look up to, like it's something to be proud of.

"Well, since you were comparing what happened to me with how I'll act in the future, I figured it was only fitting."

"*Damn. You're right, I'm sorry, I wasn't thinking.*"

"You clearly have to think before you sign, right?"

"*Not always, not anymore. Now it's second nature to just sign what I'm thinking.*"

"So what are you thinking right now?"

"*I'm thinking you're one of the most difficult people I've ever met.*"

"Oh, great. So now I'm difficult?"

"*And passionate. And wild, maybe a little--or maybe a lot--damaged. Good thing that's exactly how I'd describe myself.*"

"Well, now I'm definitely flattered."

"*You're lucky I don't know how to use sarcasm through sign language yet.*"

"That's easy. Just really exaggerate every movement and roll your eyes like you're thirteen and your mom just grounded you."

"*Like this?*"

I followed her tips and was positive I looked like an absolute moron, but it got her laughing again instead of staring at me with that blank glare she'd had on.

"Definitely. You should just sign like that every time from now on. Maybe it'll get you more sympathy points if people think you have a head injury too."

God, was that an actual easy, wide smile on my face?

When had I laughed and smiled like this after my attempt?

"You'll need to sit with me at lunch everyday to keep the assholes that want a front row to the freak show away."

"What makes you think *I* don't want a front row to the freak show? You've heard my sad life story. Maybe I want to size up the 'freak show' competition."

"Are you kidding? With my clothes and attitude, there is no competition. Just look at you--you're not freak show material."

"And what's that supposed to mean?"

She rose up high to make herself seem bigger than she was, dark brown hair glinting with streaks of auburn in the lamp glow.

Her face grew considerably suspicious, but in an adorable way that had me questioning why in the hell I just thought the word 'adorable'.

"It means that you're too...normal looking to be part of my freak show entourage."

"What was that last word you signed?"

"E-N-T-O-U-R-A-G-E"

I spelled out the word individually and watched as her eyes lit up when she recognized the word.

"Oh, so now I'm not cool enough to be part of your...entourage?"

She signed the word as she spoke but fumbled the sign for the word, but I didn't feel like correcting her on it when she looked so accomplished after trying to use it the right way.

"No, you're too cool for my entourage."

"Okay I definitely signed that wrong, show me how to do it."

I placed my hands on her own and had her hold one hand out like in a high five and then positioned her other hand where her pointer finger was pointing straight up with the rest of her fingers in a fist.

Then, I took the open hand and nudged it into the other and moved them both twice until they traveled forward.

Her hands were warm, silky smooth on my own, and a chill ran unbidden down my arms as I forgot completely about teaching her the new word, and instead focused on the feel of her skin on mine and the small space that we shared breath.

She exhaled minty fresh breath near my mouth, and my lips started tingling as I imagined how it would feel to have hers on mine.

Some old intrinsic part of me that hadn't been stoked in years started to come to life, flooding my mind with images of our bodies tangled together as hands and lips became one; as her light fused into my own.

She moved just the tiniest bit closer, and this space between the here and now--the waiting from one moment to the next--became unbearable.

I wanted the next second to pass quicker and then to slow immediately to a snail's pace.

I wanted to stay here until the sun came up and crested atop the reddish brown of her long hair until it glowed in the air gilded with the light that took up the space where the moon used to be.

A breathy exhale, an inch closer, and suddenly we were nose to nose, sharing space, breathing in each breath, an unrequited magnetic field pulling the two of us together, closer, closer, closer still until hopeless we should decide to close that minuscule space between us.

But we never did, because it suddenly was criminal to look any-where besides those caramel eyes, imploring me with an emotion I'd only seen staring back at me in the mirror.

And as my fingers rose to brush back a stray strand of shining tawny hair from her face, the spell was broken.

She flinched.

It was like a light had gone off behind her eyes and everything that we'd shared in the moments before was inconsequential; like I was a stranger once more, and she the same to me.

I supposed that was how it ought to be. Someone like that with someone like me was surely a recipe for disaster.

The loss of her warmth and light so immediately was a shock to the system; like I'd been punished for wanting someone I shouldn't have allowed myself to want.

Parker clearly had eyes for her. It wasn't my place to want her to, to feel her presence to fiercely it was as if I'd known her ten lifetimes over.

It wasn't fair.

It never was.

But that didn't mean that it was right or wrong, either.

I'd hurt my family enough that starting a war over a girl...a beautifully wild and fierce and passionate girl...I wished I could've said that it wasn't worth it but--

but as she shook her head and looked off to the side as she attempted to gather her bearings and convince herself the connection she felt between us was wrong or misplaced with the night mist seeping into her skin and coloring her in a fog of shimmering light, I realized with a sinking disparity that yes, she was definitely worth it.

I didn't know if that comforted or terrified me, but it was the truth of the matter.

I knew my brother didn't deserve someone so effortlessly delicate and yet so fiery at the same time; someone who could match him word for word and was just as--if not more--intelligent than him.

It didn't assuage my guilt over what happened in the past.

Sure, he'd had eyes for her first, but she was her own person.

She probably didn't even like Parker, especially after the show he put on tonight in front of her and my mom.

She *did* like Maria, that much I could tell from the small interactions they'd had together at home.

Speaking of my mother...

"Are you...gonna get that?"

I contemplated it, I really did. My mom usually only called when she was absolutely at her wit's end and completely terrified that I'd crashed my motorcycle on the side of the road.

I'd answer, give a little grunt and hang up and then she'd text me until her fingers went numb telling me to get my ass home or else.

She didn't know the extent of things that I did, although her imagination probably conjured things a million times worse than what they actually were.

Street racing might've been illegal and dangerous, but it wasn't going to kill me. Probably.

She probably thought I had taken Cami.

Shit. Of course she thought that.

I pulled my phone from my pocket, arm brushing against Cami as I did so and she quickly looked away, no doubt trying to hide the bright pink blush growing on her cheeks that hadn't gone away since I'd first grabbed her hands to help her sign that word.

"Grey. If you took Cami with you to what you do almost every night then you're going to receive the same punishment I just slapped Parker with. All his friends are gone; you can come home now. Grunt once if you understand me."

I grunted, and she sighed into the phone.

"Good. Your father will be back late tonight, and I want everything in the house to be somewhat normal so that he can adjust to the idea of a new houseguest. We'll talk tonight. Get home now."

I hung up before she could lecture me some more.

"You just got the third degree. What punishment was she talking about?"

"Just the usual. Fire, brimstone, all out prison if we treated you badly tonight."

"Fire and...what was that sign? And you definitely didn't treat me badly. If I'm being honest, this is the nicest first night I've had with a new placement in a long time."

"B-R-I-M-S-T-O-N-E"

"Also, I'm sorry you were treated so badly at all your other homes. If I have anything to say about it, it's not going to be like that at our house."

"I hope not. Haven't met your dad yet. Usually it's half and half with the different homes; it'll either be the mom or dad who treat me like absolute shit while the other is just neutral and doesn't care. Here's to hoping he's as good a person as your mom."

"Don't hold your breath."

"Great. Can we stay out here forever, live in the trees? We can be tree-people. No freak-show entourage to watch us and no parents to threaten us with fire and brimstone."

I laughed as she included both words I'd taught her tonight in her sentence and signed them at the same time as she spoke, correctly.

"You're a fast learner, I see."

I stood from the bench of the picnic table and held out my hand for her while also holding my breath.

She only hesitated a moment before placing her own in mine.

"Have to be if I want to beat Parker out for top of the class. I honestly should've just gone up to my new bedroom tonight and studied until my brain bled but...this was a nice break from all that and everything. Thanks for bringing me here."

"You're his competition for number one? I like you already."

I pulled her up to stand in front of me and suddenly we were inches apart, her body flush with mine, and I couldn't find it in me to let go of her hand.

"So. Where do I buy my ticket for the front row to the freak show lunch table?"

I pulled my hand from hers so I could sign back to her, and god it was the first time in a while I wished I could speak with my voice instead of my hands, just so that I could keep holding her hand.

"You're looking at the ticket master right now. How do you plan to pay for your entry?"

"Hmm...that depends. How much am I looking at? Do I get a housemate discount?"

"For a lifetime membership, you can have a front row seat for the low price of never using all the hot water in the shower every morning before school."

"That's pretty steep, however, I will agree since I take all my showers at night anyway."

"Perfect. Then make sure you use it all, and every night, too. That's when Parker showers."

"Thank god I'm not sharing a bathroom with him, then."

"Nope."

"That would've been a nightmare."

"You're sharing a bathroom with me."

"And you shower..."

"Every morning."

"Oh, okay. Good."

She was definitely blushing again, and she was definitely thinking about something going on in the shower.

She couldn't even meet my eyes.

"Come on. My mom said she'll massacre me unless I get you home now."

"Okay."

"*What, you know the sign for massacre but not brimstone or entourage?*"

"My foster sister watched a lot of true crime. Massacre was definitely in her daily vocabulary."

"*Noted.*"

And then the crickets began chirping once more, the locusts began singing their malignant screech, and the world was turning on its axis once more.

She stepped out of my magnetic field and I felt the pull as intrinsically as I felt the need to scratch an itch or feed myself.

She was a need now, not an intrigue.

And as she swung herself on the bike behind me and wrapped her delicate hands around my waist, I couldn't wait to get back home and be able to breathe again, but--

I also cursed the moment her hands would leave mine and she'd go up to her room and I'd go to mine and I'd spend the night dreaming about getting those hands back on me again.

I kicked the engine on and then we were off on the road again.

Time laughed in my face and circumstance was the bane of my existence because once we were out of each other's orbit, I'd go back to the damaged boy and she'd be my housemate.

Maybe she'd actually cash in her ticket at school the next day.

Maybe she'd be something different than this pessimistic and damaged person had ever met.

Maybe I could defend myself to Parker about this want and need for her; because maybe he'd see just how worth it she was and how in the end, he would just destroy her.

Just like I would.

But I'd savor her every moment on the way down.

Chapter 13

My thighs cradled Grey's as the motorcycle came to a harsh stop in front of the driveway, and I was terrified that this was going to end.

This easygoing dynamic that flowed so easily between the two of us...I couldn't bare it having to end so soon.

I was spared being alone with him and having to bear an awkward silence when Maria came bursting outside with her hands on her hips and two mugs of what I sincerely hoped was coffee in her hands.

I wanted to get ahead in my AP Literature course before tomorrow, so that left either tonight or tomorrow morning for researching topics for our final paper.

I preferred doing my studying at night, however, so if that was coffee...and if one of those mugs was for me, Maria was going to become my new favorite person.

Or my only favorite person. I didn't even know if Mori had that qualification yet.

The slow decline of my mind started the moment I slid off Grey's bike, however.

Like somehow, being in Grey's presence and the absence of triggers had allowed my mind to be fully free and clear, but now as reality was coming crashing back down, so, too, was the sinking realization that I could never escape the fact that my life was not my own.

My life was in the hands of others who, more often than not, did not care about my own wellbeing, but the money lining their pockets from the state for taking in a foster kid.

It didn't matter how hard I studied, how much I kept myself out of trouble. It didn't matter if I got a job to make extra money to squirrel away, because somehow they all always found where I'd stashed it and took it for themselves.

It didn't matter that I was in an apparently welcoming and wholesome home now. It didn't matter; because the worst thing that could've happened to me already had, so what was the point in even trying anymore?

Because who would believe me?

The police hadn't.

Maybe Maria had, or maybe she was just biding her time until I turned eighteen and maybe would use her legal prowess to somehow make herself the beneficiary of my trust if she was my legal guardian at the time I turned eighteen.

Maybe behind all the stainless steel appliances and granite countertops and manicured perfection she'd concocted in her home, they were secretly bankrupt.

Maybe it was all Grey's fault and the expensive surgeries to bring back his voice to blame for it, too.

Because what was I besides someone to use and defile for someone else's gain?

What was I besides an empty hollowed out vessel of a person who mattered less and less each day, the world taking chunks and pieces and bites out of me each and ever moment I survived.

"Cami? I asked if you wanted some coffee?"

Maria was suddenly right in front of me, Grey standing off to the side with his hands crossed in front of his chest staring at me with a hint of concern dancing behind the gilded amber of his irises.

How long had I been staring there silently, staring at nothing? Let the numbness sweep in and invade the pain creep in under the surface, beneath the usually unthinking facade I always kept up to stop me from the breakdown always a thought away?

"No, thank you."

My voice was a monotoned robot, and Grey flinched at the sound as if I'd physically slapped him with it.

Maria only frowned in concern at me, the small crow's feet crinkling around the corners of her eyes the perfect mirror image of the son standing at her side.

A sharp breeze ruffled the long expanse of hair on my head, sending it flying in each and every direction, but I didn't feel the chill, even as Maria hugged herself and shivered.

"Come on, let's get you inside--"

But I had already started walking ahead of her, not sparing her or Grey a single look backwards.

Their concerned or judgmental stares pierced hot daggers into my back.

I could only think of the next day at school and facing everything that would soon come crashing right back down on me.

I cut the tether off to the impending doom circling over me.

I didn't care. No, I didn't care at all.

It was midnight by the time my eyes grew weary and strained from staring at my school-provided laptop, essay topic chosen and sources picked out, outline complete and quotes arduously chosen.

All that was left was to write the actual paper and implement all the research I'd painstakingly gathered over the past two hours.

When the aching of my mind tried to escape past the barriers I'd created to keep the shadow pain at bay, from taking over my waking thoughts and turning me into a zombie like what had happened earlier with Maria and Grey.

It hadn't happened in years; that was how tight the leash had been on the demons in my mind.

I thought I'd had it under control.

Apparently the stain Colton had left on me was stronger than I thought.

It wasn't that big a deal, in the grand scheme of things.

Girls were hurt like that every day--worse, even. How was anything that he had done to me comparable to what they'd gone through?

What right did I have to wallow in this sharp and overwhelming pain?

What did I expect, anyway?

Why would someone like me expect respect, especially from someone like Colton?

They were all the same; guys like him...

His friends, Carter, Nate, Alec, maybe even Parker.

But not Grey.

I could tell there was something different about him. There was something so completely different about Grey, and it wasn't just the trauma that colored him anything but the lackluster color of his namesake, but in stripes of deep, bleeding red and shadowed, broken black.

Grey was a myriad of colors; least of all the shade between black and white.

My parched throat led me from the spacious and brightly painted bedroom I'd been gifted next door to Grey and pushed me downstairs toward the kitchen where I found myself filling up a glass of water, grateful that I'd torn through the drawers Maria had stocked with brand new clothes while I'd been off with Grey otherwise I'd have been sleeping in my underwear and traipsing around the Hartingrove home half naked.

It was still a shock to be in the household of the infamous family. No, it wasn't like they owned the academy we all attended, but it was as close as you could get.

Their father was the dean.

Richard Hartingrove was the dean of Hartingrove Academy, and the school had been in their family for generations, though the ownership was placed in the hands of members on the board so that all the power wasn't solely in one person's hands.

At least, that's what Mori told me when I asked why the Hartingrove's just didn't own the whole damn place.

Maria was a lawyer and their father was a dean of a prestigious school; no wonder these people had so much money.

I was halfway through filling up my drink with their smart fridge (that actually had a touch screen on its front) when the front door slammed open and creaked on its hinges.

In through a narrow strip of moonlight strode who I assumed was Grey and Parker's father--Richard--carrying a briefcase and running a hand through already disheveled hair.

As with the light he brought in with him, so, too, was the wafting scent of liquor that I distinctly remembered from my time with the Peterson's and their alcoholic mother.

I could even pinpoint the type of liquor he'd been drinking: Bourbon, and a stout brand at that.

This man wasn't instilling any confidence into me about this home at this point.

It was sad, really, watching as the tall and thin statured man ambled into the kitchen and his brown hair caught on the sliver of moonlight shining pale through the still half-open door.

Suddenly a sharp memory I thought I'd repressed down deep in the far corners of my mind jumped up and slapped me in the face, seizing my body and nearly toppling me over as I clung onto the countertop, water forgotten in the memory's haze inducing pull.

My mom had just tucked me into bed, but I was still thirsty. I didn't want to bother her; she'd been so tired lately and I didn't know why. We hung out every day.

She always used to tell me that I was her job, but it was one she didn't mind doing, as long as I was happy, she was happy.

I didn't want to make her unhappy.

I slid my slim twelve-year-old legs through my blankets and hopped down off my bed and wandered into the kitchen, the quack of the ducks on my slippers echoing throughout the airy house with each step I took.

Quack. Quack. Quack.

I shouldn't have worn the noisy slippers, but I didn't know what I was going to walk in on, either.

"No, I just got her to sleep! Quick, out the door."

A man was trying his hardest to be sneaky, but I didn't know why my mom wanted to hide someone from me. Was he her friend, my dad's friend? Surely not if she was hiding him away like that.

Was my mom cheating on my dad? I was old enough to know about it, especially since Bryson's parent's got divorced because his dad cheated on his mom.

My mom loved my dad, though.

She couldn't be cheating on him...

The man slid through a crack in the doorway barely a few inches thick, his thin body angling through quickly and he sighed as he escaped, not bothering to close the door behind him, like he'd gotten away with it.

I just caught sight of his side profile--black sideburns and a huge sloping nose with a big bump in the middle--when my mom scooped me up from the floor and planted me on the kitchen island.

"Hello? Do we have another mute in the family now? Jesus, what has Maria gotten us into now."

The man was speaking to me, directly in front of me and staring at me like I was slow in the mind.

I shook my head once, twice, three times before clearing my head and noticing my surroundings.

The water was on the counter, and my hands were shaking.

"S-sorry. I'm Cami. Nice to meet you."

"Cami? Nice to meet you too. I'm Richard. Now don't you have school in the morning?"

I tried to study his facial features in the dim light but all I could make out were deep set brown eyes that seemed like they were scowling along with the rest of his entire body.

He was just one giant scowl.

"Right. Goodnight."

I quickly turned on my heel and ran up the stairs, heart thumping and about to tear through my throat.

I didn't waste time getting ready for bed and praised Maria for already stocking the bathroom with everything a teenaged girl might need, from high end moisturizers to lotions and facial cleaners and serums.

I scrubbed my face with soap and water and brushed my teeth before grabbing the unopened hairbrush package.

I tore into it and was just about to start taming the unruly mess on my head when I heard a noise coming from outside my bedroom door.

Setting down the hairbrush, I tiptoed over to the door and pulled the soft robe I'd been wearing tight around my waist.

I inched open the door a sliver of an inch to see Parker standing there before me, something akin to torture swimming around in those blue eyes of his.

"Cami."

"Parker."

"We need to talk."

Chapter 14

Her hair was messy and her robe was light pink, a fluffy cotton contraption that hid her curves underneath that tugged a smile to my lips.

She usually always wore such dark clothes that seeing the opposite, cheerful color on her was...well, different.

"What do you want to talk about?"

Cami's eyes were glazed over, almost like she'd had the most exhausting day of her life and she could fall asleep standing if she were so inclined.

The haze of a bright lamp in the corner painted her in a backlit silhouette and tossed sprays of warped shadows along the off white walls.

She stared back at me impassively, like this was the most uninteresting conversations she'd ever had--and I wondered what had changed so drastically since the last time we'd spoken to each other.

When had that been, even? Was it the day of the field trip? Could it really have been that long ago?

I'd been so wrapped up in Colton's drama and Alec's mental health crisis that I'd barely given a second thought to Cami, save for when Colton had complained about her, over and over again.

"Look, I'm sorry for how my friends acted earlier. I just wanted to say that I don't hold any hard feelings or anything against you."

"Hard feelings?"

Her voice was a monotone symphony of unfeeling boredom, almost like the interested girl I'd met on the school bus at the field trip was completely and totally gone and in her place was a cold hard shell of a person who refused to give even an inch as for what she was feeling inside.

Her brown eyes were dull and dead inside, the expression not unlike the one Alec had been sporting of late.

The same expression that Grey had on his face the last few months leading up to his attempt.

Was that what this was? Was this breakup with Colton something that had thrown her over the edge?

I'd known she'd lived a life of hardships...maybe this was her last straw.

Who knew how Colton had treated her, or how he'd dumped her.

With the way he spoke about her in our group...I just knew that it wasn't pretty.

He'd been telling everyone at our table that he stood her up after she'd done the same to him as payback. He said she was too easy, and that he preferred to chase girls rather than the ones who just gave it up so willingly.

I hated how he spoke about women, but I couldn't find it in me to shut him up--Alec had been sitting right there, flicking his lighter up and down and staring into it like he was tempted to light his entire hand on fire just for fun.

He had the exact same look on his face that Cami had on in this moment.

Flashes of a football game brawl shot through my memory like a torpedo, momentarily knocking me off my train of thought.

There was a flash of near blinding light, searing pain, and then a beautiful girl's face smiling at me, talking to me, getting to know me...

I had just caught sight of her deep set brown doe-like eyes before Cami snapped her fingers in front of my face.

"Hello? Anyone in there?"

I shook my head and rubbed my eyes, surely that hadn't been a hallucination or anything, right?

Ever since my concussion during our first scrimmage game earlier in the year, I'd been having more and more flashes.

Most of them were gruesome--flashes and images of Grey hanging from that belt in his closet and swinging limply back and forth, back and forth, back and forth, his face a bloated and purplish mess as his neck was turned at an unnatural angle.

Some of the images didn't make sense--some showed Grey with more blood around his neck than there had been, some even came with auditory aspects, as well--like the sirens blaring in the background as I rocked back and forth, back and forth, back and forth on the ground in a ball as tears fell from my eyes and splashed onto the carpet beneath me.

But this one was different, less cloudy, more crisp and real, like it had just happened yesterday.

Was I regaining the memories of the night of the scrimmage game? And if so, who did I meet that made my mind focus on that one moment of speaking to that girl?

"Sorry, uh...headache. But yeah, since you and Colton broke up, I just wanted you to know I wasn't taking sides, and that I was sorry for inviting him over here only for him to act like such an ass. I don't know what all went down between you two but--"

"Nothing. Nothing happened between us. We weren't dating or anything."

"But...you were together at one point, weren't you?"

If it was possible, she shut down even further, eyes unfocused and a distant glaze in her face that hadn't been there moments before.

"Cami?"

A tremor went through her body and...didn't stop.

"Are you cold?"

She wouldn't stop staring at that spot above my head, so of course I turned to inspect just what it was she was staring at so intensely.

It was nothing. Not even a picture frame behind me.

I waved my hand in front of her face and that seemed to do the trick.

"Are you alright?"

"Yeah. I just zone out. Are we done here? I need to go to sleep."

"Shit. Uh, yeah, I guess we're done. Sorry if I bothered you--"

But she'd already slammed the door closed in my face.

Pre-dawn light filtered in through the curtains covering my windows and I quickly shoved them aside so that I wouldn't go right back to sleep.

I launched myself out of bed and immediately set to writing down my dream that I'd just had.

The dreams were getting increasingly ridiculous.

Last night, I dreamt I was getting chased by an evil clown and no one would do anything to stop it, thinking that it was part of a comedy show. The worst part was at the end, when the clown took off their hideous makeup and it was Parker underneath it all.

At least it wasn't another nightmare, though it had been close.

My last dream I'd turned into a short story that I'd submitted to our local lit mag and was still under review.

'The Abyss' was my first attempted publication, so my fingers would be crossed, if I actually ever bothered to do that.

I had just finished pulling my pants on and t-shirt for the day when there was a knock at my door and my mom entered sheepishly, half a hand over her eyes in case I was indecent, like she wasn't already peeking to see anyway.

One of the many downsides of not being able to talk--basically no privacy because people will just barge in after knocking instead of waiting for you to come answer the door yourself.

I'd lost the rights to lock my door whenever I pleased after I tried to off myself.

Apparently that's where parents drew the line.

"I need you to stick by Cami today. She's going to need a lot of help adjusting."

I lifted my eyebrows in silent question, not feeling the need to sign to get my question across.

"I know she's been at school for a few months, but...well, I can't tell you. She could just use another friend. Keep an eye on her. Don't let anyone bother her. Please."

I gave her one solitary nod in response and she sighed out a big whoosh of air that seemed like it had been collecting in her for hours.

More than once, I wondered what my mom knew about Cami that I didn't, considering that she'd told me almost her entire life story the night before.

Whatever it was, it was enough to have my mom spooked, so that meant it was serious.

I wasn't planning on letting Cami out of my sight the entire day, and I didn't care what she had to say about it.

The shower in the bathroom that was connected to both mine and Cami's rooms turned on and I couldn't stop the grin that flew onto my face.

She definitely hadn't lost her spirit, that much was for sure.

I thought back to the night before, when she'd promised to shower at night and let me have the mornings. I wondered if this was just to test me and see if she could get a rise out of me, or if it was a shower out of necessity since she couldn't get one last night.

Her mood from the moment she got off my bike was concerning. It was like she'd become a different person entirely.

Mom left my room and I couldn't help but test my boundaries even more; to see if that spunky girl from last night was still in there somewhere.

So I turned the doorknob to the bathroom, and sure enough, she hadn't locked it.

These Jack and Jill bedrooms were meant for me and Parker, but we continuously fought over every little thing that it was easier to put Parker in the larger guest bedroom with its own bathroom down the hall than to let the fights continue on much longer.

Steam so thick I could barely see my hand in front of me almost suffocated me as I eased my way inside.

Jesus. Did she have to have it hotter than a sauna in here?

That temperature couldn't have been good for her.

The soft whimper of pain that came from the shower alerted me to the fact that the temperature was definitely not good for her.

Without thinking, I shot my hand into the shower where I knew the temperature knobs were and blinding felt for the single handle that you turned one way for hot and one way for cold, finding it completely turned on the hot side with nowhere else for it to go.

She was going to give herself third degree burns with the water this hot!

I yanked the water completely over to the cold side and almost started to regret my decision when Cami's loud yelp of surprise and fear had her peeking her red, flushed and dripping wet and most likely the most magnificent sight I'd ever seen in my eighteen years of life.

Her dark hair fell in curled wet strands around her face and in a large clump behind her, though most of it I could tell fell down in front of her chest even though the white shower curtain hid her chest from view.

Not like that was what I was trying to see, but...

The burning, fiery passion smoldering behind her eyes almost turned the brown shade golden, the color of flames that danced under her skin.

"What the hell are you doing in here?"

Chapter 15

The steam was fogging up all my senses, clouding out all the intrusive thoughts and suffocating them under a blanket of hot air so thick I could barely see.

The shower knob was turned as far as it could go, but it still didn't heat the chill lingering beneath my bones; it didn't erase the past two weeks and everything that had broken me in the meantime.

The heat from the water wasn't enough to do what needed to be done, but it did enough.

It didn't soak the fire down past my skin to the muscles and veins beneath. It didn't destroy the monster hiding under the surface, roiling and pacing and begging to be let out to let the world hear its beastly roar.

I kept it on a short leash, unable to escape and terrorize, but sometimes--like that night--I let it out.

I let it shine through behind my eyes, let it bare its teeth at those who could hurt me and who do so without thought of consequence or reason.

Sometimes, I wish the beast would take over and reduce the rest of me to the shell of a person I'd become without it.

But I knew that I was nothing without it.

Was I nothing *with* it, too?

Was I still even here?

Was I already nothing, already the blank emptiness my mind craved to un-feel each and every day to stop this madness from creeping in and swallowing me whole?

If I couldn't climb out of the despair, maybe I should've just found a way to cease to exist.

Maybe this steaming, burning water would show me the way.

I stepped into the spray, letting out a whimper of pain that barely reached my ears.

I reveled in the pain, letting the flames of water lick up and down my spine and shoulders until I could feel the skin blistering beneath its heat.

The sound of my skin boiling and bubbling was almost audible until the water immediately turned to ice, hissing pelts of icicles where I wanted wrath and fire and flame to reside.

Pulling back the curtain revealed Grey, hand still partly in the shower where he'd turned the temperature gauge to freezing.

"What the hell are you doing in here?"

He didn't look guilty, or ashamed, or even particularly too out of place, which was a given considering this was--and has been--his bathroom for his entire life. Why would he seem out of place?

But then, why would he feel the need to interrupt my shower time?

He tucked his hands into his back pockets, an easygoing smirk on his lips as he leaned back against the countertop, acting for all the world like he was reveling in a prank on his new housemate.

"That wasn't funny, asshole."

One dark eyebrow raised, and I noticed that he'd put in a piercing on the edge of the left one that hadn't been there the night before.

Just like the piercing that adorned his lower lip, the small silver hoop interrupting the expanse of otherwise smooth and plump pink skin that I would've fantasized about on any other day, before.

Before...

The clouds jumbled up everything in my head, like there was an overcast day happening in my thoughts, and every so often, the sun shone high and bright and gave me the blessing of clearheadedness.

But then, the clouds came. Then, the fog took over.

"Sorry, but I thought I told you I took showers in the morning. Maybe you shouldn't have been using all the hot water."

He definitely did *not* look sorry.

His dark as night hair was strewn messily across his head and strands of it brushed across his cheeks and forehead, a slight stubble adorning his otherwise flawless skin.

How he managed to not have a single breakout astonished me.

I was almost jealous--of the perfect skin, of the long and pitch black eyelashes adorning his midnight eyes.

Almost--because being jealous would've been an admonition of feeling anything for Grey, and I wasn't ready to acknowledge any feeling pertaining to him. Not yet...maybe not ever.

"I didn't get a chance to shower last night."

"And why not?"

"I had...homework."

His lips pulled up into a knowing smirk, and if my eyes were working properly, I would've noted that it was most likely the sexist thing I'd ever seen.

Though his style screamed 'Stay Away', his body was clearly honed in the gym, all hard cut lines and muscle visible through the thin black cotton of his long sleeve t-shirt.

His denim jeans? Black.

His shoes? Black.

His hair, his piercings--even the ink I peeked crawling from up out of the neck of his shirt--all black.

"Well, maybe this will work out for the both of us, after all. You and I can shower together every morning, conserve the water."

My face dropped in shock. Surely I didn't understand what he'd just signed with his hands. There was no way he'd actually just said that...well, signed...ugh. There was no. way. I had that right. Right?

"Excuse me?"

I turned the shower off, seeing as I'd already washed my body and was in the middle of an existential life crisis when Grey had come in and interrupted what was most likely me self harming in an attempt to feel something other than the drowning nothing-ness I was staring into the face of.

"Naturally, I wouldn't want to burn myself, so we'd have to keep it at a decent temperature."

My eyes narrowed as I realized where he was going with this.

"Is that so?"

"Yes. I like it at a very mild temperature. Wouldn't want to burn myself."

"Oh, no you're totally right."

I turned the water back on again, at a normal temperature this time.

"Alright, it's ready. Aren't you getting in?"

"What?"

"The shower. You said you wanted to shower together, right? Come on, its ready for you."

I noticed as the gleam in his eye turned wicked.

"You think I won't do it, don't you? That's where you're so wrong."

I watched in a strange trance as Grey undid the laces on his black combat boots.

His deft fingers worked in a concentrated fashion, expertly untying quickly until he was onto the next boot.

I let the shower curtain drop as I disappeared into the shower again and placed some more body wash on my hands just to make it seem like I was still busy, even though I'd already washed myself before he'd so rudely interrupted me.

He thought I wouldn't go through with it? Typical. I was calling him on his bluff.

He'd be the first to back out, I just knew it.

The sound of his belt hitting the tiled floor of the bathroom filled the air, and suddenly I was wondering if this was a good idea after all...

The suds from my body wash came into contact with the skin of my back and my shoulder and I hissed out in pain, the throbbing and mind bending pain momentarily blinding me as stars and black dots assaulted my vision.

I had to get the soap off these burns that I'd given myself in the shower, but the thought of putting my injured skin in the pelting water was enough to make my knees sway with terror.

Grey tapped on the shower curtain, probably to see if I was alright, because it wasn't like he could just yell out, 'Cami, you good?'

"I'm fine, just...hurt my back earlier."

He grunted before the telltale sound of a zipper being undone echoes off the bathroom walls.

Okay, this was definitely not a good idea.

"Are you really going through with this? It was a joke..."

Even I could hear the panic in my voice as it trembled out.

I was just so stupid, stupid stupid.

I'd let Grey draw me in and bring out my stubborn pride. I'd let him bait me and my idiotic attitude and personality had fallen right for it.

I placed my back into the spray of water after a silent countdown from ten and the guttural cry that came out of my mouth was almost as painful as the first impact of the water itself.

Suddenly, Grey's hand appeared again, but this time it was holding a towel.

I shut the water off and gratefully took the towel, wrapping it around my skin before pulling the curtain back to find...something I wasn't expecting to see. At all.

Grey had pulled the vanity chair out and motioned for me to sit as all different arrays of moisturizers and lotions and bandages were placed on the counter.

The zipper I'd heard? It was from the bag filled to the brim with first aid products.

The belt I thought I'd heard hit the ground? The handle from the metal kit.

"How did you know...?"

"You're not the only one in this house who's done that before."

I was intensely aware of the shame crawling up my neck and resting in a blush along my cheeks, but still I dragged my dripping wet body clad in a pristine white towel to the vanity chair and sat while he inspected the wound.

I stared back at him in the mirror while he used his hands to tell me what I'd done.

"Looks minor, might not even blister, but we'll use the bandages anyway just in case. First, aloe, then bandage. This isn't going to feel good, so get ready."

I closed my eyes. I didn't want to see it coming; I wanted to feel the shock of the pain when it happened.

His touch was feather gentle and light--a stark contrast to the stinging pain that the salve brought to the skin.

But suddenly--that burn eased and the pain turned aching, and the sting from his fingers turned into a tingling chill that rose bumps along my arms and down my spine.

I shivered beneath his touch.

His hands left me and I looked up to him trying to speak to me.

"Is this alright?"

"Yeah. It doesn't hurt. Thank you."

There was some kind of unspoken, tangible thread between the two of us that I was scared to wonder if he felt, too. It was like some kind of mutual understanding that we could be as fucked up with the other as we wanted because we'd both seen it all.

His touch became firm as he placed the two thick bandages on my body, one on my upper back and the other on my left shoulder where my neck met the rest of me.

Already, I could feel whatever he'd put on me start to get to work.

"What did you use on my skin? Aloe?"

"No. Burn cream."

"Oh. Well, thank you."

"Just don't do it again. You're already making me relive memories I don't want to remember."

"Oh. Sorry."

"It's fine. But seriously, don't do that shit again."

"Fine, fine. I won't."

His demeanor had chilled, and suddenly it was like staring into a reflection of myself from the night before--someone hostile and half emotionless and fully done with this moment.

"Sorry I stole your shower time too. I didn't think it would bother you this much."

I stood and tugged the towel tighter around my frame, and I realized with sudden fear that I was shaking. Shivering and trembling from the cold or from the emotional upheaval--I wasn't sure which it was.

"Whatever. Get dressed--I'm taking you to school."

And then he left with a moody door slam that made me flinch from the sudden noise of it all.

Driving me to school, my ass. I was going to take advantage of the new Mercedes out in the driveway that Maria had let me use for the time being until they got Parker a new car.

"Cami! Yo! If you're not ready in fifteen, I'm taking the car without you! Better hurry, don't want helmet hair with grumpy driving you, do you?"

I silently cursed under my breath while I locked the other side of the bathroom door that led to Grey's room and got to work with the blowdryer, praying that I had time.

And then I remembered.

I'd be driving Parker to school.

Shit. Well, at least he was the lesser of two evils, right?

Right?

God, I hoped I was right.

Chapter 16

Parker preferred the radio to play the popular rap playlist on Spotify the entire ride to school.

Normally, I wouldn't have minded; it used to be his favorite kind of music as well, but today...

Today I was not in a rap music kind of mood.

There were two ways my musical genres could've gone today:

1. Heavy death metal where the singer is actually a screaming banshee yelling about death and destruction and hell and devouring your enemies and drinking their blood while slaughtering everything in sight.

2. Haunting melodies with heady orchestral production and heavenly vocals with lyrics detailing love lost and hearts broken and a pain unending.

Not songs with thumping bass bragging about a lifestyle they probably didn't even live, men objectifying women and women objectifying men.

When the third song came on, the singer droning on about drugs and ass and I was about done.

"Okay, how about no."

I snagged Parker's phone from the dash, thankfully unlocked and already on the Spotify page, and typed in my favorite playlist. 'Chill and Atmospheric'.

I was worried he would've had me committed had I put the other playlist on my mind, 'Death Metal Classics'.

"Really? You listen to this? It's so slow and boring."

"I don't listen to music for just the beats and the fact that it's what everyone listens to at house parties."

"I don't just listen to music for that reason either. I like rap music because of the beats and the lyrics, too."

"'I won't love a ho, after we fuck she can't get near me, only bitch I give a conversation to is Siri,'" I quoted back to him from one of the songs we'd just listened to.

"Okay, maybe that's not a very good lyric, but..."

"Yes? I'm listening."

"Okay, yeah, the lyrics are shit, but it's a good beat."

"Well then, let me introduce you to one of my favorite songs with more than just a good beat."

The song swelled and the orchestration grew in the background, the production bringing chills to my arms.

Parker bobbed his head to the music and seemed to be getting into it, and then the woman's voice cascaded in a lovely inter-woven melody that never failed to pull me out of whatever I was feeling.

"Holy shit. This sounds like it would be on Lord of the Rings or something. You just listen to this randomly?"

"Yep. It's fun to listen to it and get lost in that instead of my head."

"Why do you need to get lost in music? Everything alright?"

Jesus. His head had perked up from where he had been slouching against the steering wheel and was staring at me with intense scrutiny from the driver's seat.

Why did he care so much?

"It's fine. Everything is fine."

"Really? You know, you could tell me if things weren't. Fine, I mean. If you're in some kind of trouble, or--"

"I'm fine. You can stop your interrogation now."

I turned the song all the way up until its final finish, but it didn't give me the goosebumps I was waiting for. It did nothing for me at all.

We pulled up to the school and the only thing I'd accomplished was making yet another Hartingrove boy suspicious about my behavior.

At least I could (partly) trust one of them not to spill my secrets.

I was glad when Maria and her husband were gone by the time I descended the stairs in my uniform (which had been a bitch to put on with my burns) and met Parker in the foyer exactly fifteen minutes after he'd yelled at me through the bathroom.

I'd simply told him that he would be driving, and Grey who'd been set off to the side eating a banana and scrolling mindlessly through his phone hardly looked up.

So much for demanding that I ride with him to school.

I should've listened to him.

We pulled up in Parker's normal parking spot, which of course was settled around the rest of the expensive cars, though his friend group were all huddled around one in particular.

Colton's large Jeep Wrangler sat in the middle of the group of students all passing around what was probably a joint.

I couldn't believe my eyes when I saw the girl draped under the arm of Colton's best friend, Carter Jennings, though.

Mori Catawnee, my best friend since joining Hartingrove, was laughing and smiling her brightest triumphant smile at Carter like he was the sun and she was just revolving around him.

Shit.

"Oh hey, isn't that your friend? Come on, why don't you go over there and we can just say the past is the past with Colton, it'll be awesome I promise. He's probably already moved on anyway and doesn't even care that you ditched him that one time."

"Uh huh. Right."

I was frozen. Completely.

A damn popsicle in the passenger seat, unable to move, unable to think, unable to feel.

Hot terror tore through me at the thought of what happened to me happening to Mori at the hands of someone else, someone even more vicious or rough than Colton.

Of course, admitting to myself that what happened to me was horrible enough to endure the presence of Colton himself just to get Mori away from those people was hard enough, but it was time to face it.

I had been hurt. Assaulted. Defiled. Whatever you wanted to call it, just not that word. I couldn't think that word. Not yet.

But I wouldn't let it happen to Mori. It wasn't fair, and it wasn't pretty, but one way or another I was going to get her away from these people and beg her to forgive me for ever putting her on their radar in the first place.

Was this Colton's revenge, then?

Get Mori involved with his best friend and then use her like he'd used me? Or would he tell the best friend to do it instead?

They were all despicable, each and every one of them.

I shouldn't have ever thought Parker was a good person, some-one crush-worthy.

I was clearly a terrible judge of character if I'd let myself be Colton's plaything for so long, practically whoring myself out to him for a warm place to sleep and food in my belly.

I was pathetic. A useless worm who'd be better off gone.

Who did I have in this world? A dad in prison who'd murdered my mother, a social worker who couldn't care enough about me to make sure I'd been placed in good, loving homes before now, a broken, damaged boy who couldn't (or wouldn't) speak, and his mother--a seemingly lovely woman who'd I'd only known for less than a week.

Sure, I'd had Mori, but how was it going to go over when I told her she couldn't be with Carter, without any reason why?

I couldn't tell her. Would she even believe me if I did?

Parker was at my door, holding his hand out to me, and the rest of his group were staring.

Mori was waving, a brilliant smile on her face, and I wanted to puke.

My heart wouldn't stop beating in my chest. God, what I'd give for a heart attack right now, for my stupid fucking heart to just skip a beat, then two, then just give out completely in my chest.

What a headline that would read.

Otherwise Healthy Seventeen-year-old Girl Dies in School Parking Lot From Total Heart Failure.

What a cautionary tale I'd be.

"Cami. Come on. Aren't you gonna go over to your friend and say hi?"

No. no no no no no no no no no no no no no no no no no no no no no nononononononononononononono

Fucking. NO!

"Yeah. Let me grab my bag from the back."

He stepped back while I reached behind me and winced as my burns rubbed against their bandages.

My legs and body moved of their own accord.

My mind was screaming, begging, pleading for me to turn around and run into the school, or better yet--steal the keys dangling from Parker's hands and make a mad escape from this shit show that was soon to go down, but before I could convince my body that it was a good idea, I was already walking in short, staccato steps towards the group.

Four guys and four girls including Mo, they watched us with a strange look on their faces, like they'd smelled something bad. Everyone except Mori of course. And Victoria. She just looked confused. Okay, and Parker's best friend Alec, who looked like he didn't give one single shit what was happening around him.

"Hey guys," Parker called, and then my feet stopped. We were standing in a tight circle, and Colton, Carter and Mo were standing to my right.

Nate, Alec, and the three girls were to my left, with Parker standing partially behind and to the right of me.

I might've subtly angled myself toward Parker's body to shield me.

Don't look at him. Don't look at him. Don't look don't look don't look don't--

"Cami. Surprised to see you here." Colton's first words to me since *it* happened.

I inhaled air, but it scorched down my throat like smoke.

"Yeah, heard you were too good for us to show up last weekend." One of the girls, maybe Leah.

Don't look. Don't look. *Don't look.*

"That true? You too good for us?" Colton again.

They laughed, but I stared down at the pavement that I wished would open up in a sinkhole and swallow me down whole.

"Cami's actually staying--"

Parker was cut off from telling everyone where I was staying by the voracious sound of a motorcycle pulling up directly in front of everyone, like a raging beast come to save the day.

Grey was darkness and danger incarnate--his helmet sliding off his head with perfect ease, and some long forgotten part of me stirred awake at the sight of him climbing off and leveling me with a deep look that only I could discern.

"Here we go," someone muttered to themselves, causing some of the girls to giggle.

"Wonder what emo-boy wants." There was no mistaking Leah's voice on that one.

They all held their breath once Grey signed to me, though. Their mouths hung open, agape.

Was this the first time he'd ever signed at school?

"What are you doing with these assholes? Come on, let's go."

"I have to make sure my friend's alright first," I signed back, not wanting the others to know what we were talking about. I didn't wonder if any of them knew ASL. I frankly didn't care if they did or not.

"She looks fine to me."

"She's not if she's with him."

Grey shook his head and strode to the group he'd just pulled up beside, though they all moved back like he had something wrong with him.

Everyone except Mori, the one nice girl Victoria, and Parker's best friend Alec, who was so lost in his own world with his foot up on the tailgate flicking a lighter that we could've turned into mermaids on the spot and he wouldn't have noticed.

Grey didn't stop advancing until he was directly in front of me, blocking me from Colton's searing gaze.

"Then get your friend and let's go. You're a part of the freak show now baby, you can't take it back."

I scoffed out loud, wondering what the others were thinking about this silent conversation until I realized that they were whispering to themselves. And then I remembered--I honestly didn't give a shit.

"Hey Mo, can I borrow you for a second?"

"Uh...yeah, I guess."

Grey went to-to-toe with Parker who widened his eyes and stepped away from me, Grey taking his brother's spot to my right as we both walked away from the group, every single eye trained on us, even Parker's friend Alec who couldn't be bothered before were staring.

"What was all that about?"

Mo's eyes were wide and questioning, and I couldn't blame her.

"We need to talk."

Chapter 17

A few students were splashing a girl in a puddle nearby. Someone was FaceTiming with their grandma while being made fun of by their friends at the picnic table next to us.

I swatted at a fly that flew too close to my head.

The faint scent of weed hit my nostrils and then everything besides Grey disappeared.

He was at my side, strong and protective, his inviting cologne dripping with hints of woodsy balsam a heady mixture nearly crumbling me on the spot.

Grey herded us over to the outdoor picnic tables, one arm coming around my waist and guiding me there. Shit. That wasn't supposed to feel warm and comforting, was it?

No. Not after that confrontation that almost left me as mute as Grey. I wasn't supposed to feel safe and warm right after that, but somehow...he *made* me feel it, like he pushed back every wall and boundary I'd placed to keep that very thing from happening.

The faint echo of my words 'we need to talk' hung on the dew drops still steaming in the foggy air around us.

"No shit. You haven't texted me all week, you've barely been at school. I was starting to think you were friend-ghosting me."

It was a testament to Mori's personality that she didn't even question Grey's appearance once.

"I'm sorry. I had some...personal things going on."

Mo cocked one black eyebrow as her brown skin shimmered dark gold in the rising morning sun.

I'm waiting, her posture screamed.

"I...I don't really know how to say any of this," I started, slinking down onto the bench seat of the picnic table we'd decided on, the old wood of the table biting into my palms as a stray splinter caught in the tights I was forced to wear per the dress code at Hartingrove.

If I never had to wear another plaid skirt again, it would be too soon.

"When did you start hanging out with Carter and his friends?" I started, not knowing how exactly to steer this conversation but assumed that asking this was the doorway to unraveling what was going on.

"Uh...the day after Colton asked you out on the bus in front of everyone. Maybe I should be asking *you* when you started hanging out with them?"

It all fell down on me like a lead weight pressing down on my chest, but I didn't show it. I didn't breathe in and suck down the flames wanting to light me up from the outside in.

"Carter came up to me and invited me along to whatever they were doing that Saturday, and I said yes because he said you and Colton would be there, too. So I was pretty surprised when you fell off the face of the earth afterwards. I still went and hung out with them though in their basement. It was pretty fun."

Pretty fun.

Maybe Carter wasn't just like Colton, but could I take that chance? Could I let one of the only people I actually cared about in this godforsaken place get caught up in the same mess that I had?

Would I ever be able to forgive myself if I did?

"And look, I'm not judging. Whatever you had going on with him is..." she paused, looking pointedly at Grey before continuing. "Clearly over. I was just trying to keep up with you. But now, I got to really know Carter and he's actually really sweet and nice to me. Can you believe he actually helped me with my chemistry homework? Apparently he's some closeted genius."

"So you've just forgotten about all the 'scholarship pussy' remarks? All the times they made fun of us almost to our faces?"

I could tell the moment she started pulling away from me. I'd gone too far, but I didn't know how to put it all back together again.

"And? I could ask you the same exact thing. According to Colton, you guys have been together for months under the radar, not telling anyone. If anyone should be asking those questions, it should be me. Especially considering the fact that he kept up his actions while you two were supposed to be together. I don't know what I'm supposed to think, Cami. One minute we're as close as two friends could be, and then the next it's like I have no idea who you are. You have a secret boyfriend, you don't live at the address you gave me anymore, you're hanging out with a different guy now, and...I don't know. That's the whole point; I just *don't know* anymore."

"I'm sorry, Mo. I got placed in a new home, it's temporary, but it's--I'm staying with Grey and Parker, that's why everything has been so crazy lately. I just got moved to their place last week, right after Colton told everyone about us."

"Oh. So that's why emo-dude keeps following you around?"

"Uh, you do know he can hear you right?"

Mori sucked in a gasp and her eyes widened exponentially, gaze darting to where Grey sat beside us idly rolling his lip ring in between his fingers slowly, almost sensually, his focus anywhere but on us--almost like he could still see all the way out to the parking lot and directly into his brother's eyes.

"I am--so sorry, I honestly thought you were deaf and--"

"And that makes it cool to talk shit about me while I'm right beside you anyway, just because you thought I couldn't hear it?"

Grey scoffed and draped an arm across his leg propped up against the picnic table.

He pulled a lighter and cigarette out of his pocket and lit it up.

"Wow. Cliche much?"

"Fuck off. Not like I can smoke weed here."

"Thank god I know the sign for weed."

"What are you guys talking about?"

I glanced to Mori, still looking sheepish and a little bit guilty.

"Sorry, I guess I forgot not everyone knows sign language...bas ically--he said it's not cool to talk shit about someone right there even if they couldn't hear it."

"Well obviously, I wasn't talking shit, just stating a fact. I mean, he's basically himself goth or emo or whatever you want to call it with his outfits. Don't get me wrong, I'm all here for it--it just doesn't scream 'uniform appropriate' but I guess you can get away with it when you're the dean's son."

Mori's words drifted away as the wind shifted the leaves still clinging onto the scraggly trees in the courtyard, blowing an au- tumnal breeze by in a whispered song telling the story of a chang- ing season.

That very same breeze tinted with notes of crisp cool air and the decay of summer ruffled the dark-as-night hair atop Grey's head, and I was struck with the irony of his name versus his appearance and personality.

Grey was the antithesis of the lack of color; a vibrant splash of darkness across a rainbow background desperate to taint him with their bright and eye-catching hues.

Grey was gloomy and bathed in shadows, drenched in darkness and drawn to life with a steady hand.

His canvas was a background of whorls of pink and purple sunset shades, but his outline was an ink stain blot against it.

The ground of Grey's portrait was verdant green and lush with wildflowers--like the artist was trying to regain the beauty in the pigment but forgot that the sun can't shine without the night--that you can't feel the heat without its absence.

His face, though expressive and full and entrancing was left blank. Unformed. Unfinished, untouched.

It could've been swathed in tan neutral shades to match his warm olive skin tone. It could've been cut with dark shadows to highlight his sharp jaw line and light stubble crawling across it.

It could've been painted with delicate strokes to capture his black metal piercings and slight peeking of tattoos reaching through the collars of his shirts like arms outstretched around his neck, as if their spindly, ink-wrought hands could erase the damage done to his throat.

It could have depicted the light pink fading scars around his throat that I'd been far too scared to glimpse up close, until now.

Until this moment in the buttery sunshine rays, lost in a stolen figment in the fracture of time, in the space between one breath and the next, when our eyes locked and refused to let go.

When his fingertips brushed against mine and that portrait suddenly came to life in my mind, all those rainbow colors lost their pigment but never lost their vibrancy--like they all turned perfectly translucent and effortlessly grey--the color of peace before a sunrise and the shroud of mist over a calm rippling pond.

Suddenly, the color grey wasn't nothingness—but the absence of pain yet the refusal to accept happiness—some kind of in between limbo where happy and sad didn't have a name, where 'good' and 'bad' were only words in some forgotten dictionary in a language no one knew how to speak anymore.

Grey's throat bobbed up, that scar moving up right along with it, and my mind suddenly conjured another figure in that portrait of Grey's, one that I was too scared to give color to. A figure that my brain could only outline, because her insides were empty and her soul a muddy brown color mixed up with too many others and indistinguishable from the brilliance of the serenity of the painting she was ruining with her presence.

Mori cleared her throat, and the painter in my head erased the second figure from Grey's figurative painting.

It would've destroyed the picture in the end, anyway. Grey was better off a solitary, lone figure. Perfect and peaceful and calm.

"Sorry. What'd you say?"

I didn't break from Grey's eyes until she spoke to me again, and then met her dark eyes and their confusion filled depths head on.

"Bell rang. You ready? We can talk more at lunch, but I'm sitting with Carter. You good with eating with his friends, too?"

And then that panic was back, rising up in my gut with such effective lucidity that for a moment, I was suddenly there in a darkened room with a forceful hand on my naked back, pressing, pressing--*pressing down on me* and I couldn't breathe.

Why can't I breathe?

"Sorry, gotta run. See you at lunch!"

She hadn't given me time to speak, because I couldn't catch my breath.

Maybe that was a good thing.

Because I didn't breathe in the scent of Colton's cologne as it became lodged up in my nose once more as he strode by with his friends in tow--

and I couldn't tell if it was relief, or...

some kind of twisted morbid disappointment that he didn't look back.

Didn't stop to see what a mess he'd made.

Didn't put the final nail in my coffin, didn't throw the last knock-out punch.

I was

right

there.

I'M RIGHT HERE!

Can't you see me?!

Can't you see what you've done?

Don't you KNOW this is wrong?

Do you think you've done NOTHING WRONG?

But then Grey's hand was on my back instead of that searing print tugging me down deep into an abyss darker than the empti-ness that I'd imagined encompassed the outline of my soul on that painting I wished I could've been drawn next to Grey in.

It was that shock and that reminder that we were both a little too fucked up for our own good that had me pulling away, turning from him so that he couldn't try to sign to me.

I didn't turn even as he gripped my shoulder.

I didn't even breathe as I ripped up that painting in my head and threw it in the trash where my good memories went, and cursed my brain for not allowing me to do the same with the bad ones.

If everything I know and remember is terrible, then it won't hurt as much if I can't remember a time when things were different.

You can't feel pain without first having felt joy or peace. Right?

So what would happen if I just forgot it all, and sunk myself down into the misery once and for all?

Would I drown? Or would the sting of the dark keep me afloat long enough to get my head above water?

I should've known that I was already breathing water into my lungs.

Chapter 18

S chool was a blurry figment of daily monotony that could drive even the most stable person mad.

It was a wonder anyone ever escaped alive.

I almost didn't.

I was determined to make sure she survived, though.

Something had happened to Cami—something unspeakable that forced her to retreat into her mind and shut out the world.

She was a billowing tuft of sunshine in a broken cast—a fragile paper doll with the eyes carved out and shadows left to replace them.

She hasn't let me speak to her I'd gotten lost in her eyes; fuck.

Those damn eyes.

They haunted me even when I closed my own, following me down deep into the depths beneath my conscious thoughts.

She was there the night before in my dreams, laughing and talking with me like she had when I'd taken her to the lookout.

She was fiery and wild and argumentative and utterly uncaring about the way I dressed, the piercings, the attitude...

the scars, physical and otherwise.

She was unlike anyone I'd ever met—and maybe it was because some of our traumas matched like twin flames burning in a tunnel of malcontent, but she called to me in a way that had my grip on my surroundings fading and falling away.

We were in a deadly game that danced and sang to the tune of our pasts, and I didn't know what would happen once we reached the final note.

We had two classes together before lunch.

It didn't matter how hard I tried to pay attention to the class, though. My eyes were always on her.

Cheeks flushed and eyes wild, she drew mindless circles on her notebook with red ink—the lines so thick and stained it colored the page like scarlet blood against pale white skin.

Cami was staring off into space for the next class, hands clenched so hard her knuckles were white with the force of her stress.

Parker was staring holes into the side of my head, but I didn't care. I didn't give him a second thought as Cami's breathing increased and a lone tear slid down her cheek.

What was going on in that mind of hers, locked in a death-grip by her traumas and thoughts that must've been drowning her?

What had caused her so much pain, so much grief in her young life?

I knew the answer wasn't all that simple.

Most probably thought the same of me—what had happened to me that made me want to take my own life just a few short years ago?

The answer wasn't simple. It never was.

Sometimes, there were never really any answers, either.

Sometimes, the *not* knowing was knowing enough to make sure that what you were doing wasn't just for the pain of it all, but for the escape and the freedom that felt like flying when you finally fall asleep.

That blissful, deep black abyss.

Sleep, if only for eternity.

Colton stood minutes before the bell rang pulling out a note excusing him for an academic advising appointment before lunch and his bag slammed into Cami's shoulder as he ambled down the aisle toward the door.

"I'm so sorry, are you okay?"

Colton was crouched by Cami's desk, eyes staring intently into her own, but she refused to look back at him.

Her eyes were pinned to the blackboard ahead, where the teacher fumbled around with different books on her desk.

We were supposed to be reading the new chapter we'd just been assigned for 'Of Mice and Men' and while everyone else was focusing on the book in their hands, or rather, the phone they were hiding behind their book, I was more interested in what was happening at Cami's desk.

"Cami? You alright?"

Colton waved his hand in front of her face, but she didn't move.

She was a statue, unmoving, unblinking.

Motionless, save for the shaking of her thin, delicate frame.

He placed a hand on her back, and she flinched like the touch had burned her.

A drop of blood dripped from her palm onto the floor, and I suddenly realized just how hard her hands were clenched.

My legs rocketed me upwards quickly, like they had a mind of their own.

I was at Cami's desk in an instant, grabbing Colton's arm and yanking him upright while pushing him back simultaneously.

"What the fuck, dude?"

"Language, Mr. Wright. Grey—oh, uh...please, go back to your seat."

I didn't move an inch.

Though, neither did Colton.

"Mr. Wright, why don't you head on to your advising appointment."

Every eye was on the two of us, though not Cami's. From my peripherals, I could tell that she sat still, the shaking becoming more and more noticeable. Soon, everyone would understand exactly what I was beginning to realize.

Heat and anger and pure fire burned in the gaze of my eyes, and if I'd been gifted with the power, Colton would've been a smoldering pile of dust and ash in this moment.

"Dude, sit the fuck down. What's your problem?"

Parker was at my side, though I wasn't sure when he'd gotten there.

I stood tall at my large height that towered over Colton's shorter frame.

Cold, hot fury roiled through my veins at the thoughts of what he could've done to receive such a visceral reaction from Cami, and all of them were enough for my mind to start begging me to end this motherfucker right here and now.

I could've sworn I saw a bead of sweat appear on his forehead, but he wasn't backing down as he bowed his chest up, but his head barely reached my shoulder.

It was comedic, really.

"What's wrong, Greylon? Cat got your tongue?"

I stiffened at the use of my full name, but didn't let it show.

"Or wait...was it a noose?"

He didn't get another word out of his mouth before my fist was buried in his face.

The pain stung so good, I almost wish I could've relished it longer, but then he was rearing back to get a clip in against me.

Parker's hand caught Colton's fist before it could be directed toward me, and then I watched in amazement as my brother laid out one of his friends and tumbled to the ground with him, punch after punch after punch until Colton's face was nearly unrecognizable, blood dripping all around mixing with the one single drop of Cami's that had fallen on the ground.

Not even a single drop of her blood drawn from her own hand—or anyone else's— was acceptable.

I'd make sure anyone who tried to fuck with her got exactly what they deserved; Parker just beat me to the punch—literally—on making sure Colton received his fair share.

I didn't stop to watch on any longer than I needed to.

The crowd had formed, the resource officers for the school were being called and the teacher had already ran out of the room for help.

I dropped to Cami's side and pried her slim fingers from her palm and winced at the bloody mess she'd made of her hands.

I didn't waste time grabbing up her things before helping her up and holding her tightly against my chest under my arm, her bag slung over my other arm as shouts and yells echoed throughout the small classroom.

Mori walked up to us, frantic and panicked, but I brushed past her. Now that I had Cami under my arm, I wasn't letting her get caught up in this mess. I was getting her out of here as fast as I could, and then I would get answers as to what really happened.

Or I wouldn't.

I deflated as I realized I couldn't force answers out of her, especially in the state she was in currently.

Students and teachers usually avoided me and gave me a wide berth in this school, but with Cami attached to my side and shaking like a leaf, we attracted more than enough curious glances as I picked our pace up in the hallway as Mori was still running after us, a vengeance in her voice that I was surprised could come out of such a tiny person.

It didn't matter; I was getting Cami the hell out of this school.

"Grey! Where are you taking her? What the hell happened?"

I had never wished to be able to speak more in that moment than I ever had before.

What the fuck does she think happened?

Did she not have eyes?

Colton was clearly harassing her, right in front of everyone.

What he must have done to her to get that kind of a reaction out of someone so full of wild, passionate light...

I could barely stop the bile from rising up in my gut at the thought of the things that he could have done.

I was strangely protective of Cami, especially after only knowing her for such a short amount of time.

Maybe it was the fact that from Parker's stories about her, it felt like I'd already known her before we officially met, but it was something different than that, something deeper and more intrinsic.

She was like my fellow soldier in the foot war of life; sitting there in the trenches with me while the gasoline skies doused us with artillery fire.

She was a haunted and anguished duplicate that reflected the person I stared back at in the mirror each morning and night; a battered warrior desperate for the fight to finally end.

Cami didn't hesitate when we reached my bike and I handed her the helmet. She'd need it more than I did.

She had more to live for than I did. I just wished I could convince *her* of that.

This would be my one last purpose in this meaningless life. Maybe I could make it mean just a little bit more for someone else.

I could make her realize just how much life was worth living—for her.

I could show her the truths and the highs and lows, the elegance and the madness, the beauty in the face of despair.

I could do for her what I could never do for myself—and then I'll have accomplished everything I needed to.

"Where are we going?"

Her voice was a melancholic zombie rendition of the once colorful chime I'd grown used to hearing.

I wanted to hear that voice scream and rage against the unjustness and depravity of the world.

I wanted to listen to her sing and cry and yell at me with that same fervor and passion she'd barely shown to me the night before at the lookout.

But instead, I settled for something that would hopefully wipe that lethally calm expression off her face and replace it with one of peace instead.

"It's a surprise."

She didn't question me as she slung her leg over the side of my bike and ignored the blatant stares of every single student who'd filed outside for the mandatory drill that followed in-school fights.

Her arms clutched my waist so tight I was afraid she'd crush my ribs, but at least she didn't wince when her hands made contact with the leather of my jacket.

I kicked the leg stand and balanced our weight, the engine roaring to life underneath us as Mori and some of Parker's friends started power-walking their way toward us, like they had any reason that would make me stay.

They were in the rear view mirror by the time I peeled out.

Cami rested her cheek across my back, and I could've sworn she breathed a soft, whispered "Thank you," against me.

She stopped shaking the moment we hit the highway.

Chapter 19

"So you hit him because he said something offensive to your brother, and then you just didn't stop because…?"

On some accounts, having the dean of your school as your father was something some kids would take advantage of.

Not me.

I took it as a challenge to prove to others that my accomplishments were my own, and I intended to make sure that I earned that Valedictorian award all by myself with no kickbacks or preferential treatment.

"Because I was still pissed."

"I see. And why was he having a confrontation with Grey in front of the entire class in the first place?"

My dad paced from one side of his spacious office to the other, and I was grateful that this was the first time I'd ever been sent here.

It was fucking intimidating.

"I don't know, I guess he was making some girl…Cami…he was making her uncomfortable in front of everyone. He wouldn't leave her alone, so Grey tried to make him stop, but it only pissed

Colton off even more. Look, if anyone's in the wrong here, it's that asshole—"

"Language, son. And it's my job to hear every side of the story—including you instructor's side—to make sure that everyone's telling the truth and figure out what really happened. You said he was bothering Cami—is that the same Camille that's staying with us? Camille Astor? She wasn't mentioned in any of the other reports made by the students or even by Colton. She seems to have disappeared along with your brother. Know anything about that?"

"No."

And the bitter resentment in my voice was the indicator that I wasn't emotionless about the topic, either.

It was like the universe thought this was some big cosmic joke.

I wanted her, my ex-friend had her, and now my brother got to keep her. Just like with what happened in the past, Grey always gets handed things the easy way because of what happened to him. Because he's 'damaged'.

I wish they all knew what damaged really looked like.

Maybe then they wouldn't think that I was the good kid anymore, the golden child like my friends used to joke.

I wasn't the fuck up or the suicidal kid. I was just normal, hard-working and kept my head down and did what I was supposed to do—until now.

Until I saw red after what Colton had said.

I had started to rise from my seat the moment Grey had when I noticed Colton making Cami uncomfortable. Anyone with two brain cells to rub together could tell how much she didn't like that guy, although the history there was still confusing as he'd made it seem like he had been the one to dump her when she wanted to stay together, but it didn't make him practically harassing her any better.

When I noticed my brother stand up to scare the guy off, I thought, *good. Now I don't have to deal with the drama in my friend group for pissing him off. Grey will set him straight.*

Until I watched in horrified silence as the amused maliciousness bloomed across Colton's face—something akin to violence hiding behind his eyes, and it was the first time that I'd seen beneath the mask that he wore for all of our friends and actually believed that he could be somewhat dangerous.

And then those words he'd said to my brother...

Sure, I held resentment for Grey. Who wouldn't?

What he put my family through...it was unspeakable how distraught and ruined my mom had been for months and months after Grey's attempt in front of me.

For him, though?

She was a solid, strong and steady rock, keeping a cool and calm facade of warmth and radiance that he could latch onto in order to get himself healthy enough to come home instead of the mental wellness retreat program he'd entered for six months.

He was coddled and soothed, while everyone else had to suck it up and pick up the pieces.

Still I wondered. Still I asked him, but never received an actual answer.

Why.

Why would he have done that to us?

Was his life really that bad? What could possibly have happened to make him think that death was the only escape?

To me, death was a prison, some kind of feared afterlife that would judge you on the things you did and didn't do, the person you were in this hellish landscape of the living.

Maybe this earth was the actual hell, and we were all just going through the motions, striving for greatness until an inevitable end and searching for an eternity of peace, only to wake up in another human body and do it all over again.

Maybe we were just living in hell on earth, and this was the eternity they were talking about.

I couldn't imagine it ending, though.

Death was terrifying, and I planned to ignore its existence until mine became inevitable.

"Parker?"

"Huh? Yeah, sorry."

"I asked you what Mr. Wright said to your brother."

"Oh...um. He said something about him trying to kill himself. Mentioned a noose. I don't know, it's all a little bit of a blur, but once I heard that I guess I just snapped. I'm sorry."

"You should be. Your brother can take care of himself. You don't deserve to have a negative spot on your permanent record just to defend your brother for something that he did."

"Wait—what? You're mad that I defended my brother from that asshole?"

"You didn't just defend him—you damn near beat that boy within an inch of his life. He's in the hospital right now having reconstructive surgery done on his nose. How do you think that makes us look, huh? Your brother made his choice about where he stands with this family a long time ago."

"And what is that supposed to mean?"

"Grey decided he'd rather be dead than be a part of this family. Maybe it's time to let him live with that decision."

"So you're saying if someone is coming after MY family, that I shouldn't defend them because their mental health was suffering and no one was around or paid enough attention to the warning signs? He was crying out for help and either no one cared or they just didn't give enough of a shit to see it. You're the one who failed here, dad. Not me."

He sighed out in exasperation and pinched the bridge of his nose with his forefinger and thumb, whipping his glasses off and throwing an accusatory stare in my direction.

His glare was so sharp it almost cut me with its intensity.

But I wasn't backing down. Not this time.

I was so sick and tired of my father refusing to help Grey all because of the decision he made years ago. It wasn't like any of us knew he was suffering as much as he really was, but I was trying to change things.

I was trying, actively working to see the signs for my friend Alec. I didn't want the same thing to happen to him like it almost happened to Grey.

I couldn't survive that failure again.

Grey was my brother—my other half, the person that was supposed to always be there for me, and because of my resentment after everything, I hadn't been there for him lately.

It was time to open my eyes, to step up and do better, for him, for Alec, and even for Cami.

Anyone with eyes could tell that that girl was suffering almost as much as Grey had been back then, suffering out in the open where anyone with two eyes could see what was happening.

"Just—just go home, Parker. You're suspended for the rest of the week and you're on behavioral probation. One more screw up and you're out. Just because I'm your father doesn't mean I can protect you from these kinds of things. Do you understand?"

"Yes."

"Excuse me?"

"Yes, sir."

"Good. Now, go. I have a meeting with Colton's parents to explain why my son almost put him in the morgue."

I didn't waste time escaping my father's office.

Funny how in that entire meeting, he'd been more concerned with the kid who'd bullied his own child.

It had been like that for a few years; my dad not giving a shit about Grey.

It all started after his attempt, though.

Something was nagging at me in the back of my mind, though, that it was something different than that. Something deeper, but I couldn't put my finger on it.

Instead, I made my way back to my car and hoped that Grey had taken Cami on his motorcycle because I didn't hesitate before driving to Grey's favorite place that he used to escape from his problems.

The roar of the engine and loud music drowned out everything in the world around me as I stumbled upon Grey and Cami already there, staring up at the base of the mountain as a small smile pulled upon her face.

They hadn't seen me yet. I waited, but it never happened.

Instead, they walked into the cave systems together hand in hand, and a little piece of me broke once more.

He had Cami, she had him. I had Alec, my mom had my father...

Who had me?

Was I even worth having someone there for me in the first place?

I didn't look back as I drove away.

Soft rays of warm sunlight penetrated the harsh blast of pain that threatened to suffocate me before we ever even left the parking lot.

I could still sense his handprint on my back, the weight of it shoving me down into a deep corner of my mind that I was scared I'd never crawl out of.

He was still there, hovering beside me, lingering in my mind and in the back of my head like a malignant tumor that would never ever leave, would never let me escape....

Would I ever escape? Could I?

I would. I would never escape.

I could.

It would happen.

It will happen.

Wild spring water gurgled by on a stuttered current, small fish bounding up and down as Grey pulled the motorcycle to an abrupt stop on the side of a clearing that led to a walking path.

Redding, California held hidden wonders that most wouldn't expect—I surely didn't expect to be blindsided by such beauty.

Helmet off and sunlight brandishing my sight, Grey tapped my shoulder to get my attention.

"Follow me," he signed, and I did as he instructed, allowing him to lead the way and let my mind turn into background noise while the songs of nature around us filled every aching piece of me with a sense of calm and peace that I hadn't had in so long.

It was beautiful here, painfully so.

The kind of beauty that you wanted to be able to gaze upon every day; but it was the knowing that you had to return to the real world soon was what gave it that fleeting sweet taste of temporary euphoria.

"Where are we going?"

The mountain loomed up well above us, imposing in its stature as I stared and stared and tried to imagine what could've carved something of such significance.

My history brain knew—the scientific aspect, at least.

If you believed in a god or a higher power, you'd say it was carved and cut from his or her hand, crafted from cosmic radiance.

If you believed in a more scientific approach, however, it was the forming of lands, the slamming together of plates underneath the earth's surface, the erosion of land from water and exposure to the elements.

Whatever you believed, however, it was still a magnificent sight to behold.

Grey's hand was suddenly on the small of my back, and I was drowning.

I was suffocating underneath this mountain of grief and shame and guilt that I knew I shouldn't have felt, but still did.

It was my fault.

I could've done something more to stop it.

I could've stopped him.

It wasn't my fault.

I couldn't have done anything more to stop it.

I couldn't have stopped him.

It wasn't my fault.

Grey's touch grew gentle as the soft breeze floating by us.

His impassive face morphed into something serious, and once more I found my fingers itching to draw this portrait in front of me.

In the bright and shining afternoon sun with pale tufts of clouds gliding overhead as the songbirds and butterflies fluttered nearby, he was absolutely and irrevocably ethereal, irreverent, Grey was a translucent color that was constantly seen but never studied, never appreciated.

"Follow me, Cami."

So I followed him.

I was starting to realize that there was nowhere this boy would go that I wouldn't follow.

Chapter 20

Cami was shivering, even though the sun was casting the field in warm rays causing sweat to bead up on my forehead.

It didn't matter, though. Where we were going, it was cool and dark and one of the most amazing sights I'd ever witnessed.

I only hoped that she'd feel that way, too.

I was worried that she might've been shivering for an entirely different reason than the temperature, so I didn't think twice before placing my hand in hers and linking our fingers together.

I could sign with just one hand if I had to.

She could always ask me to mouth the words, too.

I could still whisper, considering that didn't use my vocal cords, but for some reason any kind of communication with my words out of my mouth just didn't feel right.

Not now, at least.

I tucked away the dwindling time left for me to make a decision on my voice forever to the back of my mind. This was about getting Cami's mind off of Colton and what had happened with my brother.

This was about helping her heal; showing her everything she'd be missing if she acted on those impulses I knew were firing back and forth in her head.

I'd felt the exact way, too, once upon a time. And maybe even a few more times since then.

An addict doesn't magically stop being tempted by their vice once they remove themselves from the situation.

A cancer patient isn't magically cured when they undergo treatment.

They go into remission.

I guess I could say I was in remission with my mental illness.

I would be fine one day, destroyed the next.

It was what always happened, but with Cami by me, I could only hope the next flare up took longer to rear its ugly head.

I didn't want her seeing that side of me, ever, but I knew it wasn't a reality to keep it under wraps forever.

The verdant grass crunched beneath our feet and the mud tried to stick to the underside of my black shoes but still we trudged on.

Her soft, warm hand squeezed mine a few times when her breathing sped up, almost like she could feel her panic attack coming on and was tightening her grip on me to make sure she was still okay; that she was still here.

Or that I was still with her.

"You know, I somewhat trust you since the view was so pretty the last time you took me somewhere, but I still haven't ruled out that you're a murdering psychopath."

"Psychopaths don't have a conscience. I would be classified as a sociopath, but I wouldn't commit crimes against people I like or admire, like my family and friends. You need to brush up on your criminal terminology."

Having to spell out a few words on my right hand instead of signing out the entire word might've been a burden if I weren't holding Cami's hand.

If it were anything else...

"Oh, right. So you're a good murderer? What, like Dexter? You only kill the ones who deserve it?"

"Exactly. People like Colton."

She shuddered after I finished using letters to sign out the asshole's name.

"I don't want to talk about him."

We were almost to the entrance of the cave, anyway.

"Fine. We're almost here, anyway."

I didn't want to push her, but I still couldn't get it out of my head.

The way she'd acted around him, the reaction she'd had when he touched her back...

It was why I'd been so gentle in touching her back, because she'd almost flinched out of her skin when I'd done it.

Yes, something traumatic had happened to her, and recently.

I wanted to throw up when I calculated what, exactly, could happen to a girl at the hands of a guy. The visualizations in my head were gruesome and bloody and violent and I wanted to rip Colton limb from limb and string him up in front of the entire town to make others understand what I'd do to garbage humans that thought it was acceptable to hurt a woman, or anyone smaller than them to begin with.

If I'd found out he'd done anything to another girl at the school, I'd still be equally vengeful and full of wrath, but it was the thought of him touching Cami in that way absolutely blinded me to acceptable behavior in front of others.

So long as he was around me, I would not be able to control myself or my actions.

Cami stumbled a bit as we reached the rocky outcrop of the entrance to the mountain caves I'd discovered during my adventuring phase, the one where I was trying to connect with nature since humans had failed me so terribly.

I thought that if I could find the joy in the natural things that I didn't have to work for that my head would just straighten itself out.

It had worked for a bit, until my father had taken away my privileges—something he loved doing constantly to keep me on my toes.

He didn't like my clothes, didn't like my music, my refusal to 'try my hardest' at school like he did.

There were lots of things my father didn't like about me. Those were just the tip of the iceberg.

"I didn't know there were caves in this mountain. They're safe, right? Like, you're not gonna make me crawl through tiny places and get me stuck in here with a cave-in, right?"

"Don't worry. I've got you. I've been coming here since I was fourteen and never had a problem. You're safe with me."

And it was true. I'd never let anything hurt her. I'd sooner hurt myself than let something happen to her.

I wasn't sure when it happened or why, but Cami was someone I had vowed to protect, and I always kept my promises.

Except for one—but I'd keep that one in due time. It was a promise to myself, one I'd never planned to break. It was going to be upheld, one of these days.

"Wow. You've been coming here this long?"

Cami tripped over another stray rock and almost went flying down to the ground but my hands caught her around the waist. She didn't flinch.

There was a light pinch of red dusting her cheeks, but I didn't know if it was in embarrassment or something else entirely.

I righted her before moving to pull away from her waist, but something stopped me—like some kind of intrinsic need to keep my hands on her. She didn't protest.

I angled her to walk slightly in front of me, and from my vantage point, I had a direct view of her face as she took in the caves around us.

Natural light dripped down into the cavern stretching out before us illuminating her features filled with wonder as we stepped further into the systems.

Cool air caressed the back of my neck and sent chills skating along Cami's skin, so close I could smell the body wash that she'd been using. It had been clogging up my senses since I found her in the shower burning herself.

I should've reminded myself of that—of the fact that she was still in pain, still hurting, still putting herself back together after what happened, whatever *it* was, but I couldn't help myself.

She leaned herself back against my chest and fuck if it wasn't everything I thought heaven would be and more.

Her warm back pressed against my chest and soft silky hair tickling the bottom of my chin.

My grip instinctively tightened around her waist, arms encircling her in a protective embrace and maybe it was the artwork from years and years past decorating the cave walls or the old age of the caves itself, but this felt like a moment already carved out in time—like the two of us would go down in some kind of infamy together.

Like this spot, defined by tourists and graffiti stains and eroding from the elements would be forever marked because we were here—because I was always here and always alone and always something broken and unrecognizable, but now? In this moment?

I wasn't alone.

I wasn't broken.

Maybe I was half-way healed before Cami, but her wildfire and wonder gave me something more to work to, something bigger to achieve.

Maybe she was the reason I wanted to finally fulfill that old promise to myself.

Maybe she was the reason I would actually do it.

Or maybe it was just the moment talking; that I had finally found someone who could actually see me for who I was and not what I had tried to do and immediately latched onto her because our traumas matched somewhat, like two branches forked from the same tree, our spindly twigs like our shared experiences and the leaves the tears which we'd cried because of them.

Maybe she was just a sad, lonely girl and I was just a broken, damaged boy doomed to repeat the mistakes of his past.

Maybe that was all this was.

And maybe that thought terrified me more than the alternative, that this actually meant something.

And maybe I squeezed Cami just a little bit tighter at that thought, and maybe she leaned back into me with a contented sight that constricted the very heart I'd wanted to carve right out of my chest.

Grey had taken me to a cave underneath a mountain.

An actual cave, that once inside opened up into a cavernous room filled with sharp points and slate grey walls dripping with old rainwater and smelling of a cool dampness mixed with green moss and...paint fumes?

All across the once barren walls were splashes and slices of artwork; some old and faded and some as vibrant as if they'd just been painted mere seconds before our arrival.

The steady *drip drip drip* of the water onto the stone floors created a cadence of musical nature inside the cavern, and I couldn't hardly understand what I was seeing with my eyes.

The harsh bright sunlight from the outside world had become dimmed and softened as it filtered through cracks in the top of the cave, like we were in the pit of a volcano and could see out of the top.

"What...how did you find this place?"

I craned my neck back to stare up at Grey's face, but he kept his eyes forward on the cave walls ahead and didn't bother to answer my question, but I wasn't sure if it was because he was so comfortable with his hands all over my body that he didn't want to let go to sign to me or if he simply didn't hear me.

It was as if he were soaking up the beauty of the cave just as much as I was, and he couldn't bare to tear himself away from it.

His arms tightened around my waist for what felt like the hundredth time in as many seconds, but I didn't object.

There was something different about arms wrapped around me that didn't want to cause harm.

It was like I was relishing in a reality that wouldn't remain; it was the lack of permanence that made it so special.

What is life without death, love without pain...

what is a beautiful moment without its eventual end?

It was that eventual end that had me feeling no shame in burrowing myself even further into his warm embrace and gazing upon all the artwork spread out around us.

This wasn't your usual everyday overpass graffiti, no.

This was an intricate patchwork of elegant brush strokes and poignant pieces that tugged at the heart strings in your chest.

This was a monument to history and to nature and to all living things around us: a woman with flowers crawling out of her eyeball, a man whose torso was transformed into a blue stormy ocean, a child being birthed from a mountain, a smoking vehicle with the tail end covered in ivy and overgrowth returning to nature.

Each and every piece told of a story of healing, of peace, of nature overcoming the tribulations of humanity and its cruelty.

It was the story told in the painting of the girl with bruised eyes leaking blood as tears and forced the breath in my lungs to stop working.

"Thank you for bringing me here," was all I could whisper as we stood there trapped in each other's embrace and remained captives of the artistry of the walls around us.

After a while, he reluctantly let his hands fall to his sides as I moved closer to the art, wishing upon everything to capture them with my phone camera, but I knew that it wasn't how they were meant to be viewed. It was why the artist had painted them so far out in the wilderness, with not many tourists coming to visit the installation.

Before long, it was time to leave, but as the sun sank on the horizon and Grey pulled his arm around my waist and tucked me into his side, I realized that there wasn't anywhere else I'd rather be than exactly where I was, and that was the first time I'd ever had that thought since before...

And wasn't that the most terrifying thing of all?

Chapter 21

C ami was having a nightmare.

The whimpering cries started around two o'clock in the morning, but it was the gut-wrenching sobs that woke me up from a dead sleep.

I'd smoked a bit before bed, which was what had allowed me to fall into the depths of sleep and unthinking peace so quickly and easily when usually I'd had to suffer through it in the dark staring at nothing waiting for the night to drag me under, but not tonight.

Tonight it had been quick and painless—much like I'd wanted my death to be—but the waking up part?

That had been the real hell. Listening to Cami in pain was like taking a serrated knife and scraping the ridged edges against the inside of my arms.

Hearing her cries was a new torture in and of itself that I'd never subjected myself to even in my darkest moments.

So maybe that was why I'd jumped up immediately and placed my ear against the door in the bathroom that led to her room.

It was why I had pulled on a pair of sweatpants over my boxers that I'd been sleeping in and edged the door open slightly, seeing her shadowed shape writhe around in the blackness surrounding her like it was welcoming her home into its inky embrace.

I'd felt those shadows pull at me one too many times—felt the allure of their call deep in the darkest dregs of my soul—and knew that I couldn't let her suffer it alone.

She'd been different from the moment we'd stepped off my bike and she walked into the door.

She was even quieter than me at dinner—which was impossible, but somehow she still accomplished it.

Not a single grunt or hum of acknowledgement.

My mother seemed to know immediately what was wrong and didn't push her on the subject, but that didn't appease me. I needed to know if she was alright. I had to know. I had to.

Knowing was the only way that I could make sure it didn't happen again. It was the only way to acknowledge that it was in the past and it wouldn't be able to damage her the same way it once had.

I eased the door open further until it squeaked on its hinges and cursed the damn door before she shifted in the bed again, shooting straight up as her eyes flashed open and landed directly on me.

"Grey? What—what are you doing in here?"

I was grateful for some stray beam of moonlight that had cast me in a shimmering streak illuminating my motions.

"I heard you screaming and wanted to check on you. Are you okay?"

She sighed, a dark, almost resentful sound filled with years of exhaustion and something far too heavy for someone her age.

She had seen and felt too much of the dangers and ruin of this world before ever even reaching full legal adulthood.

Yet again—something that the two of us had in common.

It wasn't something I relished having in common with anyone.

"I'm fine. Just a nightmare, I guess. I get them sometimes. Sorry I woke you up."

"Do you want to talk about it?"

I could see her squinting her eyes in the darkness and almost chuckled at the sight if it weren't for the rest of her expression.

She was so tired, I could make out the deep purple bags underneath her eyes even from this distance.

"Not really."

I had enough sense to say that I was disappointed, until she spoke again.

"But I wouldn't mind talking about something else."

The edges of my mouth quirked up.

"Oh really? Like what?"

She reached over to the lamp on her bedside table and suddenly the room was awash in yellow golden light unveiling the barren landscape that was her bedroom, her sanctuary, blank save for some little wooden trinket on the dresser and a duffel bag in the corner.

Almost like she never really unpacked.

Like she could pack up and disappear at any moment.

Like she was never here to begin with.

I didn't like the direction my thoughts were taking and decided to take her up on her offer, finding the desk chair beneath her pristine white desk and rolling it up beside her bed.

She unfurled herself from the thick white comforter beneath her and crossed her legs underneath her, sitting up further and getting comfortable while pulling her long, thick and dark hair up with a spare hair band on the dresser.

With her hair out of her face and pulled up tight, she looked younger, almost more vulnerable, more alive.

The smooth, creamy white column of her neck was exposed, and I found myself desperate to reach forward and place my hands on her skin just to see if her pulse would jump from my touch.

Would chills break out on her skin like they had in the caves earlier?

Would that shimmering magic of that infinitesimal moment return and wash my blood and bones with enchantment once more? Would she feel it, too?

This buzzing electrical current that hummed its song through the bond created by the two of us from the moment we locked eyes in that empty classroom and she struck out at me with her words, uncaring of the fact that I couldn't talk.

I was just another person to her, just Grey. Just the weird brother of the golden boy. Just another human, just like her, at least in that regard.

"What do you want to talk about, then?"

"I don't know, anything. Distract me."

So she was anxious, then.

I could tell the moment I sat down across from the bed and her leg wouldn't stop its incessant shaking, her fingers picking at the skin of her nails nervously.

Although it wasn't that she was nervous of me; no, I could tell it had to do with the nightmare she'd just had.

The damn thing was eating her up inside.

So I distracted her.

"What are some words you want to learn to sign?"

"Oh, that's a good one. I don't know—maybe...discombobulated? I always used to like that word. Oh, and what about symphony? Descriptive words, oh, I don't know the sign for 'descriptive' either. I know 'describe' but not 'descriptive'."

And so we spent the next fifteen minutes or so practicing the sing language until she began using the new words in sentences.

"The cat was discombobulated so he fell off the stage at the symphony and was descriptive in his fall."

"That's the most descriptive and discombobulated sentence about a symphony I've ever heard."

She fell apart in laughter and—fuck, if it wasn't a goddamn *symphony* to my ears.

I was falling down into a hole I didn't know I'd ever be able to dig myself out of.

She was light and airy and wistful with a wild streak filled with fiery passion and angst that was enough to rival my own.

She was complex and filled with different dimensions that I was both intrigued and terrified to explore, if only she would let me.

She was a blank canvas the world had drawn upon until she became splattered with darkness and the colors got all mixed up together until she was an unrecognizable caricature of who the world wanted her to be versus the girl that was sitting in front of me.

She was new, she was good, she was broken, but in that moment, she was mine and somehow I was hers.

If only for a moment.

The nightmare had snuffed out all the light from the world.

The blood had blotted out the sun and the gunshot winked all the stars from existence.

The prison sentence murdered electricity and his final goodbye had sent a nuke to the moon.

My father's wailed cries still echoed in my ears when Grey had edged the door to my bedroom open, and I had never been so relieved to see another person in my entire life.

Here was my escape—here was the way that I could take my mind off the terror and the pain and the knowing.

The knowing was the worst of it all.

Knowing what my mother had done—knowing what my father had done to her *because* of it.

It had been five years and still I was haunted.

At least it wasn't a nightmare about Colton.

If it had been that...I didn't know if I would've been able to stand Grey's presence in that moment.

Or maybe I would have. There was something different about his gaze, his touch, his presence.

His attention wasn't lecherous, his touch not a painful reminder of everything I'd endured thus far, his eyes not hungry and filled with lust.

He'd never made an unwanted advance on me, never tried to go out of his way to make me uncomfortable—rather, the opposite.

He'd protected me from Colton when he saw what was happening in the classroom.

He was stepping into that role of my safe place, and I was scared to let it evolve into that because of what it would mean in the future. What if he left me? What would happen to me if suddenly I let him into my life and my heart in that way, and he just decided to walk right on out?

His face was open, clear, patient.

We had fun, so much fun that I wondered what life used to be like without him. Hadn't Grey always been there?

No, he hadn't.

Because if he had...Colton would never have done to me what he had.

I never would've suffered half as much as I had if I'd had Grey there with me.

"So...can I ask you a personal question?"

"Why not? Go ahead. But I get to ask my own personal question."

"Fine," I said begrudgingly to the amused and arrogant look on his face.

I scooted closer to him on the bed subconsciously, though I wasn't sure why.

"Why...why don't you have a girlfriend?"

Why was I suddenly shy, hiding my face with one of my hands while trying and failing to not look at Grey?

His dark eyes widened in half surprise and half intrigue, though that arrogant smirk still remained on his face.

It wasn't lost on me that he was shirtless.

In fact, it was one of the first things that I noticed about him when he came into my room.

There was a drop-dead gorgeous boy in my room, shirtless, staring at me expectantly with eyes of an innocent sin contradiction.

I wasn't blind; I just didn't know what would happen if I let him touch me...in that way. I was scared to try, scared that I would have a breakdown in front of him and scare away the only person who'd ever seen the real me, flaws and all, and not balked from it or ran screaming the other way.

With Colton, I'd shown him a facade. I'd shown him what he wanted to see—a simpering, sad, lonely girl who needed help and was willing to give up half of her soul in order to have safety even though she was staying with the villain the whole time.

"Well, I don't really want one. Being a part of the freak show at our school doesn't really make girls want to jump into a relationship with me."

"That makes sense, I guess. But you're like..."

"Like what?"

Oh fuck, what had I gotten myself into?

Why had I opened my stupid fat mouth and let those stupid, embarrassing words fall out of my stupid dumb mouth?!

"Ugh, fuck it. You're hot. You're funny. You're a really good guy underneath all the piercings and black clothes and 'fuck off' stare you give everyone. I guess I'm wondering why no one's ever had a shot with bad-boy Grey."

There. I'd said it. And I was immediately regretting it as my cheeks turned redder than the burning fiery scarlet of a hot sunset.

"Cami. Are you saying you have a crush on me?"

"Shut up!"

"Technically, I didn't even say anything."

"You're ridiculous. And discombobulating."

"Nice use of the word, but you need to change it if you're going to use it with i-n-g at the end. I can show you, if you want?"

I could only nod my head in agreement, and then Grey was out of his seat, leaning into me and placing his hands on my own and helping me form the right words and—

holy fucking shit I couldn't breathe.

It was a good breathlessness this time, not like I was choking on water that I could never surface from, but instead like I was panting from a nice run out in the cool air gilded in honey sunlight that had made my skin glow in effervescence.

This was the kind of breathlessness where I couldn't wait to see what happened next.

Where Grey was everything I could see and all I could feel and the only thing I wanted to touch, see, smell, hear, sense in that moment...

"Cami..."

The breath of his whispered voice blew across my temple and I blinked back at him in shock.

Had he just...?

"Did you just say my name...out loud?"

He pulled his head back a bit so I could see the wide smile brimming on his face.

The sound was hesitant, like he hadn't tried out sounds from his mouth in a very long time.

It was a harsh, rasping whisper, something not made from his voice but from his breath.

Grey had just spoken my name aloud, and I almost melted into a puddle at his feet.

"Since when have you been able to do that?"

His resulting shrug was enough to make me rear back and playfully push his shoulder, but he didn't budge, and touching him was clearly a mistake because all I wanted to do...was do it again.

So I did.

My hand came back to his shoulder and my fingertips traced the black ink of his tattoos while he stayed stock still, allowing me this little piece of exploration and curiosity.

There was an all-black bird at the base of his sternum directly in the middle, it's wings stretched wide and outwards as if in mid-flight and was perched right beneath his scars on his neck, almost like after his attempt he felt the need to ink it there on his body the truth of what happened...after.

Filler pieces of dark shadowed flowers connected with licking flames caressed his skin as they traveled down and connected with his arms, all of it a patchwork of art that told a secret story that only he knew the words to.

"When did you get all of this done?"

"The year after my attempt. Mom basically let me do whatever I wanted as long as it wasn't a danger to me or others around me. I fed

her some bullshit line about getting it done to take my power back. It worked."

"Wow. They're beautiful," I breathed, wanting him to sign to me again because then his arms would have to come up between us and I could look up into his eyes at the same time while translating his signs.

His muscles flexed underneath my featherlight touch, his skin burning from the outside in with a fevered glow that I wanted to bask in every moment of every day.

He let out a staggered breath that fanned out across my face, and then I was a goner.

Completely and totally gone in the sensations that swirled around my body and fueled the desire that I thought I'd never feel again.

Who was the girl that leaned forward on bated breath and the weight of the wings that covered Grey's tanned skin?

Who was she to bask in this early morning night and wrap it around her like a warm blanket and suffocate the demons with the comforting safety of Grey's arm?

And who was she, to press her lips against his, to swallow down her protests and throw caution into the fraying wind?

Who was this girl in my body, taking over and hitting mute on the pain that never seemed to go away...until now?

Who was I?

Chapter 22

One moment, it was only Cami brushing delicate fingers across the ink stained into my skin.

The next, she was leaning closer and closer, the sweet scent of her perfume from earlier in the day still clinging to her soft skin.

The next, she was a fluttering hummingbird, nervous and eyes wide with a question in them that I didn't know the answer to.

She was a masterpiece crafted and painted and made for my desires and wants and needs; like she was created for me, crafted from golden hands and molded into a form that was wholly her own but my biggest temptation.

Still, I kept my hands at my sides.

Still, I didn't move a muscle.

I did not place my hands on her waist nor her neck.

I did not press my body tight into hers, no matter how hard I was shaking to keep myself from doing so.

I did not dare breathe when her soft lips pressed down onto my own, like feather silk and pillowy satin brushing against my mouth.

I stifled the groan bubbling up in my throat; it would've come out sounding like a choking garbled mess, and I didn't want to ruin this moment, not as she placed her hands on my shoulders and tingles spread outward, like a seismic current sending shockwaves throughout my entire body.

In the dim lamp glow of her bedroom, Cami explored my body with her hands and lips, and I allowed her every indulgence because what else could I do but remain unmoving, terrified that she might break this contact and think it a mistake even as she had been the one to make the first move.

She pulled back suddenly, cheeks flushed and pupils blown out from desire and suddenly that haunted, lost look was completely gone, replaced by a divine need and primal instinct driven by this inch of separation between us.

"Is...is this okay?"

Her dark voice filled the otherwise silent air around us, and damn if I didn't want to snap and throw her down on the bed and show her just how *okay* this was...but she wasn't ready for that.

She might never be ready for that, and the sudden shy look in her eyes had me reaching up and pushing the hair behind her ears, fingers trailing along the skin of her cheeks and tracing the plump curve of her pink lips slightly swollen from her kisses.

I could only nod, too absorbed to pull back and sign, because this was not the time for words.

We didn't need them.

In this moment between the two of us, where the outside world didn't exist, we were floating on a cosmic cloud of stars and moon dust shooting us through the atmosphere.

And then she was pulling me closer.

I was up out of the chair and kneeling on the bed, hovering over her small body.

She was a restless balm against the burn in my chest; a galaxy of possibilities underneath the heat of my palms.

Dark brown eyes stared up at me through thick eyelashes and their intense need shone through all else.

Smooth hands traced down the bare sides of my stomach, down past my ribs and then around to my back, cupping behind my neck to pull me down further, closer, a needy whimper rising in her chest as I only barely complied.

She wanted more, more, more, and I was scared to give it all to her; scared that she might not be ready for what I had in store for her.

"Grey," she whispered, my name a beckoning plea on those gorgeous lips.

And then that mouth was on the side of my neck, kissing down my scars until I was the one trembling, until I was the one shaking on my arms placed on either side of her head keeping myself upright above her.

She placed those goddamn lips directly on the scar that I wished I could've tattooed over the most, but my mother said it wouldn't be appropriate as I would have to wear a turtleneck to keep it covered.

Didn't she understand that it was the scar that was more inappropriate; that it was the scar that I was most ashamed of?

Didn't she realize that my refusal to speak was the punishment I'd given myself for almost giving up on any and everything in this world, including my entire family?

Didn't she know...

But Cami knew.

She knew how I felt about it, even without having to ask.

Somehow, she knew, and she was trying to tell me that it was okay.

That even though I'd have to stare back at this scar in the mirror every single day and relive what I'd done to myself, what had almost happened...

It was okay.

I was okay.

I didn't need to be ashamed, because she...

She pressed her lips against the scars, she didn't run away from them or hide from the truth of what they meant, and that meant more to me than any pretty words ever could have.

That was when I finally let go, and unleashed the torrent of emotions against her.

That was when I gave her my all, and she didn't run, didn't shy away.

She took it all with a blissful smile on her face and met me.

My perfect match in darkness and in light.

When Grey finally kissed me back...

It was like the floodgates of pleasure opened and I was able to see what I'd been missing for so long.

It didn't feel wrong to have someone's weight on me, pressing me down into the mattress.

I didn't feel panicked or terrified that I would be taken advantage of.

I also didn't feel that apathy and lack of enthusiasm that I had normally felt in these...situations.

No, I definitely felt something here, with Grey, with his dark gaze staring me down with something akin to wonder in his eyes.

Slowly, ever so slowly, he dipped his body down lower, breaths mingling and energies mixing until there was nothing separating us; until we were combined, his chest on mine, one leg pressed in between mine.

One hand tipped my face up to meet his eyes, thumb underneath my chin and the rest of his long fingers curling behind the column of my throat and tangling with the hair there.

It was what I found swimming in his eyes there that had me inhaling a sharp breath and trying but failing to hide the choked sigh swelling there.

Barely contained lust stared back at me, his eyes pitch black, almost darker than the nighttime terrors that would wrap themselves around my skin late at night...but Grey's darkness was something different.

It was like he was the surety of the night, the constant reminder that there were dependable things in the universe.

The sun would sink every day and then there was the comforting reminder that I wasn't alone in the world; the night was just as lonely as me.

The night had no confidant to spill its darkened secrets to; only the comforting companions of its fellow secret keepers to watch over and listen to, forever endless and forever lonely.

His other hand was planted on my hip, fingers digging into the skin there, but not moving any higher or lower, almost like he was determined to let me lead this, and for that I was grateful.

It was my first time dipping my toes into the waters after what had happened, and I wasn't sure how much of this I could take; but it wasn't like Grey was some test run.

If anything, he was the healing energy I needed in order to push myself back in the waters.

Not the waters swelling high with storm waves, but the waters cool and calm and peaceful where I could tread and keep my head above the surface easily, a sweet swim where the water caressed and cooled instead of drowning and suffocating.

Somehow, I was healing right before my eyes, and I hadn't even known it was happening.

Maybe I would be okay in the end, after all.

Maybe Grey was all I needed to figure that out.

When his lips met mine again, he moved against me.

It was a breathtaking shattering of earths that I knew in that moment could compare to nothing I'd ever felt nor would ever feel again.

It was like Grey had completely ruined all future experiences for me...

but I wasn't upset that he'd done it, either.

I was grateful.

Because this experience erased the last.

His kisses wiped away all traces of Colton.

Every touch of my skin evaporated the handprint that had been seared onto me from the moment he'd taken advantage of my body.

Grey's fingertips replaced Colton's along my back, and suddenly it was his gentle touch that I wished to be burned onto my body.

It was his kiss that I wanted to taste in the aftermath of this moment between us.

It was Grey's fevered and inked skin that I wished to feel and see and remember in my mind if Colton tried to confront me again.

Soft lips parted my own and then our tongues were dancing in our mouths and he was the night and I was the stars dotting the black sky.

His hand had just started traveling further up when a thump nearby shocked us both out of our skin.

"I don't think it was anyone," I rushed out breathlessly, taking in Grey's wild features and expression.

"Yeah, we should probably go to sleep."

I shouldn't have felt the disappointment when he made to move off the bed.

I didn't know where the courage came from, but the word slipped out nonetheless.

"Wait."

He turned, eyes wary but intrigued, still half-filled with that lingering lust and interest.

I didn't say anything, only pulled the comforter back and scooted over so there was a space between us.

He eyed the bed and then me, and then the bed once more before sighing and easing himself back onto the bed.

I had just hit the light on the lamp and turned away from him on the bed to give him his privacy when a strong arm gripped me from behind and tugged me into a warm, solid chest.

I melted back into him and fell into a dreamless sleep surrounded in a pale light of peace.

Chapter 23

They didn't question the sound at the door.

They didn't know that I'd been coming to Cami's room to apologize—that I'd wanted to say that I was sorry for whatever it was that Colton had done to her, that I was sorry for the scene I'd caused in front of her.

To ask her if she was alright...

Instead I found her in bed with my brother.

The flashbacks came in full force, then. The reminders of finding Leah in bed with him flashed across my mind and I saw red.

I was halfway down the stairs trying to scrub the image out of my eyes when I heard the raised voices.

"She's...from the prison and...doesn't know..."

"Keep your voice down, Richard."

My parent's voices got more clear as I descended the stairs but kept to the shadows just in case.

"Cami does not need to be staying here. I never agreed with it and you still went ahead and did it anyway."

"That girl needs our help, and you know that as much as anyone else."

"You're only doing this because of the money, right? The Power of Attorney if she chooses to let us adopt her? How are you going to convince her, by being mother of the year, Maria?"

"This is not about the money! Maybe for you it would be, but I could care less. I want Cami to come into her full inheritance the day she turns eighteen and I want nothing to do with it."

"Sure. Because *Maria Hartingrove* never cared about the money, the pro-bono lawyer fighting for the under dogs."

"Don't you mock me. This girl is suffering and needed a home; what was I supposed to do—let her go to the Maynard's with the father who'd a known predator? Over my dead body. She got hurt on the previous family's watch and I refuse to let that happen to her, too. The boys are protective of her; they'll watch over her at school."

My father snorted. I could see him in my mind shaking his head and pacing like he always did when he got angry.

"Who cares? She's like a stray that we shouldn't have brought into our home, you know why?"

He didn't give her a chance to respond before he answered his own question.

"Because they bring back fleas. You want our house infested with her issues, her problems? Grey and Parker are barely keeping it together as it is, we almost got sued by the Wright's because of what Parker did, and your son was the one who instigated it!"

"He's your son, too, Richard."

"No. He's not. Not anymore. You know that. You know why."

"Don't say that. You know it's not true."

"Goddammit Maria, I've said it once and I'll say it a million more times: that punk is *not my son*. Parker's mine for sure. We both know that. But Greylin? No. Never. He never has been. Why would I want a son who doesn't even want to help himself? He could have had surgery yesterday and be talking within a month. He doesn't care, so neither do I."

"He doesn't have to be blood to be considered your son; you've raised him since he was a baby. I don't know why he doesn't want to have the surgery, but that is his decision and it's his journey! We can't force him into anything. You've been there for him his whole life Richard, how could you walk away from him now, after everything?"

"I was there because I thought he was MINE! Now he's nothing more than a pathetic excuse of a boy desperately trying to be a man, but he won't take responsibility for his actions! If he did, he would've had that surgery months ago, when it was offered to him in the first place! No son of mine would ever be so much of a coward!"

"Stop it! We've had this fight over and over again so just *stop*!"

I couldn't stop the chills from crawling along my arms. Grey wasn't my father's biological son?

"Yeah, well, I made sure we were even after what you did, didn't I? And I promise you Maria, if you try to push me any further on this, you'll see just how much more I can push the boundaries."

"You don't need to throw in my face, again, how you got back at me for what happened almost twenty years ago, Richard. Trust me. I know."

There was no hiding the pain swimming in my mother's voice at his words. What the hell had happened here?

"Good. I'm glad you know, so that way I don't have to go out and remind you again what happens when you betray your husband."

"At least I didn't cause a homicide from *my* actions!"

The sounds in the kitchen ceased, all insects outside the windows stopped chirping.

Maybe even my heart stopped beating.

"Yet another reason for us to not have that girl in our home. What if she recognizes me one day? What if she goes to visit her father and starts digging into her past? Just...give her back to the social worker and be done with her."

"I will not subject her to the outside world. She's in the system because of you—because of what I did to push you to be with her mother. So I guess it's my fault, too, then isn't it? We have a responsibility to make sure she's taken care of.   Otherwise...how are we any better than what her father, and what he did to her mom?"

Camille Astor was the girl who's father murdered his wife in cold blood after cheating on him.

My father was the man who'd started it all.

"Whatever, Maria. Do what you want. But if you don't get that Power of Attorney over her, it'll all be for nothing. She'll have the means to do whatever she wants, and if she finds out our connection to what happened, I don't see the daughter of Michael Astor being very forgiving, especially not after how she grew up. Be. Careful. Otherwise you'll have more than a vengeful teenager on your hands."

My mother sighed out and then there was the telltale clink of glasses and a wine bottle. My father had already gone the other way and out the door. Where, exactly, he was going I had no idea, nor did I care.

Instead of confronting my mother like I wanted, my phone buzzed in my pocket and I fished it out quickly to silence it so she didn't find me spying only to find that it was a message from Alec.

S.O.S.

Meet me at the spot.

I didn't waste time dragging myself outside to the carport, grateful that my father's BMW was already gone, steaming tire tracks left in his wake.

Funny. I didn't even hear him leave.

It took thirty minutes to make it to our spot, the same one that I'd stolen from Grey like he'd stolen Leah from me all those years ago.

Before, it'd been filled with half-assed graffiti and a stray penis and hairy ballsack painted on the walls of the cave, but after me?

I tugged the bag of spray paint and other tools over my shoulder and trudged inside, using my phone as a light to guide me even as the beams from the moon shone down brightly.

The crickets were chirping out in full song, the field a darkened symphonic masterpiece around me.

Alec was already planted at the entrance, curled up into a ball crying and shaking back and forth, back and forth, this whimpered howls echoing through the cavern around us.

His dark hair shone in the moonlight and his hands were shaking so badly he couldn't get the cigarette to light.

I yanked it out of his hands with little effort. He only coughed and cleared his throat before looking up at me with wide blue tear filled eyes.

It killed me to see him this way, but there was nothing I could do.

There was nothing anyone could do. It was all on Alec, but he was too scared.

So, I stayed with him. I made sure he was never alone.

I was there for him the way I should've been with Grey, but also...there was another reason I couldn't leave him by himself. Something I was too scared to put a name too. Maybe that made me as bad off as Alec, but I didn't want to hurt myself because of it.

"Come on," I said, tugging him up in my arms and pulling him with me.

We'd done this so many times, I'd lost count.

But each time, a new piece of artwork decorated the space around us, breathing life into something only my brother and Alec had truly appreciated before.

Now, I guessed Cami would be the one to bask in its entirety, too.

What had started as a 'fuck you' to my brother for stealing my first girlfriend had morphed into a way to keep him here on this earth—to make him see the beauty in all things and appreciate life for what it was worth.

I didn't believe my art really could do all of that, but after what Alec had said...maybe it could help, if only a little.

Tonight, however, I did not paint for the beauty of this world.

No, tonight I painted for the violence, for the villainy, for the blood and pain splashed across the lines connecting my family to Cami's.

I carved out lines and sketches while Alec sat and attempted a few caricatures I'd taught him last time. I didn't have the time or patience to teach him anything tonight.

Not tonight.

Not after everything my parents had been hiding from me had finally come to life in one of the most gruesome of ways.

I painted in blood red arcs and dark blues and purples that resembled bruises.

A quilted patchwork of colors and sketches and pain, so much goddamned pain.

My chest hurt.

It wasn't supposed to be this way.

None of this was supposed to be this way.

"Parker."

Alec was wrapping his arms around my back as I sobbed into the cave, paintbrush dripping in red paint that was supposed to be the blood of the mother spilling out in a puddle around the gunshot from her brain.

I flung the paintbrush against the wall and turned around to hold him back, and for the first time something in me snapped.

Something forbidden that I'd kept the walls around.

Maybe now that everything was destroyed and broken, I could let myself break, too.

Maybe Alec would help me pick up the pieces, just like I'd done for him, time and time again.

His arms didn't leave me for the entire night.

Chapter 24

Sunlight coated Cami's hair in soft golden rays and I wished for the first time in my entire life that this moment would last forever; that time would stop moving and that I'd never grow old just so that I could relive this over again and again and again.

I used to relish the fact that I would age; that I would grow old and senile and forget all the pains of my past. I used to think that life was so horrible that I couldn't wait to be eighty or ninety years old and on my death bed, waiting for death like a perfect, nice human who'd lived a perfect, ordinary uneventful life and never tried to end it prematurely.

But now, with Cami wrapped around my arms and clinging to me like she was scared I'd somehow float away in her dreams...now I knew the reason why some people said they were scared of death.

I knew why they said they wanted to live forever, when previously I'd thought it to be a punishment akin to torture to be forced to walk this godforsaken earth for an eternity.

Soft breaths escaped her mouth and she sighed out in contentment, and I never wanted to wake her.

How unfortunate for me that the sun did that all on its own.

She smiled up at me sheepishly after realizing how close she'd tucked herself to me.

"Sorry," she said but I didn't respond. She had absolutely nothing to be sorry for.

I jumped up out of her bed first and left to mine before anyone could figure out what had happened last night.

We'd...slept. After having the most intensely intimate moment of my life. I could only wonder if it were the same for her, if she could sense the power of that moment as it flowed through my veins.

We dressed for school separately, but it was when I found her waiting outside with the helmet already on her head that I almost dropped down to my knees in worship of her.

She didn't allow things to be awkward or tense between us.

She clung tightly to me on the smooth ride to school, body loose and content...because of the events of the night before, or because she knew Colton wouldn't be at school to torment her?

He was still in the hospital according to the rumors still swirling on social media.

The courtyard was bare of the 'group' that Parker always hung around. Maybe they finally realized none of them really liked each other and split up. That would've been the cherry on top of the best night I'd had in my entire life.

I hadn't had a single nightmare, even after the effects of the weed I'd smoked had worn off. No nightmares, no dreams, just peace. Just contented, sweet, restful sleep.

Was Cami my remedy?

I never wanted to sleep alone again.

Not if that was how real sleep should have felt like this entire time; not if that was what I'd been missing out on all these years when the anxiety and depression would follow and torment me into oblivion.

Cami found Mori in the courtyard and they were glued together the rest of the day as we ate lunch together, sans Carter and Parker's band of friends.

For the next two weeks, everything followed the same pattern.

Cami would either seek me out in my room at night, or I'd go to hers.

There were no more instances of kissing, though I wasn't about to rush her on anything, although we did talk.

Well, she did most of the talking and I listened while shrugging my shoulders, nodding or shaking my head in answer.

It was the night before Colton was due to return to school, and Cami knew this because Mori had told her that day over text.

She'd been a walking ball of anxiety the entire day, and anything I'd tried to do to calm her wasn't working.

"What's wrong?" I asked, finally caving.

She sat up on the bed a little higher where we'd been camped out. She'd been preferring my room lately. She preferred anything that had my mark on it, really.

My hoodies, my sweatpants, my long sleeved shirts, even my side of the bed.

I'd gladly give her anything she wanted, the moment she asked. Hell, she didn't even have to ask.

Not Cami.

"Do you think...do you think when the cops don't believe what happened that it's not as bad as what you thought?"

"What do you mean?"

"Well...like, you know what happens when a girl reports...*that*."

I did know what she was talking about, but suddenly I was on high alert. Had she gone to the police, and they hadn't believed her?

What had happened?

"Yes. I watch Law and Order with you every night. I don't think a murder didn't happen just because they couldn't find enough evidence to put away the murderer. I don't think an assault didn't happen just because they didn't have enough evidence. The police not choosing to go forward with a case doesn't mean they didn't believe in the victim, it just meant there wasn't enough evidence to get a guilty sentence."

That answer seemed to appease her as she eased back onto my shoulder and curled herself around my frame, cuddling closer until she was practically glued to my skin. I had to stop myself from sighing out in happiness. I didn't want her to know how much I loved it when she did that.

It would ruin my 'touch guy' act.

"Your mom's been so nice to me lately."

I tried to hum out in interest but it came out scratchy and sounding like a cat coughing up a hairball.

"I'm starting to interpret your sounds, you know? That one meant, 'hmm, interesting.'"

I huffed out another sound to see if she'd decipher that one, too.

"And that one means, 'oh really?' but like really sarcastically. But anyway, like I was saying, I think your mom is trying to make me her actual daughter. You know she took me shopping for a prom dress? I didn't even want to go to prom but I guess I am now."

She was laying on me and I was too comfortable to move to sign my thoughts back to her, which she already knew, so she kept going, talking and talking and it was music to my damn ears.

I'd been used to the silence for too long. Maybe it was time to finally call my doctor and make the appointment. I think Cami would like my voice, no matter how distorted and wrecked it might sound.

"I wonder what it would've been like to have had a mom growing up. What would've happened if my dad didn't do what he did. Would I still have gone to that stupid prep school in L.A. or would we have moved out to the country? Would I have ever met you?"

Of course, the answer to that was 'no', but she wasn't asking that.

She was asking herself if the price of meeting me was worth it. The cost of losing her mother wasn't worth meeting me, I knew it, but she didn't say it out loud. Instead, she kept it light.

"I like to think the universe likes to make us work for things. Like...if you want to be happy, you have to try first, at least a little. If you keep looking at the negative things, then the world will be negative. If you want the real things, like love...you can't just sit back and wait for it to happen to you. You can't settle for things that feel good, you have to wait for something to come along that feels perfect."

I suddenly got the feeling she was talking about someone else that wasn't in the room but was stuck in her head.

"You know when I first met you, I thought you were an asshole with a superiority complex, even though you couldn't talk."

I couldn't help the snort that escaped from me.

She laughed at me, of course, but that didn't stop her.

"I'm glad you stormed into that classroom that day, Grey."

I was about to lean up and say something equally sentimental, until she had to go and ruin it.

"I'm glad you stalked me so hard that you made your mother basically adopt me just so you could be close to me. You must be so obsessed with me."

The closest thing to a laugh fell out of my mouth, and then I was half choking, half bark-laughing as Cami started laughing hysterically, which only made me choke on my voice even harder.

"You're a bitch," I signed to her.

"You love me."

"Not even close."

She had no idea how close to the truth she really was.

It was after seven o'clock the Sunday evening before the school day where everything would change.

It was all getting better—Colton wasn't around because he'd been suspended and in the hospital due to his fight with Parker. The group of friends that used to torment me with Carter and Colton had dissipated almost overnight and none of them even sat together anymore, so Mori had taken to sitting with me and Grey every morning and afternoon at school.

No more teasing mockery of us being on scholarships.

My grades that I'd let slip had risen, and I once again boasted all A's in my classes. Grey was a good study partner—he couldn't distract me by talking aloud, and even when he could communicate, he usually just let me do the talking.

I had a feeling that even if he could talk, he'd choose to be silent.

I'd just entered the bathroom for a shower when my phone began ringing with an unknown number.

Chills shot through my body as I thought of who could be on the other end of that line, but...

You know the old adage about curiosity and the cat.

"Hello?"

"An inmate by the name of Michael Astor from Sentry Penitentiary is attempting to reach you. Please press one to accept the charges."

Charges? My father?

I pressed the number one with the blood roaring in my ears. What was I doing?

"Hello? Cami? Baby, it's Daddy. Are you there?"

"D-dad?"

My voice caught and broke, a scratchy, hollow reminder of the fact that I hadn't said that word to him in over five years.

He'd never even gotten to say goodbye.

Had I even wanted him to?

"It's so good to hear your voice. Listen, I don't have much time. I need you to get in touch with your social worker. She's my lawyer, and she's working on a reduced sentence for me, to cut my time in half. If she does that, then the inheritance can revert back to me. Won't that be great? You'll be over eighteen and I'll be out and able to take care of you."

"What?"

I didn't know what he was saying.

I couldn't comprehend this.

I hadn't spoken to him since he'd killed my mother, and this was what he'd wanted to talk to me about?

Money?

My inheritance?

"It'll be just like old times, baby. I'll even take you on that ski trip we always promised, before..."

His scratchy, deep voice didn't sound like my father's.

This man's voice was desperate, with a tinge of madness and insanity lurking in its depths.

"I...I don't want to talk to you."

"Cami? Come on, just contact your social worker, and tell her you want to give her Power of Attorney over your guardianship. You have to be the one to ask, and you'll go in front of the courts.

They'll give it to her, and when I get out it can be transferred to me and we can live together again."

"I don't want to talk to you."

"Cami, I—"

"I DON'T WANT TO TALK TO YOU!"

I kept repeating it, over and over again, as the blood flashed in my mind.

The walls in the bathroom weren't white anymore, they were red and splattered with brain matter.

The floor was a puddle of scarlet that had flowed out of my mom's head.

There were holes in the walls where the rest of the bullets had sprayed and punctured through drywall and the pretty pale blue of our large living room.

One of the bullets had gone through a picture, directly through the eye of a little girl in a unicorn dress on the mantle.

He'd killed that little girl and her mother that day, she just didn't know she'd been a dead girl walking these past five years.

Not until this phone call had finally twisted the knife in a puncturing finality.

I don't want to talk to you I don't want

to talk to you I don't want to talk to you I don't want to talk to you
I don't want to talk to you I don't want to talk to you I don't want
to talk to you I don't want to talk to you I don't want to talk to you
I don't want to talk to you I—

"Cami?"

Parker was standing in the open doorway of the bathroom, but
I couldn't see him through the tears leaking down my face like the
blood that had dripped down the sides of her head when I walked
in on her.

"Grey!"

He was there in an instant, picking me up in his arms and
cradling me against his chest.

So warm. He was so warm.

I was so cold, so tired, so fucking tired of it all.

When would it end?

I'd see the light at the end of the tunnel, I'd reach for it, only to
get dragged right back down to the fiery pits where hope was only
an illusion; another form of torture.

There was a reason they said to abandon all hope in the depths
of the Underworld.

It wasn't allowed.

Hope was for fools.

The world was nothing more than fire and death and agony and
anyone who tried to think differently would wind up with a dagger
in their back or a bullet in their brain.

Chapter 25

It was midnight and Cami had been a catatonic shell of the lively, passion filled person she once was.

She hadn't spoken a word to me, only murmuring near nonsense to herself after Parker had alerted me to what the hell had happened.

At first, I'd stared at him in accusation, pushing his shoulder in an attempt to get him to tell me what the hell was going on—but he'd been adamant that this wasn't about him.

Her warm brown eyes were devoid of all life; cold, hard, iced over pain staring me down deep into the pits of my soul.

I'd pulled myself from the room when she'd finally settled enough that she was no longer shaking, curled up on my bed in the blankets and staring at the wall as if her eyes were lasers that could burn a hole directly through it and aid in her escape.

"Is Cami alright?"

I startled as my mother came to a stop at the top of the stairs; her warm blue eyes filled with concern for the daughter she'd never got to have.

"She's fine; laying down in Grey's room. It's the only place she wouldn't freak out again. I don't know what happened, I just heard her on the phone and then she had a breakdown, basically."

"Oh, no. I was worried this would happen."

I was left out of the conversation even though my mother knew sign language. I didn't attempt to interject myself into this one.

"I checked her phone and saw that it was from the prison. Her father contacted her. It must've triggered her PTSD from finding her mother as a child."

"Finding her mother? You mean Cami had to see her after..."

"Yes, after her father...did what he did that sent him to prison for second degree murder."

"And you just conveniently left that information out of the 'welcome' packet?"

"I'm sorry, we tried to keep it as quiet as possible. Your father ...he used to work with Michael, Cami's father. When I found out that she was in the system and going to the same school as you two, I knew that I had to do something."

"Yeah, he 'worked' with Michael. Sure."

My head turned to Parker's at the same time my mother's hands started to shake ever so slightly.

"What do you mean?"

"I heard you two talking the other night, mom. I heard everything. Everything. The truth about Cami's mom—how dad only cheated because you did, first. Why don't you go on and tell Grey *that* truth, huh? And while we're at it—why don't we discuss how Grey could've been able to talk this entire time if he'd just suck it up and go have surgery? Or how the entire reason that Cami's mother is dead is because dad stepped out on his marriage with you because you were the one to do it first?"

You could hear a pin drop in the room.

Parker's anger was palpable, a building escalation that rose and rose until there was nothing left in its wake—the world decimated by his words.

My world...destroyed in an instant.

My eyes were accusatory, but my mother wouldn't meet them.

I'd always felt a distinct shift in my relationship with my father a bit before my attempt. I was eighteen, but my father didn't pull away at fifteen after I tried to off myself.

No, this had happened two years before, when I was thirteen.

He'd suddenly stopped coming to my guitar lessons, so I stopped bothering to practice or show up, too.

He'd refused to help me with my homework, though he was quick to jump and do Parker's for him if he'd been too tired at football.

It was part of the reason why my mental health had declined so drastically and at such a young age.

I know, I know—poor little rich boy, doesn't have his father's love anymore, his brother is the favorite. What gives him the right to try to kill himself?

Sometimes, your mind likes to play tricks on you.

"The world wouldn't even notice if I were gone," it whispers in your ears. "Who would even miss me? No one."

No one.

No. One.

"Parker, I—"

"Don't. Unless you're going to tell Grey who his real father is? Or you—"

He turned to me, then. That anger swimming and swirling and festering under the deep blue surface of his darkened eyes.

"Schedule the fucking surgery. Quit punishing yourself for something that happened three years ago. Just—stop being a goddamned coward. It's just making things worse for everyone else. You think this is fun? You think it's cute to just refuse to talk to us? I miss my fucking brother!"

"I—I'm n-not—"

The air was lodged in my throat, the garbled sounds straining and burning and so utterly painful I could've passed out from the attempt to speak, but it had to happen.

I had to say it.

I had to make something I said actually count.

Maybe this time it would stick.

"I'm n-not your b-brother."

I was practically wheezing on the ground, hands on my knees and sucking in great lungfuls of air that squeezed and squeezed until I could see nothing except for the stars clogging up my vision.

"That's enough. I'm going to check on Cami, boys we will talk about this later. Grey, go get some water."

Except I didn't move from my spot in the hallway.

"Parker, I thought you said she was in Grey's bed—oh, wait. She's in her room, nevermind."

She'd left my bed? Had she heard everything, heard about my cowardice, and been disgusted?

She finally realized what I'd known all along.

I wasn't worth the gum she scraped off her shoes—let alone her beautiful, star speckled smiles that lit up my darkness.

I wasn't worth the beauty in her dark eyes that matched the blackness of my own, if only in color.

I was not worthy of Camille Astor, but I was going to make sure I would be.

Maybe Parker was right about one thing—I *was* a coward.

And maybe it was time to prove to myself and to everyone else that I could be worthy of something.

I would apologize to Parker later...but then, after what I'd heard in the hallway, I wasn't sure he even deserved one.

Parker's car drove like a dream beneath my hands, and while school was the last place I needed to be after what had just happened the night before, I couldn't avoid my grades.

They were my escape plan, after all, in case the state somehow delayed my inheritance.

With my luck, that was exactly what would happen.

I'd end up on an academic scholarship at an Ivy school in a different state and my social worker would somehow figure out a way to get ahold of the money that was supposed to be mine.

The money that was supposed to pull me out of this nightmare I was living.

The money that as supposed to save me and get me far, far away from the place my mother had taken her last breaths.

The place where my father had been the one to steal the oxygen from her lungs.

The school parking lot was devoid of Grey's motorcycle; it made sense.

I had woken up an hour early and escaped out of the house long before the rest of them had stirred from their sleep.

I'd spent the extra time driving around aimlessly, searching for the cave Grey had taken me to weeks ago.

I'd found it. Archived the information in my mind. Kept driving.

And driving

and driving

...and driving...

Until there was nothing but tire tracks swallowing the hole left in my heart from what I'd found out the night before.

Their father...Parker's father, at least.

His familiar profile had been stuck in my head for weeks, but I didn't understand why.

I didn't know why the dean of my new school resembled someone I'd caught a glimpse of so many years ago.

I couldn't have figured out he was the man my mother had been having an affair with so long ago.

I couldn't have known...

Could I have?

Or was I still in denial of the things that my mind refused to accept?

And Grey...

God, Grey.

He was stuck in a punishing cycle of self-hatred that he wouldn't even go to the doctor for the surgery that would save his voice.

He felt he didn't deserve it.

And I understood it completely.

Wholeheartedly.

Because I felt unworthy, too.

Undeserving of justice for what had happened to me.

Undeserving of the satisfaction of seeing Colton in jail, rotting right alongside my father.

The students traversed the campus grounds like insects infesting somewhere full of life and happiness, diluting it until it soured and became infected with their filth.

Colton was standing there along with the rest of the insignificant insects.

He was just...standing there.

Laughing.

There was still bruising and slight redness around his left eye and nose that was noticeably more swollen and crooked than it had before, but it somehow humanized him in some way.

It made him seem vulnerable—like he could be hurt.

Because he had.

Because Parker had punched him into the ground until he was almost oblivion on the wind.

Would I have even wanted him to stop if he had?

No.

I didn't.

The thought was almost as sickening as what he'd done to me.

No, it was worse.

It was the proof that I'd been corrupted by the anger and violence swarming around me my entire life.

There wasn't Parker or Grey here to save me now.

There was no one that could save me besides myself.

I hadn't been able to save my mother—I was only a young, half clueless twelve year old who believed the sun rose and fell with her parents.

A little girl who thought it was so achingly true that her mom and dad loved her more than anything in the world.

They didn't, though.

They loved the superficial things more. They loved their selfishness more.

My father loved his pride and damning wrath more than he cared to protect his young daughter at home.

My mother loved sneaking around with one of my father's friends more than she cared about her daughter 'sleeping' upstairs.

She didn't even wait until the lightbulbs had cooled in my room after flicking them off and saying her goodnights before bringing that man...the dean of my school into our home.

The moment I put the car in park and opened the door, the group that had fallen apart in his absence who were suddenly huddled together again as if nothing had ever happened turned their necks in my direction—no doubt thinking it would be Parker instead of me.

Upon noticing I was alone, Colton's eyes widened and his smile became feral.

He was a beastly animal—fangs dripping with blood and eyes a scarlet so deep they were almost black.

His poison tipped talons stretched out with his hands as he flexed them, preparing for a feast on his favorite prey.

Mori was nowhere to be found, though.

Good.

I didn't want her anywhere near me when this happened. When things finally reached the peak they'd been climbing to.

I was ready, though.

There would be no freezing this time.

If Colton came for me today, I would not shrink back.

I would not cower. I would not cry.

I would face the beast with a smile on my face and claw his eyes out with claws of my own.

Because what he did to me?

It had sharpened me into something almost unrecogniz-able—had broken and shattered me into pieces that were round-ed and soft and I had glued them back together and reformed them into something powerful and strong—with the help of Grey and a stable roof over my head.

He'd taken advantage of me, my situation, my entire life...and he was not going to get away with it.

Not this time.

No, this time, I would be ready.

And he would have no idea what hit him.

Chapter 26

"**G**rey slow down! We don't have to do this today—I know we have the resources to pay for the surgeon right now but it doesn't have to be rushed!"

I ignored my mom—like always—and pushed through the glass double doors of the out-patient center.

I'd spent many afternoons in this very building receiving stern lectures in a back room offset from the surgical rooms.

The doctor my parents had hired privately to handle the trauma to my vocal cords had a very experimental procedure that would give me up to ninety percent of full vocal use back, and my mother's money was a guarantee that I would have the best of the best.

The surgery had been set up for almost an entire year, but I had never set a date. I had never decided when to do this, despite the ticking clock on the procedure. The more I let it go untreated, the worse it would become.

I had to try. It was now or never.

"Mr. Hartingrove, I wasn't expecting you today—oh, Maria. How can I help you today?"

"Grey is adamant about having the surgery today. I don't want him to lose his enthusiasm for it, but I told him you would be too busy. Isn't that right?"

The doctor must've taken pity on me.

Must've seen the burning desperation on my features, the pain etched onto the writing on the silver strands of my soul that were seeping out of my pores.

I couldn't handle the news—all of it.

My mother and father, the secrets they'd been keeping from me almost my entire life.

Cami...her family and my family's own involvement in the downfall of them.

When would it ever end?

When I finally stood up and took responsibility for my own actions and decided to let the past go and forgive myself. That was when it would finally end...

When I would be able to control the things happening around me would be when I stopped allowing the past to dictate my future.

"Actually, I have availability for this afternoon. Grey, we've been waiting for you to be ready for this surgery for a long while. Are you ready? I'll just have you sign some paperwork since you're over eighteen. Right this way."

My mother had no more arguments.

This was happening.

I'd finally be able to speak again without excruciating pain.

Would it be enough to pull me out of the depths I'd fallen into?

Would it make me enough?

For Cami, I'd try. For Cami, I'd do anything.

I followed my doctor through the doors under the bright fluorescent lighting and stepped into the triage room, ready for my future to finally begin and to put my past where it belonged.

I was starting to regret the fact that I'd eaten with Mori every day at lunch for two weeks straight.

All my classes had gone off without a hitch—even the class I'd shared with Colton—but when it came to lunch time?

Mori was desperate to sit with me.

And she wasn't alone.

I should've turned and ran the other way.

I should've told her I was sick; 'I'm so sorry, maybe next time,' or 'I really don't think I'm up for it'.

I should've...should've...should've...

Instead...

Instead I walked with her, arms linked together and my feet were hitting the ground like a death march, each and every stomp of my black shoes against the ground a reminder that I was one footstep away from seeing him again, willingly.

Maybe it was some kind of test of my sanity.

Like I could prove a point to myself that I could survive this.

I'd survived this villain in my bed...so why couldn't I face him in real life...after the fact?

After what he'd done.

After...

"Where's Grey today? And Parker? You're living with them still, aren't you?"

"Oh, I don't know. I left before they did, and I didn't ask if they'd be in today. Hey, about that..."

Excuse, excuse, excuse....I needed a damn good excuse for this to work.

"I'm getting so creeped out by their dad, Mo. He's making me so uncomfortable in their house. Is there any way I can stay with you at your place for a little while, just until my social worker can find me a new replacement? It's hard for foster kids to have a voice in the system, so I don't even know if they'll move me just because I asked, but I still have to try. If your grandparents can't do it, I totally understand—oof."

I was cut off mid monologue by Mori slamming her entire body into mine in a hug that I wasn't sure I was ready for.

I mean, sure, I was used to Grey and his affection, but this? This was so filled with emotion and a sense of regret from her.

It filled my eyes with tears.

"Of course you can stay with us. I don't care what they say, either. I'll just say you're having a sleepover with me, and you'll just never leave. I hate that he's making you feel that way. There's no way that I'm letting you stay in that house a minute more. God, and to think I actually liked Mr. Hartingrove."

I could've told her the truth.

Could've come right out with the ugly words that wanted to dance across my tongue.

But I couldn't—not really. Not when I knew she wouldn't look at me the same way again.

I shivered in disgust at the thought of pity for me crossing her features even more than the emotion was already on her face.

I couldn't bear anymore.

"Thank you," I whispered into her dark hair that was tickling the bottom of my chin. I'd never hugged Mori like this, not really. She was much shorter than I'd thought.

That thought brought a slight giggle to my mouth but I quickly tamped it down once the sight of the cafeteria doors loomed in the distance.

Mori continued on in excitement like she couldn't sense the anxiety seeping through my pores.

I supposed she couldn't sense it—I'd done such a good job of locking my thoughts and emotions in an air-tight vault that she hadn't even known about my 'relationship' with Colton or the fact that I'd practically been living with him for the majority of the semester.

"We need to star talking about college applications. What are your top three?"

I quickly listed off my list of Ivy League schools and her eyes widened exponentially.

"Well, I'm going to have to work a lot harder to get a better SAT score if we want to go to the same school. If we can't, I'll settle for the same state. What are you thinking, New York City or are you wanting to stay in California?"

"I want out of this state. I don't ever want to come back here again."

Her dark eyes softened as she realized the subtext of what I hadn't spoken aloud.

Even though she didn't know the context surrounding my descent into foster care, it was obvious I'd had to go through some dark things in order to survive. No one got out of the system unscathed.

Mori kept the conversation going even as she pinpointed her spot: directly in the middle of 'the group'.

They were all there.

The three girls: Leah, Victoria and Kennedy. All three wore identical masks of expensive makeup.

Carter was joined by Alec, Parker's close friend, and then Nate who I'd never actually spoken a single word to.

Then, finally, the 'star of the show' surrounded by his adoring fans—Colton sat on the other side of the bench table right in the middle.

Right across from where we would be seated.

Why was I doing this?

Was I begging for an altercation?

Was I desperate for the pain, because I needed some other form of it to distract my brain from the news I'd just uncovered about Grey and his family, from the phone call from my father the night before?

Was I just a glutton for punishment, and this was my own personal type of self-harm?

"Well well well, look what we have here? Cami, nice of you to finally join us. Mo, come here babe. I have a seat right here for you."

Is it bad that I wanted to vomit when he pointed to his lap and Mori just...giggled? Like a little schoolgirl...

"Hi, Cami."

"Hi Victoria."

She was the only one I actually liked. The other girls didn't speak up. The cat probably had their tongues, but I wasn't about to be the first person to say hello after their behavior toward me in the past.

I was scrunched between Carter with Mori on his lap and Victoria on my right.

That seating arrangement wasn't the problem. I could handle that.

It was the evil sneering grin Colton had painted on his face that was pointed directly towards me that had me completely on edge, my heart rate skyrocketing until I was sure my pulse was going to go haywire and my veins would explode right under my skin.

"We were just talking about how Marcus from our remedial algebra class got arrested last night. Can you believe that?"

Mori was the one to become immersed in the conversation, and I wondered how she'd assimilated into this group so quickly.

Maybe Alec wasn't so bad, and Victoria was a sweetheart, but the rest of them? I couldn't see myself being friends with any of the rest of them.

My phone began going off in my pocket incessantly, but I ignored it in fear of what would happen if I took my eyes off Colton.

It was like trying to look away from a car wreck in motion—seemingly easy in theory, but impossible to do in the moment.

"Yeah, I heard that earlier, but no one would tell me what happened. What did he do?"

"Apparently—and you did not hear this from me," Leah started, pulling everyone in closer like she were their co-conspirator.

"*Apparently*, he got caught putting a crushed up Xanax tablet in Christina Coor's drink last weekend, and he only just now got arrested after all the interviews and everything. She hasn't been back to school since. Everyone says he did it, though."

Victoria had stiffened into a cardboard cutout beside me, her face pale forcing the reddish brown freckles on her face to stand out.

"D-did what?"

Victoria's voice was a hollowed out imitation of what it had once been. Did she know this Marcus or Christina?

Colton was staring laser holes into my head, but I did not waver in keeping his eyes pinned with mine. He wouldn't win. Not yet.

"They said he...you know...sexually assaulted her."

Leah spoke the news like it was some juicy piece of gossip and not some poor girl's life being broadcasted for entertainment.

But when she'd said those words...I wasn't the only one who'd flinched, but Colton didn't miss a thing.

His grin grew once he realized how affected this had made me.

"What evidence do they have? Some girl's word against his? How do they know she's not just making it up for attention? Or what if he rejected her and she got pissed and decided to claim she did that when he's actually innocent?"

I could practically feel the heat of anger radiating off of Victoria beside me, though she wouldn't look Colton in the eye when she spoke again.

"They have tons of witnesses that saw him put that in her drink and watched as he carried her up the stairs completely sober. Her friends tried to go get her, but he'd locked the door. They have her rape kit, you asshole. That's their fucking evidence."

Victoria didn't look back as she gathered up her things and escaped from the cafeteria like it was on fire.

Some inkling of knowing prickled at my scalp, but I didn't want to assume someone else's trauma.

But I knew the stats.

Most abusers didn't only stop once, and they had to start with one victim.

These people had been friends since birth—was I Colton's first victim, or just his latest?

"Don't mind Victoria, Mo. She's just a little moody. Probably on her period."

Mori's head snapped in Carter's direction, which was hard considering she was placed on his lap.

"Oh, really? So women can only be passionate about a topic when they're on their period? That's pretty sexist of you to say that, Carter."

"I—it's not sexist, it's the truth! Women are more emotional, especially on their periods."

"Actually...men are technically more emotional than women...like, do you not realize that anger is an emotion? Do you see how often guys get angry, and how violent they can get when they get mad?"

I could've kissed Mori for pointing that out. The guys at the table stiffened, brains working in a way you could tell they hadn't before trying to find a way to dispute what she'd just said.

"Hah, she's totally right. Maybe we should take the nuclear codes from the men, they're unstable."

Kennedy and Leah dissolved into laughter at her joke and...I didn't *not* agree with her...

"God, men are such babies. I heard that women sit so much better for tattoos than men, too, because they can't handle the pain."

"Right? Like, women are conditioned to ignore our pain or we're criticized. Like...pretty sure my period hurts more than your cross tattoo, Chad."

The more Mori, Kennedy and Leah joked about men, the angrier Carter and Colton became, though Alec at the end of the table didn't seem to hear a single word.

With each joke and jab about men, Colton's staring, creepy smile turned more sinister until I was crawling in my skin.

My phone vibrated a call one more time and that was when I decided to get up and accept it, especially considering the energy at the table was growing more and more unstable as the moments passed.

"Where are you going?"

"Someone keeps blowing up my phone. I'll see you after school? I need to drop the car off at Grey's but after that can I ride with you to yours?"

"Wait. You're driving Parker's car. You're always with Grey. What's going on, are you like...living with them now?"

i turned to answer Leah, but Colton beat me to it.

"Of course she is, she's homeless, you know that right? She's jumping from couch to couch, paying for her room and board with sex. It's what she did with me. Isn't that right, Cami?"

The entire table was silent for a moment, like they couldn't believe what had just come out of Colton's mouth.

"I—that's not what—"

"Oh, come on now. Don't go trying to change the tune, now. You did live with me for about two months, right? I mean, you practically pimped yourself out for a roof over your head and a hot meal."

He wasn't wrong. No, in fact, he was absolutely right, and that was what made my eyes water.

That was what made the hairs stand up straight on my arms and stay there.

It was what made my stomach fall to the floor with the confused and almost betrayed look on her face.

"Cami? What the hell is he talking about? I thought you guys were just talking and you ended it. What is going on?"

My phone chose that moment to ring once more, and though I needed to pay attention to one of my only friend's perception of me completely falling into the gutter at that moment, my brain decided to read the phone number flashing across my screen.

Parker had been calling, and calling...and calling.

So had Maria.

Alec suddenly spoke up into the group once my phone stopped flashing.

"What the hell? He did what? Is he okay? Shit...okay, I'll be there soon. I will. Stay there, don't move. I mean it, Parker."

"What's going on?"

My heart almost came up through my throat.

"It's Grey, isn't it? Did he...did he—" I cut myself off. I couldn't bear it to ask the question.

I was ready to sink to my knees in agony if Alec gave the answer I was dreading.

"No, no, he went in for his surgery today, but there were complications. I rode to school with Carter, you said you have Parker's car? Can you take me to the..."

"To the where? Come on, let's go."

"Cami, wait."

Mori stood up off Carter's lap and latched onto my arm.

"What is going on? You're not telling me everything."

"I know and I'm sorry. I'll tell you everything you need to know, I promise, but I need to make sure Grey's okay. This...it's probably all my fault, and—"

"How is Grey having surgery and having complications from it your fault?"

"Because I—" I cut myself off, all the listening, nosy ears interrupting my almost word spew that would've told them everything, everything I didn't want them to know.

"I'll tell you later, once I make sure he's alright."

"Okay. Let me know how he is."

"I will. Thank you Mori."

Alec stood impatiently, his dark leather jacket already on and black satchel bag already slung across his shoulders.

"Yes, I just have to get my stuff. Here, take the keys."

Alec didn't waste time catching the keys I threw him, and I didn't spare the rest of the group another look as I darted down the hallway to the room where I'd placed my things for the lunch hour, fully intending to come back with the last thirty minutes and finish up the editing on a paper due.

That wasn't going to get turned in.

There were a lot of assignments I wouldn't be turning in that day.

Grey.

Why would he jump into surgery so quickly, and how was it available on such short notice?

Had it already been planned, and he just hadn't told me yet?

I didn't know the answer, but I knew I needed to be there for him, even if he didn't know that I would be there.

The door to the classroom banged shut with a menacing *thud*, and chills erupted on my skin.

"Finally. I thought we'd never get to be alone."

My neck nearly snapped in half as I realized who stood in the doorway, blocking my only exit.

He leered at my body like he owned it, and I swallowed down the bile rising up in my gut.

So, this was it. This was my final demon to face before I could get to Grey.

"Colton."

Chapter 27

My throat bobbed once, twice, three times.

Sweet, sweet bliss entered my veins as I remembered a different time. One with sunshine and rainbows and happiness and the beautiful shine of my mother's love that radiated down on me like the luminous stars in the dark night sky.

Those stars winked out the night she died, and they only just started coming back to life.

"What do you want, Colton?"

He stalked forward a step, a predator circling in, sizing up his prey. But I wouldn't be an easy target—not this time.

Fuck this asshole.

Who was he to try and threaten me—to try to make me cower in fear and tremble beneath his punishing gaze?

I'd allowed him to victimize me once before, and I wasn't going to let him do that to me again.

"What do I want? Well, I'm looking at it."

I sharpened my gaze, the only tools in my arsenal being my attitude and my words, so I made sure that they didn't miss their mark where I threw them.

"I'm not sure I understand what you mean. I'm a person, not an object. Try again."

"Shit, you got feistier since the last time we were together. What, you not enjoy yourself one time and then you're suddenly not into me anymore? That's rude, Cami. Really rude."

"That's unfortunate that you feel that way."

He could've growled with the amount of menace in his voice, with the volume of frustration swimming in his dead eyes.

He'd grown less terrifying in the past two weeks; like the happiness and contentedness that I'd been surrounded with basking in Grey's glow had eradicated the memories of our last encounter.

Like I wasn't powerless anymore.

He stalked closer and closer, and I knew I shouldn't have done it—knew I should've stood my ground, but the instinctual fear took over and that damn fight or flight kicked in, and I took one small step back.

Colton noticed. Of course, he did. He noticed everything.

Because he thought he was in control, but he didn't know that I wasn't going to take it anymore. I wasn't going to lie down and take it.

I would no longer freeze.

No, I would fight until every drop of blood left me and covered him in the evidence of his evil.

"I'm tired of you playing games. You walking around with Parker's freak of a brother at school and all around town, like I wouldn't find out? Do you know who my father is?"

Another step forward, one step back.

He kept gaining on me, and I kept letting him win, but I couldn't stop my brain—couldn't make myself stand my ground.

"Cami. Camille. Camille Astor. You know, I read up on you."

And that was when the freeze happened.

I couldn't control it—it was like I was floating outside of my body and I was screaming at my corporeal form with a vengeance, 'MOVE, DO SOMETHING, GET AWAY, FIGHT!!!' but she wouldn't listen.

That weak, powerless girl from before had infiltrated my body, and I couldn't stop it.

He finally took that final step and then we were toe-to-toe, staring at each other straight in the eyes.

They say the eyes are the windows to the soul.

Grey's was warm and irreverent—ethereal and magnificent and full of wonder like the break of dawn over a new day.

Colton's soul was black and withered and shriveled up—such a sad excuse of a soul that I wasn't even sure if it was there, anymore.

Almost like all the light had been snuffed out of his body and that was what allowed him to be so callous, so careless, so unfeeling toward the others around him.

Maybe he didn't even understand what he was doing was wrong.

And that was even more terrifying, because that meant there was no reasoning with him.

There was no explaining to him that he should stop, because why should he? If it felt good to him, what use were feelings or empathy if women were only his punching bag, a hole to use and abuse until he got what he wanted and then he could abandon them until they were needed again.

"Your mom, shot right in front of you by your dad. They found you in a puddle of her blood, all covered in it like you'd been rolling around in it with her."

It was everywhere. Red, red, red, suffocating me, covering my hands, all over my clothes. The knees of my jeans were stained scarlet and I ran my hands through my hair to get it out of my face, but—oh, it was in my hair, then.

He bared his teeth. He was an animal, unrecognizable, smoking gun in his hands.

He wouldn't stop shooting.

My hands flew up to cover my ears, and I kept screaming, screaming, screaming...

STOP

STOP

STOP

stop

stop

stop

please, please please—

He was shaking me, then he had one hand over my mouth, and that was when I lost it.

My hands flew to his shoulders and then my knee was coming up to slam into his favorite part of himself.

The piece of himself he'd used to violate me, and probably others.

It felt so good to hear his groan of pain that I almost got lost in it, swimming in a deranged sort of ecstasy that didn't allow me to see straight.

One moment, I'd been having an out-of-body experience, and then the next I'd been slammed directly back into my body and had gathered up enough energy and anger to finally put my thoughts to action and hurt him right where it counts.

Only I didn't account for how strong and angry he would be after such a painful hit.

They always told you to kick them there.

They said it would incapacitate them.

They didn't say they would recover quickly, that they would reach out with their poison tipped talons and reach into your skin and pull your soul right out from your insides and gnaw on your flesh and bones until you were a pile of skin and tissue, sinew and muscle and—

"What are you doing here, Cami? Get out! GET OUT!"

The gun went off again, a POP ringing out so loud it felt like it could've burst my eardrums.

He seemed to like the power and the sharp sting of pain that occurred after a shot.

He fired again, at the family pictures above the fireplace on the mantle.

He shot my picture directly through the eye.

There was blood everywhere.

everywhere

everywhere

every

where

The gun kept popping and exploding the furniture and walls around us until he finally ran out of bullets.

They were shot through the walls, decorations, the black, shattered screen of the television above the couch.

They were embedded in my mother's dead corpse on the ground beside me.

Her blood ran in a single line down the floor, leading directly to my father's standing figure.

He wasn't my father in that moment. No, he was something else, something different.

Something absolutely monstrous.

Colton flashed between himself and the vision I had of my father in my mind that kept taking over my body.

One moment, I was sitting in a puddle of my mom's blood, brushing her dark golden hair back from her head and streaking it auburn with her blood, and then the next I was pushed down to the ground below Colton's towering form.

"Why the fuck did you do that?! You fucking bitch, you didn't fight me this much before."

He fumbled with the zipper on his jeans, and I realized with a terrifying sort of clarity that he was going to do it again. He was going to take advantage of me right here and now, if I didn't do something to stop it.

He had my hands pinned beneath me on the ground, the cold laminate of the school flooring biting into my skin.

One of his knees was pressed down against my stomach, keeping me thoroughly and effectively subdued, but he couldn't use his other hand to pull himself out if he was busy trying to keep me quiet.

"HELP! HELP! Somebody HELP ME!"

When his hand came back down over my mouth, I didn't waste time.

I found whatever purchase I could on his skin and I *bit*.

Hard.

The coppery tang of blood washed into my mouth as he hissed and pulled away.

I used his distraction to my advantage to let out the most blood curdling scream I'd ever uttered, and the response was immediate.

His hand came flying across my face, but he'd let go of my hands.

The sting was nothing compared to the feral smile that fell onto my lips.

I was sure my eyes resembled a wild animal who'd contracted rabies, teeth stained red with my prey's blood.

I used my last remaining energy to swing my legs up and somehow bucked him off of me, but just as I was running to the door, he grabbed me around the waist and tried to grapple me to the ground once more but I held firm.

He resorted to clasping my elbows to my sides tightly so I couldn't use my hands and used his other hand to squeeze my air way.

It was poetic, in a way.

That Colton was choking me to death, just as Grey had tried to do to himself.

I would've laughed at the irony, had the pain not been so immediate and intense that I started seeing spots in my vision.

Spots that resembled stars in the pitch night sky.

Stars that had lost all their luster and shine the moment my mother's own light had been snuffed out by an evil man.

How fitting, then, that I was to find my own end at the hands of another evil man?

"Cami? You in there?"

I tried to get the air in to scream out at Alec's voice to help find me. I tried.

I really did.

But Colton's grip was too strong.

I closed my eyes.

I didn't want his face to be the last that I saw on this earth.

No, instead I conjured the images of Grey that I'd tucked away for safe keeping.

His soft reserved smiles.

His eyes when the light hit them just right and I realized that they weren't pitch black like the night sky without its stars or the moon.

They were actually a deep caramel, rich with vibrant swirls of gold and amber that gave them a depth that made me want to drown in them when I saw them for the first time—really *saw* them.

Someone was jiggling the doorknob.

Footsteps.

Yelling.

I almost succumbed to the darkness, to that sweet, numb abyss where I could live with Grey forever in the night sky, the stars to his forever expanse of eternal, comforting darkness, never alone again.

I almost joined my mother, floating around out there somewhere.

Someone's hands ripped Colton's from my throat, though, and I dropped to the ground in a vicious coughing fit.

Alec was there, his face blurry and distorted.

"Cami? Are you okay?"

Someone was restraining Colton, but I couldn't see them. I could only think of Grey.

"We're going to take her to the hospital."

Yes, the hospital. Then I could be with Grey, I could be there for him.

"Yeah, I need to go there too. I'll ride in the ambulance with her."

"Alright. I'm going to have to notify her parents when she regains consciousness."

"I think she's a foster child. I'll try to get her guardian's contact information."

"I'm here, I'm here. What in the world has happened?"

My eyes were closed, but the action hadn't stopped around me.

"We need to contact this girl's legal guardians."

"I'm one of her legal guardians. She's a foster, and we're having her at our home. What's all this about?"

"It seems your foster child was attacked by one of your students, Mr. Hartingrove. We're transporting her to the hospital right now."

There were hands touching me, but I couldn't flinch to swat them away.

"Alright, I'll follow behind the ambulance. I was just on the way to the hospital as well."

There was shuffling, then we moved somewhere else. I was weightless, then crashed back down onto something like a bed on wheels.

We were outside. It was cold.

"Mr. Hartingrove? I'm Alec, Parker's friend...is Grey...?"

"I don't know how Grey is right now. Last I heard, he was coding. I don't know if he's alive or dead."

He sounded like he didn't care.

I suddenly wished I were dead, too.

At least then, we'd be together.

Chapter 28

There are moments in everyone's life where the narrator of your own story has to take a step back and look at the finished work and evaluate if it's actually worth telling.

My 'finished work' wasn't so finished yet.

I opened my eyes.

The atmosphere was serene and so, so clean.

Everything was white.

"Cami? Are you awake, sweetie?"

My social worker's voice cut through the calming fog, however.

I jolted at the sound of her voice, angry that she was still allowed to be anywhere near me after hearing my father tell me over the phone that they were basically in league together to take my inheritance money.

Her honey blonde hair assaulted my eyes and the sickly sweet smell of her perfume attacked my nostrils.

Joanie Grant—the worst social worker in the entire state of California, and she was mine. How lucky must I have been?

"I—I can't—"

I couldn't talk.

I'd sustained the same injuries Grey had during his attempt, it seemed. I could still make certain sounds, though, so maybe they weren't necessarily as bad as his.

The thought of Grey there, dangling from his belt strap hung on the doorway of his closet...

I couldn't motion for the trashcan before I was hurling my guts up onto the floor beside us.

"Can I get some help in here, please!"

A nurse in sky blue scrubs came rushing into the room with a small puke bag, almost like she'd been expecting this to happen.

My social worker came up behind me and rubbed her hand down my back as I continued hurling into the small plastic bag.

I hated her touch. I wanted Grey's instead.

Grey...

"Is—is he ok-okay?"

"Who?"

"Grey."

My throat was angry with me. It was scratchy and irritated and ready to give out on me at any moment, but still I pushed the words out.

"Grey Hartingrove? He's in another hospital, your foster mom called me after he had some complications, but it looks like he's doing better. She wanted me to be here for you since she couldn't be."

I admired Maria for doing the next best thing, but wished she hadn't sent anyone at all.

A boy with dark blonde hair poked his head in the door.

Alec.

His appearance was rough, hard edged, bedraggled. Almost like he'd been waiting a very long time for me at this hospital.

"Cami? Are you okay? Can I come in?"

I nodded my head, if only because I'd wasted my talking capabilities asking about Grey.

"I was so worried. They arrested Colton right after they took you to the hospital. I think...I think it's actually gonna stick this time, the charges."

"I'm sorry, Alec is it? Cami is resting and she needs her privacy, so if you don't mind—"

"No!"

I didn't know where I found the strength to speak up against her, but I knew that I didn't want to be alone in the room with her.

Alec edged around the puddle of puke still on the floor and sat in the chair to my left, completely ignoring Joanie.

Good, I'd ignore her, too.

"Grey had some kind of reaction to the anesthesia and Parker's been with him the whole time. He slept in late for school but when he woke up and his mom said they were at the hospital, he took off on Grey's motorcycle and he's been there ever since. Grey coded once, but they got him back. He's stable."

I nodded my head. Good. Some of my anxiety lessened, but it wouldn't ever really go away until I could see for myself that Grey was actually okay.

"Do you want to hear what they arrested Colton for?"

Another nod. I wanted to make sure the charges stuck.

"Aggravated assault and attempted sexual assault. We'll see how well those charges will stick, but with all the girls coming forward, he's probably going to be facing a lot of time."

He must've sensed the question in my eyes. Other girls?

"Victoria and a few other girls from school went to the police station after he was arrested and began giving their statements on how he assaulted them at parties. It's been so long since most of them, but one of the girls had a ton of evidence, photos, videos, that kind of stuff...It was Leah."

Leah?

Leah, as in the girl who'd been with him since he'd thrown me out like day old trash.

Leah—the girl who'd helped him bully both me and Mori?

I only wished I could figure out what was going through her mind—what had happened between the two of them that had allowed her to gather so much evidence against him.

I could only hope that it was enough to send him away—for good.

"Anyway, I didn't want to leave you here since I rode in the ambulance with you. I had to lie and say I was your brother. I didn't want you to be alone."

My eyes watered. I only wished I could've said my thanks, but with the state of my voice, I doubted I could squeak out another sound.

"Anyway, I'll let you get some rest and let the nurses talk to you. I was going to call Parker and ask him for an update on Grey and how he's doing too. I can grab your assignments from school, too, if you have to miss a few days...no one would blame you if you did. Alright, well, I'll talk to you later I guess."

I stopped him from leaving by reaching out and grabbing onto his arm as he passed.

Our eyes locked and I sent him a meek smile and nod of grati-tude, squeezing his arm with my hands in goodbye.

Once he was gone, though, my social worker turned her sky blue eyes on me and narrowed them, almost in irritation.

"Your father told me he called you last night. And then this happens right afterwards...I only hope this isn't some kind of a cry for help. All you have to do is sign the papers that I give you and we can have your guardianship and Power of Attorney transferred to me. What do you think about—"

"Excuse me, are you Miss Astor's legal guardian?"

The nurse who'd been in to clean up my puke and give me the barf bag had reappeared, and my respect for nurses had suddenly gone through the roof as she eyed Joanie beside me with a keen suspicion.

I shook my head vehemently.

No, she was most definitely not my legal guardian.

"I'm her court appointed social worker."

"Ah, I see. Well, I need to speak with her legal guardian, who I have on the phone right now. If you wouldn't mind leaving so I can let Miss Astor here in on her condition as well as her legal guardian, Mrs. Hartingrove."

Joanie brushed off the intrusion and flicked her blonde hair behind her shoulder. She pinned me with a look in her eyes that told me that this conversation wasn't over, but if I had anything to say about it—it definitely was.

"Thank you," I whispered to the nurse, realizing that I could still whisper even though it scratched my throat with a vengeance.

"Of course, sweetie. Maria, can you hear me?"

"Yes I can hear you. I would be there if I could, but with my son in the ICU here..."

"No I understand. I have Cami here listening so I'm going to go ahead and list off the injuries she came in with. Cami, does that sound okay to you?"

I nodded my head and she began.

Slight bruising around my windpipe. Bruising on my ribs and around my wrists from when I'd been pinned down on the ground by Colton.

"Overall, you're in great health and once the swelling around your throat goes down, it should be easier to talk and swallow. We can release you today, I don't see any issues with your discharge. We can send the papers to you virtually through your email, Mrs. Hartingrove, since Cami isn't eighteen yet and can't sign them. Does that sound alright?"

"Yes, that sounds wonderful. Thank you for your help with this, I would be there if I found some way to split myself in half and be there for both of them at the same time."

But...why?

Grey was her child, not me. She didn't owe me anything.

After what Parker had said about her true reasoning for fostering me, I had just assumed her caring and sweet nature was all just an act to trick me into wanting her to adopt me.

I didn't ever stop to think that it could ever be...authentic.

"Of course Mrs. Hartingrove. Alright, I'll give the phone to Cami in case she has something more to say."

The nurse handed me the cellphone just as my own sat on the chair beside me began buzzing incessantly.

"Cami, are you alright?"

"Yeah, I'm okay," I whispered, wishing that I could just speak normally. Was this what Grey was going through?

"Good. I can't believe that happened at school, but you know he's been arrested, and he won't be getting out on bail. We're going to make sure they set it to an amount his family can't pay."

"Thank you."

My whispered words barely broke the barrier of the sounds bouncing back to me through the other end of the phone.

Beeps and scattered conversations and muffled yells from across the room could all be heard. She must've stepped out of Grey's hospital room to talk to me and the nurse.

"How's Grey?"

"He's—he's going to be okay. They think he had some kind of a reaction to the anesthesia, but with all the other surgeries he's had, this has never happened. We're keeping an eye on him now, but they're telling me he—"

Someone was yelling, loudly.

"Call a code!"

"What? What's going on? Hello, this is my son's room, what's going on!"

I could only sit in stoic silence as the blankness wrapped around me.

I curled the comforting bliss of numbness around me with trembling fingers as Maria dropped the phone on the ground.

There was running, shuffling, crying.

"Get a crash cart in here, now!"

"Please, please, PLEASE! This is my son! That's my SON!"

Her voice broke the sound barrier, but I stuffed my ears with cotton and stuck my head underwater.

Still, her shattering cries made it past my defenses.

"Grey! GREY!"

"Someone get the family out of here please."

"NO! No no no no no no no!"

"Ma'am, please—"

There was nothing else on the line but static.

And then I handed the phone to the nurse calmly.

"She said she signed the documents you emailed. She said it might take some time to send because of the signal in the hospital. Can I be discharged please? I just want to go home and lie down."

"I—"

The nurse hesitated, but noticed the withdrawn and pathetic look on my face.

"Just this once. I'll let you get dressed. Do you have a ride?"

I nodded my head. Talking was so, so painful.

"Alright sweetie. Let me get you some papers on how to take care of your throat and your rest instructions and doctor's notes to miss school for the next week. Wait here."

I didn't wait.

I didn't wait because Alec appeared at the door again.

"Parker just called. He left the hospital and...wait, are you al-lowed to leave? Already?"

I only nodded as I pulled the thin, scratchy hospital blanket away from my legs and waited for Alec to continue explaining what was going on.

"Parker needs a ride. I was going to take him to the hospital again, but...do you need a ride, too?"

"Please."

Alec turned away as I stepped into my uniform skirt underneath the hospital gown, then slipped the white button up over it and tucked it in.

Next came the socks, boots, jacket.

I was a mechanical robot incapable of feeling.

There were clouds in my brain, fogging up my thoughts and filling my head with sweet, blissful nothingness.

I knew there was somewhere I needed to be. I knew something had happened to me, and to Grey, but I just...didn't care anymore.

At least Alec was taking me out of this god awful hospital.

I could still feel grateful, apparently.

I didn't ask why Parker had left the hospital when his brother had almost just died—where his brother was likely dying at this very moment.

I didn't ask why he couldn't just drive himself back, either, or why Alec had to go pick him up.

I didn't ask a thing at all, only ripped the hospital bracelets I'd been given off my wrist and grabbed up my backpack from the collection of my belongings in the corner and followed Alec out of the building.

No one stopped us.

The drive was shorter than I'd expected.

The area was familiar. So, so familiar.

Green pastures and an imposing mountain in the distance grew closer.

The sun sprayed down onto the ground and reflected off a few stray pools of water in refractory diamond light.

I did not ask Alec why we were there.

I followed him out of the car on foot, trudging through dirt and weeds and wildflowers up to my knees.

I did not react when he reached the mouth of the cave.

I did not breathe as Parker came into view, shouting obscenities at the walls and slinging paint darker than a Stygian Sea.

I *did* sink to the ground, knees scraping against grey rock beneath me.

I *did* inhale a shaking, slow breath that stained my lungs with the scent of paint fumes and still water.

"No, you didn't hear anything, did you? No..."

"No, Parker I haven't heard anything. I think he's still in stable condition."

Except he wasn't.

Grey wasn't okay. Grey wasn't in stable condition.

I'd been on the other end of the phone when Maria had collapsed in on her grief and anguish.

Like a tether to the other side, I felt his connection to this world snap like the branches of a tree in a howling windstorm.

He's gone.

He's gone.

Gone.

gone

gone

gone

gone—

Someone was shaking me by the shoulders, spitting in my face and asking me, how, how, HOW DO YOU KNOW and then—

But then his body fell forward, his forehead brandishing a fire onto mine and then his arms were around me in a punishing hug, punishing me with pain for the things I'd done and what I'd said and—

and then my arms were around him, my eyes leaking onto his shoulder and none of us moved until pain splatter drip drip dripped down onto our shirts and mixed into our hair and painted us the color of night and grief and an anguish so deep it bellowed out into a yawning abyss of eternity spooling out before us.

He's gone.

Grey, Grey, Grey...

Gone before I ever really knew him at all.

Chapter 29

They are all wearing black.

It's very depressing.

Why couldn't he have left instructions for his funeral; for them to all be dressed in bright rainbow colors instead?

This wasn't supposed to be a dismal, wretched kind of funeral.

No, in his mind, it was supposed to be a celebration of the life lived and the eternity that would follow in everlasting night, finally free of the shackles and pain filled prison that was life on earth.

His father stands, all dry eyes and stony expression.

The gathered crowd on the verdant grassy knoll turns toward him in anticipation; almost like they're expecting it now, at any moment.

'Soon', they think to themselves. 'Soon, he'll show some emotion. Soon, he'll actually prove that he did care about his son.'

But he doesn't.

He stares and stares and stares at that open casket.

He must believe it still has his son inside.

It doesn't.

His son is watching the proceedings from somewhere *above*, somewhere that he cannot reach, and the place his father will not be able to follow.

He knows the contents of his father's soul.

He will not be joining him at *Peace.*

Peace is exactly as it sounds; just as the word describes, it is thankless and wondrous and an absence of the kind of pain that used to wrap around his neck and choke the life out of him, just like it had done to him on that earth.

The pain had finally overwhelmed him.

He'd let go, succumbed to it. Drowned in it.

Reveled in it.

The light wasn't bright, but a beautiful diluted ray of sunshine devoid of all color—almost as if it were...grey.

Pale and effervescent, translucent. The conduit for a myriad of kaleidoscope colors to traverse through and paint the rest of the world in its beauty, but this...

this lack of color...

This was the real thing.

Perhaps he should've left instructions for them to all wear grey that day, in honor of his namesake.

It sounds ridiculous in his head.

'In honor of'.

Like *he* deserves any kind of honor.

At least in death, Grey Hartingrove understood his place in the world.

He understands it just fine, as his father approaches the podium to deliver an emotionless eulogy.

His mother couldn't have done it—she was too busy weeping and wailing over the loss that she could hardly form words. He doesn't understand why—his wasn't a loss that should've been felt deeply and profoundly; rather, it was a loss that should've only scratched the surface, made way for their perfect child to shine.

Parker is off to the side, alone.

Sad. Despondent. But he'd be okay in the long run. In the end.

There is no friend of his in the crowd. No one there to comfort his mother. Not even his brother would do her that favor.

Instead, his brother stares at their father as he begins his speech.

"Grey was an emotionally complex young man. He always said what was on his mind, and it didn't matter how you felt about it—he was going to tell it to you right then. He was kind, but other times, he could be a little devil."

The crowd gets a kick out of hearing of his mischievous ways as a child.

"Grey was the kind of kid you always knew was going to grow up to be smart—too smart for their own good. He was so interested in writing stories...but they had to mean something. One time I remember, he was twelve years old. He came up to me with a story about a giant spider that could talk. The giant spider wanted to befriend the humans, but they were all terrified of him because of what he looked like.

"He said that's how people saw him because even then he began dressing differently; wearing darker clothes and wanting to shave his head. He felt different, I suppose, because he *was* different. I don't want the way my son died to define his life and the works he created. That's why I'll be starting up a center for Creative Writing at Hartingrove Academy. In honor of Greylin Hartingrove, and his stories that were never told."

It is like his father expected applause after his eulogy.

He doesn't understand that everyone is sad for a boy that none of them knew; sad for a family that should've known better and seen the warning signs.

It doesn't matter that they tried to cover up the way he passed; it is a small town. Everyone finds out eventually.

Finally, Parker stands to walk to the podium.

Instead, he bangs a fist on the coffin off to the side.

The coffin is closed; his parents not wanting to show the world the scars around his neck.

"Dammit, Grey. Why would you do this? Why? Tell me!"

He flips open the black stained wood of the coffin, but his body is no longer inside.

Instead...

His body is underneath a plush kind of bed...and there is beeping somewhere far off in the distance.

Someone is weeping nearby.

"Grey! GREY!"

Someone is screaming his name, but they are so far away.

If only he could cling onto that bright pale light a moment longer, then the scene would begin to feel real again. The funeral would really happen.

Except...

Someone is missing in that scene.

He can't put his finger on it, but—

a girl.

There was a girl missing from his funeral that should have been there. She should have been the one to deliver his eulogy, not his robotic, unfeeling, uncaring father.

She...

She was soft lines and the remnants of a beauty he'd forgotten long ago.

The weeping intensifies, but he does not listen. He closes his ears, eyes, nose, mouth, senses...holds it all in until—

"You all need to get out of here!"

"Doctor Sloan, I'm the code RN. We just shocked him at 150 for a V-fib arrest—could still be in V-fib. Last shock was a minute and a half ago."

"Have we given any meds yet?"

"No meds yet, we have IV access."

"Alright let's push Epi. Someone get the family out of here, please."

Something tethers himself back into his body.

It feels like acid flowing through earth-bound veins.

"One milligram of Epi in."

Something is concaving his chest in and out.

"At pulse check we're gonna change compressors."

"Alright, looks like its V-fib. Let's go ahead and shock."

"Charging at 200 joules."

"Everybody stand clear."

"Shocking—"

Colors. Lights. Sounds, smells, and touch—all of it is delivered to him back into this body until he is no longer a floating entity above the heads of nurses and doctors, but a patient lying in a hospital bed in a flimsy gown with electrical wires connected to his body and needles sticking out of his arm and fluid entering through the tubes connected to the needles and—

"Shock delivered, resume CPR."

His heart is slamming into his rib cage, the pain near excruciating.

"10 seconds til pulse check."

"Pulse check."

"He has a pulse with compressions."

"Hold compressions."

The breath he finally inhales on his own that isn't being forced down his lungs is one of sputtering, choking oxygen.

"We have a pulse. Good job guys, let's secure the airway and let's call ICU."

Grey Hartingrove opens his eyes.

Chapter 30

"Cami? You've got a visitor."

"Coming."

Mori moved out of the doorway of her front living area and stepped aside so that I could be confronted with the reality of what my hiding away had done.

I hadn't seen Parker Hartingrove in two weeks.

Hands in his pockets, he turned to face me and I was hit with it all at once—the memories, the moments, everything.

The shock of it all.

Seeing his face, his eyes opened and filled with such a precious life that I had to look away.

It was torture seeing that on his face and knowing that his life had almost gone out completely.

"What are you doing here?"

"What am I doing here? Cami, are you serious?"

Mori cleared her throat and I stepped outside onto the front porch of her grandparents small home that I'd been staying in for the past two weeks.

I hadn't even had to go to school after the trauma of it all—Mori had been able to bring me all of my schoolwork and, of course, I'd gone above and beyond to finish it all ahead of time.

Nothing like a failed attempt on your life and the boy you loved almost dying to force you to want to dissociate by doing schoolwork.

Now, staring at the brother of said boy, however...I was starting to regret my decision for the radio silence.

"What the hell do you think I'm doing here? He's...he can talk, Cami. He finally has what he's been punishing himself over since his attempt. He's finally got what he was too scared to admit that he wanted, and he's miserable. Do you know why he's miserable? I'll give you one guess."

"Stop it, Parker."

His eyes were blazing with a fury I hadn't seen in them before.

His clothes were snug on his frame, filled out and healthy and glowing—Parker was absolutely glowing.

I could only imagine the shell of a person looking back at him.

"Why should I stop? I understand what's all happened, but pushing him away—pushing us all away? That's not helping. I can promise you that."

"How you do know that? I met you at your game and you pretended you never even met me, so why should I think that you'd ever even cared about me to begin with? Is this all about Grey, or are your feelings just hurt because I'm ignoring you?"

The confusion on Parker's face gave way to irritation.

"What are you talking about? We met on the bus on the way to the senior field trip to the museum."

"No. We didn't. We met at that scrimmage game at the beginning of school when you and *Colton* got into a fight. You don't even remember, I was insignificant to you then, just like I am now."

The vehemence in my tone that I spat *his* name out caused Parker to jerk back a step, but the bewilderment never left his eyes.

"Cami...I had a concussion. I was missing time for that whole day. There's a lot I can't remember, but that does not make you insignificant. I always thought you were so familiar to me, that was why I wanted to be your friend, to talk to you...and yeah, maybe I even wanted something more at the very beginning but you were drawn to Grey. I get it, I'm not bitter about it or anything—"

"Oh, thank you for not being bitter about a decision you never had any part of whatsoever."

"Okay, Jesus, Cami. Why are you so mad? What is wrong with you? You were fine that day you came to see Grey in the hospital, until you saw him. Then you just...you just booked it out of there like you were on fire. What the hell is going on with you? He needs you—"

"Okay and what about me?! I need someone too but I can't ask that of him, not after what he just went through! Not to mention what I just found out about your father. It's too much Parker it's just all too fucking much. Do you not get that? I needed to get away from that, from it all. I was so overwhelmed. Fuck, I almost died, too, Parker. He almost got away with it, too."

"What?"

There was that damn confusion playing out across his features, again.

"Colton. He almost got away with what he did to me the first time, and he almost got away with it the second. If Alec hadn't been there..."

"What do you mean, the first time?!"

"Parker, you cannot tell me you're this clueless. Please tell me you're joking."

"Cami. What happened the first time?"

His voice was lethal, filled with spikes and barbed wire.

"What the fuck do you think happened, Parker?! He. Hurt. Me. Rub two brain cells together and you'll get the answer."

He started panting, taking in deep, wheezing breaths.

"No. No no no no no..."

"Oh, yes. I've come to terms with it."

Mostly.

Two weeks of therapy three times a week was a start. I was getting there, but most times the memory was a sore, scabbed and bloody mess in my mind that I couldn't stop picking at no matter how much it hurt.

Therapy was telling myself that it was okay to let it heal and scab over, just a little bit.

And then the nightmares would rip it right off again.

"He was...he was in my friend group. I subjected you to him, at our house, at lunch...in the parking lot. I found out later what happened with the other girls, but I thought he'd just *tried* with you. Cami I—I am so fucking sorry I couldn't protect you."

Something broke a little bit inside my chest at his words.

"No one's ever said that to me."

No one had ever protected me before.

My throat burned as tears tumbled down my cheeks, but I didn't move to wipe them away.

"If you need him and he needs you, then why can't you just come back—for the both of you?"

"Because it's—"

Because it was too hard.

Because it was terrifying.

Because I was worried that since he could talk he'd say he didn't want me anymore because of what happened to me.

Because I'm scared he'll think I'm damaged goods and not worth it.
Because I don't think I'm worth it...

"I can drive you over there right now, Cami, I swear. He just got the all clear to go back to doing what he used to—going to school, exercising, anything he wants. You're going to see him."

He was going back tomorrow, just like me.

"Thanks for coming to let me know, but I'm staying here."

"Cami—"

"Thanks, Parker. I'll see you tomorrow at school."

He didn't get another word out before I closed the door in his face.

Mori didn't bother me for the rest of the night, but I didn't know if I appreciated it or hated her for it.

I was on fire on the way to school, riding alongside Mori in her grandmother's tiny two-door Mazda.

Kids were clustered around the cars in the parking lot, just like always.

They stared when we got out.

Pinpricks danced alongside my skin as each and every eye pinned me in place.

"Come on," Mori whispered encouragingly to me, but I was frozen.

Rooted to the spot.

A familiar motorcycle rumbled to life in the background and my heart stopped beating.

My thoughts stopped swirling.

My stomach dropped into my gut.

The chirping of birds filled the air with a symphony of song calls, bathing the atmosphere with a brevity of permanence.

Grey was here.

Grey was pulling into the school parking lot, and I hadn't seen him in weeks.

Hadn't cried with him. Hadn't spoken one word to him.

I'd only gazed into his open, alive eyes in that hospital bed, so similar to the one I'd just been lying in not hours earlier.

Because we'd gotten the call: Grey was alive. He was stable. He was in the ICU, but he was okay. He was going to be okay.

That life tether that I'd felt snap in my bones had come back to life, just like him. His soul returned to his body, and he was back, he was safe, he was there, there, there...

and I'd taken one look and left.

He reached out for me with a slow, steady hand, but I was already gone.

And now he was here, pulling up on the other side of the parking lot with an ocean of space and unsaid words hanging between us—a sea filled with what-ifs and broken promises to always be there for each other.

He was here and I had left him and—and suddenly I was hyper-ventilating, because there he was.

Bathed in sunshine.

Gilded in yellow light.

Dressed head to toe in black.

Shaking out his dark hair from the helmet and raking his fingers through feather-softness that I'd once had the pleasure of touch-ing...before.

Kicking the stand up on his motorcycle and pulling the key out and pocketing it.

There he was...

Striding forward on sure steps.

There he was—

embracing Parker in the middle of the lot, and those were his lips...

speaking. Aloud. To his brother.

I wasn't the only one staring anymore; everyone's attention had turned to the golden boy and his shadowed brother.

The clouds parted as my feet took one, two, three steps forward.

His head snapped to me, and then,

and then

and then—

he was sprinting toward me and I couldn't control the sob that tore from my throat.

He was running and not looking back and I was flung into his arms before my brain could ever register the shock of it all.

His warm scent enveloped me and this was it—this was everything I'd ever wanted.

This was it.

I was home.

Chapter 31

It only took ten seconds.

Her eyes were silver lined and filled with unshed tears.

But that wasn't the only thing that I noticed about her.

She was absolutely terrified, and I wasn't sure if it was for the fact that I'd almost died—twice, or because she was feeling things she didn't want to feel...but it only took ten seconds.

One.

Her head popped up as soon as my eyes met hers, and the relief that filled through my veins with undiluted joy was something I wasn't expecting to feel.

Two.

The smile stretched over her features. It was shaking and filled with fierce emotion that I would have to be in denial to try and explain away. The smile—it was the one she only used with me.

Three.

I let out a breath quivering with anticipation as I tried to sit up in that damned hospital bed—but that was when she broke her gaze and took in the wires and the IV pole and the bandage around my neck and—

Four.

She sucked in a sharp breath that forced a lone tear to slide down her face.

Don't cry...please, don't cry, not for me. I wished I could've told her that. I was okay, I was alright. Why wasn't she coming forward, why was she still rooted in place in the doorway, like she was nothing but a stranger here, to me?

Five.

Somehow, I knew this was coming. I knew I wasn't good enough for someone to stay for me. I knew my family was only there because they were blood. I knew...I knew this was too good to be true.

She took a step backwards, hands searching for the doorjamb while her eyes flitted around the room in what seemed like a blind panic.

She was having an anxiety attack.

Six.

More tears slipped down her cheeks, and my mother took a step toward her to help steady her, but she put a hand up to keep her at bay. Her eyes met mine once more, and what I saw in them devastated me.

She couldn't do it. I knew it the moment we locked eyes the first time, but it still felt like an anvil dropping on my heart.

I almost died, and she was bailing. This was it. It was over.

Seven.

But—no. Those were bruises around her neck. There was something wrong. Something that I couldn't ask because I still couldn't fucking talk!

Talk, you dumbass, get the words out!

"C-c—"

Eight.

Choking on my own air. Of course this was how I acted in front of her after the surgery.

Her eyes widened in something that resembled pain as she took a stumbling step toward me, almost like she was desperate to get near me to help.

"Grey, do not try to talk! You heard the doctor, if you do, you'll ruin all the progress they made and then all this that you just went through will have been for nothing."

No, it wouldn't have all been for nothing. I knew that I didn't want to die, I knew what I wanted in life and I was done beating around the bush in order to get it.

I was done letting life happen to me.

If all you do is sit around and wait for the clock to run down on your life and there's nothing after, then you just wasted your time living waiting to die. I wasn't going to let that happen to me. Not again.

The funeral I'd dreamed of had been the one I imagined after my attempt. I had it all planned out in my mind and everything. It would unfold just like I thought, and I wouldn't be surprised, wouldn't be disappointed. It was just how it worked.

I would be at peace and I would be fine. Not happy, not sad, just peaceful. Not black or white, but grey.

The in between place between heaven and hell—purgatory.

I didn't want to live there anymore.

Nine.

Cami took another small step toward me, but stopped herself at the last moment. Our eyes locked again, and I knew there was no keeping her here.

I would find out what happened to her, and then I'd figure out a way to help her, just like she'd helped me.

Ten.

An apology flickered across her face for the barest of moments, but then...

she was already gone.

"Alright, now let's try some higher inflections in your voice. We know your voice is going to be much deeper than it would've normally been, but I want to see if you can still speak in different tones and have tone shifts."

"What do you mean by that?"

"Mimic me—oh, no, a turtle!"

I almost cracked a smile at the doctor's ridiculous voice and phrase, but still I repeated what he said and how he said it.

"Good, very good. And do you feel any residual pain when speaking in a higher tone?"

"No. It all feels fine. I haven't had any pain since the first time I tried."

"I will say I'm very impressed with your recovery, Grey. I might call you up one day and ask you to come to a conference on this surgery to show my success stories. Would that be alright with you?"

Success story? After I'd flatlined not once, but twice on the table?

"Sure."

"Perfect. I'll have the nurse schedule you a follow-up appointment in six weeks, but other than that...if this were a disease, I'd say you were cured."

"Thank you."

Cured. Right.

It was true.

I could speak.

There was no pain.

So then why was I so unhappy?

My motorcycle rumbled out of the parking lot and drove me to one of my least favorite places: the county jail.

He hadn't been transferred yet, or bailed out.

Apparently, with the abundance of evidence, his parents were disgusted of him. Either that, or they weren't as rich as they claimed to be and couldn't afford his bail.

Officer Murphy was at the desk when I strode inside.

"Ah, no. Not you again. Let me guess—you passed the bar exam since we last talked and you're his lawyer now?"

"Whatever you want to tell yourself."

I slipped him three hundred dollar bills.

He looked the other way.

The first time, Colton just stared at the wall and refused to talk to me.

The second visit, he yelled and threw his pillow at me—or rather, at the bars in his jail cell.

This was the third, and the last.

I was returning to school tomorrow, and I needed to get a few things off my chest.

I hadn't spoken the first two visits, so he had no idea I could talk again. I'd kept that a secret on purpose.

"Great. You again. Let me guess—the officers either don't give a shit who they let back here, or you're using your Dad's money to bribe them."

I cringed as he said I was using my 'dad's' money. That's where he was wrong. It was my money that I'd earned for racing my motorcycle every other weekend before Cami came along.

Parker's father was not my own. I was still wrapping my head around that one, but thankfully my relationship with my mother hadn't suffered after learning this information.

It had been repaired, actually, and she was on her way to helping me figure out who my birth father was.

"Oh. I know. You're here to stare at me for two hours in silence because you can't fucking talk. Well, guess who's fault that is, huh?"

He crept closer to the metal bars separating the two of us.

They were gunmetal grey, gritty, and most likely hadn't been washed since they'd been placed in this jail cell.

The dank fluorescents flickered and zapped above and illuminated the white uniform Colton had on that had turned a strange shade of light brown since the last time I'd seen him.

I was lucky the bastard didn't have a cellmate, and that there were only three cells in the county jail. They were currently empty.

He'd remain here until his trial in a week, and if convicted, he'd go on to the state penitentiary. With his violent crimes, he could even end up at the exact same prison as Cami's father.

What strange irony that would be.

Still, not realizing the danger standing in front of him, Colton moved like a snake in the grass, sliding closer, closer, closer still until he was right there, right in front of me.

He pressed his face to the bars, hands going to rest upon them, and that was when I snapped.

My hands encircled his throat, and I yanked him so close I almost pulled his entire head through the bars.

"I'm only going to say this once: if you *ever* come near Camille again, I will personally hunt you down and slit your fucking wrists to make it look like you did it yourself. I'm good with the topic of suicide, you know. I can make it look like you did this on purpose. Blood doesn't scare me. I've almost died three times, so I've got nothing left to lose, but you do, don't you *Colton*?"

I spat his name like a curse, but I wasn't done yet.

Even as the urine dripped down his leg and created a foul smelling puddle on the floor spilling out around us.

"Or maybe you'd like me to knock you out and tie you up, just to wake you up as soon as I kick the stool and let you realize you're dying, hanging there by a belt...single gunshot wound to the forehead? I could just put the pistol in your mouth, place your fingers over the trigger and...

BAM!"

Colton flinched so hard it felt like his body was at the start of having a seizure.

I couldn't stop the dark laughter from rolling off my tongue.

"That's what I thought."

One final shove and he was on the ground just as Officer Murphy came storming through the doors, no doubt having watched my little show on the cameras.

"I'm done, I'm done. And if he knows what's good for him—he's fucking done, too."

I was *really* fucking nervous.

Parker had told me the night before that Cami would be returning, among other things, and I was sweating bullets.

I'd already gotten my anger out on Colton last night, so my emotions were on a tight leash.

Until I pulled into the parking lot, and then everything rushed right back into my head.

What if she wasn't ready to see me? I hadn't tried calling or texting, just in case she wasn't ready for that either.

She hadn't reached out to me at all.

I was beginning to ask myself if that was the wrong move as I swung off my bike and slung the helmet across the handlebars and locked it there so the clowns who liked to pick at me wouldn't try to steal it.

Parker was there, an encouraging smile and steady hand, but then, he wasn't really what I needed at that moment despite all the help and support he'd given me since I'd returned from the hospital.

It was this strange sense of knowing, of this gut feeling that had me whipping my head to her.

It was like the skies parted and the clouds made way for the sun to shine directly onto her, where the light always should have been.

Her face crumpled into a half sob, half grin, and then I wasn't thinking anything anymore—only the sudden need to get to her, to hold her close to my body, to crush her against my side and never let her leave there again.

Her sweet vanilla scent hit my nose just a half a second before she was there, right where she belonged, and then I wished my arms never had to let go ever again.

"Cami."

Her head whipped up in surprise, eyes wide and brimming with unshed tears.

"Grey," she choked out, her voice a melancholic whisper of everything I could tell she wanted to say but couldn't.

We were attracting a crowd, but it wasn't like either of us were bothered even a little bit by it.

"Want to get out of here?"

She nodded before burying her face in my chest, arms tightening around my waist, and damn if I couldn't find another memory more perfect than this one.

One more second, I'd pull away in one more second. Just to let this feeling linger and soak into my bones all the way down into my soul where she'd nestled herself a place amongst the shadows and spiky walls I'd created.

But then I was leading her away from that crowd in the parking lot, away from my brother with a satisfied smile on his face, away from the rest of the world and everything that came with it.

Onto my bike, with her arms around my waist and her legs tightening around mine.

On the road, it was just the two of us and the open air and everything we'd never been able to say to each other until now.

Until I drove her directly to the place where I'd first taken her, to the lookout hidden in the trees in the silence of nature swimming with an orchestra of life.

I was the first one to swing off the bike, as Cami was left half dumbstruck on the motorcycle.

Goddamn she looked good on my bike.

"You can talk."

I came up to her as she slung one leg around so that she was facing me.

I edged my way in between her legs and placed both hands on either side of her on the leather seat.

The sun threw a stray beam through the trees and it flickered in her eyes, turning the dark brown in them a pure amber; so light they almost seemed golden—not brown, but gilded in light and sparkling with beauty.

"I can."

"You...your voice is so deep."

I was aware how much deeper it was compared to everyone else, but it was a result of the trauma to my vocal cords. My voice held a distinct smoky quality, almost like I was a singer and had overused it my whole life, but it was better than nothing.

"I...I didn't come to see you."

I couldn't help the chuckle that came out at her words. She was just staring at me in shock, like she couldn't actually believe that I was really there.

"No, you didn't."

"But—you're not mad at me?"

"Why would I be mad at you, Cami?"

"Because...because I just...left."

Somewhere nearby, a blue butterfly fluttered onto a low hanging tree branch. A squirrel darted up that very same tree. A songbird chirped its call into the serene, still air.

I reached up to push Cami's hair behind her shoulder, threading my fingers through the strands and cupping the back of her neck.

"I am anything but mad at you."

My voice was a hoarse whisper, but then her hands were wrapped around my shoulders and pulling me into her and—

the first brush of her lips against mine was a symphony of joy and triumph unparalleled by any drink, any drug of choice, any vice I could've used to hide the pain.

My mouth drank her in and pulled her soul out to dance with mine in the clouds while our bodies surged forward and came together in a tangle of limbs and kisses flush with an emotion we were both too scared to name.

She was the sun and I was the shadow swirling around it, blinded by her brightness but cast in gilded darkness.

This was what my body and soul had been craving for so long, but after what she'd gone through I wasn't going to push her. She'd been the one to grab me and hold on like she was never going to let go, and I wasn't going to object to that when it was what I wanted, too.

Those legs wrapped around my waist and pulled me closer, impossibly closer, until the only space between us was from the barriers of our clothes.

Her hands were in my hair, tugging like she thought she could pull my soul from my body and drink it down until it mixed with hers.

"Grey," a whimpered whisper falling off swollen pink lips.

"I'm sor—"

"You have nothing to be sorry for. I know why you stayed away. I understand."

"You...you know?"

"I know."

The weight of those two words seemed to undo her, and those earlier unshed tears slipped down her unmarred cheeks drawing lines of pain down her face.

"Hey," I started, reaching for her, but she buried her face in my chest instead.

I held her through her shaking, through the hiccuping sobs, through the pain flowing through her body until my own absorbed it as its own.

"How—why are you still even here with me, then? If you know?"

"What the hell are you talking about?"

"Don't make me say it, Grey. You know what happened to me, what *he* did to me. It's disgusting. I'm dis—"

I cut her off mid-tirade by placing one soft, featherlight kiss to her forehead.

Then, one to each of her cheeks even as they came away salty with her tears.

"He is the one that's disgusting, not you, Cami. Never you. What he did changes nothing about who you are or what you mean to me."

"I'm scared."

The truth of that emotion in her eyes was almost enough to knock me off my feet, but somehow I stayed steady, strong for her, strong like I wished someone would've been for me so long ago.

"That's okay. You can be scared. But one thing you'll never have to be scared of is me leaving. I'm here for good. I am all fucking in, good days, bad days, days you don't want to see my face, days you don't want to get out of bed, days you almost burn yourself in the shower because you're too numb to feel anything else—I'm going to be fucking right here, Cami. Right by your side."

"But...but why would you do that for me?"

"Haven't you been listening?"

"No, I have, I just—it's hard for me to believe someone could ever be there for me like that. All anyone ever does in my life is leave. That's why I couldn't see you after what happened with your surgery. I was so sure you were going to think I wasn't worth it, that you were going to break my heart...so I guess I just decided to break my own instead to save you the trouble of doing it yourself."

She could barely look me in the eye after what she'd said, so she grabbed the front of my shirt to tug me closer and rest her cheek on my chest.

I immediately began rubbing soothing circles onto her back, my breath hitching as she tightened her grip on me, like she was scared I'd disappear if she let go.

"I was so scared because I think—no, I know that I was falling in love with you. The thought of you dying, and leaving just like everyone else...it was all too much."

I was frozen. A still statue that she was clinging to, but she was waiting for me to say something, to respond to what she'd just said.

"Was? As in, past tense?"

She pulled back and faced me with a bravery I hadn't seen on her face since the last calm night we'd shared before her father had called her. The night everything had gone downhill.

She pulled her arms back, and while my body missed her touch, everything else inside me lit up as she signed three words to me that she couldn't say with her voice, which somehow made it all the more perfect for us.

"I love you."

We'd spent nearly every waking minute with each other for two weeks before everything blew up in our lives.

I knew her favorite color, food, the name of her favorite shampoo.

I knew her favorite Marvel character (Mantis, which made a strange kind of sense), her favorite movie, tv show, the name of her childhood stuffed animal (Pinky).

I knew she moaned out loud when she bit into a particularly delicious piece of food (most notably bacon), I knew she clipped her toenails in the shower, I knew she did one-sock-one-shoe instead of sock-sock-shoe-shoe, and I knew...

I knew that I was desperately and hopelessly in love with her.

So when I held her hands in mine and leaned in to her ear, I made sure she knew just that.

"I love you, Camille Astor."

She shivered at the sound of her name on my tongue, and then the world went from black and white to unflinching pigment, and suddenly the color grey wasn't so bad anymore.

Suddenly, her golden hues mixed with the pale colorless aura dancing around me and shimmered like the pale light of day breaking over a new world, and this was only the beginning.

Epilogue

"**S**eriously? I'm trying to run a tight ship here. This isn't free labor."

"Uh, technically it is free. You're teaching us how to paint cave art."

"Smart ass."

Ever since he'd gotten his voice back Grey had been nothing but a smart ass. It wasn't like I was actually complaining, though. I would've given anything for him to talk back to me the way he had been just six months ago. Now that it was actually happening, it was hard to believe sometimes.

"Cami, try to use a relaxed hand when you're spreading the paint."

"Yeah, babe. Relax your hand."

Grey sidled up beside her and slipped his hands around her waist and she giggled. She actually fucking giggled.

Jesus, these two were disgusting.

I hid my smile though. I didn't want them to know their PDA actually made me happy.

It wasn't the PDA in itself that made me happy. No, that I could do without seeing constantly. It was the happiness shining clear and true on both of their faces that forced the smile from hiding and back onto my face where it belonged.

Cami and Grey could finally relax. Colton was sentenced to seven to ten years in the state penitentiary where her father was currently doing time for the murder of his mother.

Normally when a man was accused of sexual assault or harassment, it went either unpunished or completely ignored, but in this case with dozens of women coming forward after he'd attacked her at the high school on camera, the case had garnered national attention.

His trial was publicized across the world, and he wasn't given the option for parole. He was going to serve his entire sentence, and be on the sex offender's list for the rest of his life when he got out. *If* he got out. Sex offenders didn't do well in prison with other inmates who'd committed different crimes.

Alec came up to my side and I pulled back to look up into his brown eyes. There were stars in them, floating through his irises in the dim amber light of the cavern.

"Abstract this time? What's this one supposed to be?"

"A monster...confronting his own inner demons."

I didn't tell him what it was actually referring. The monster was me, and the demons were the people in the world around me.

Though I wasn't nearly as conflicted as Alec, I still had my own issues to work through before I could be truly happy with the turns and twists my life had taken.

I finally remembered the reason I'd gotten into a fight with Colton the night I'd met Cami at the football game and my concussion had kept me from remembering the events.

He'd told me that he was the one who'd basically cat-fished Leah Maren into my brother's bed. He'd been texting her from

an unregistered number pretending to be Grey. He even gave her
the code to our garage for her to slip into our house with.

She'd been waiting half naked in my brother's bed when I went
inside knocking. I hadn't even realized Grey's motorcycle wasn't
in the driveway. I'd only blamed first and asked questions never.

But that wasn't the entire reason for the fight...

He'd been on my phone looking at a video from a rival high
school, the players on the team trash talking our school and
promising a beatdown the next time our schools met on the field.

It wasn't the video that had his attention, though.

It was the text from Alec that he pulled down and started going
through our entire thread while I'd been gearing up for the scrimmage that was where we'd eventually come to blows.

It was the photos we'd sent back and forth to each other that
had him ready for the mocking.

It was the messages he'd sifted through and the privacy that
he'd invaded and it was the words coming out of his mouth that
I'd thrown the punch for.

It was Alec's identity that I'd kicked his stomach on the ground
for.

It was the hit I'd taken to my skull and lost my memory for.

The only person I'd ever told was Grey when he was in his coma,
and in those texts with Alec.

"And are you ready to do that?"

"What?"

Alec's words had pulled me out of my reverie.

"Are you ready to confront your inner demons?"

"I am if you are."

He didn't waste time slinging an arm over my shoulder and
turning me to face the newest mural I'd painted with delicate

purples and deep forest greens, splashes of deepest black cutting through the middle.

"I've been ready for a while, I think I've just been waiting for you."

"Parker! I don't think Grey's doing this right."

I sighed out and pulled myself from Alec's warmth and went to see what Grey's painting issue was.

"That's because you mixed too many colors and now it's all just poop brown."

"I don't think I've ever heard you say the word 'poop'. Say it again."

Grey leaned in Cami's ear and whispered something to her which made her erupt into a fit of laughter.

I couldn't wait until I could have something like the two of them. Ever since they'd escaped from school their first day back, the two of them had been inseparable even despite the fact that she no longer lived with us.

Apparently it would be considered inappropriate for the two of them to be dating and living together because of her foster placement.

Not like my father had any say in what happened in our home anymore after my mom filed for divorce.

Apparently she was working with Grey to find his birth father, too.

Things were looking up.

I glanced back over at Alec who stared at my latest mural in silent contemplation.

Yes, things were definitely very much looking up.

Grey wrapped his arms around Cami's small frame as she picked up a can of spray paint and aimed it at Grey's sludge colored base.

"What are you going to do with neon purple?"

"I don't know, but purple always makes everything look better."

She sprayed the paint out in arching circles, and only then did I realize that Grey had covered up the monstrosity I'd painted in my grief over his flatlining only three months ago; the woman with her lifeblood dripping from the bullet wound in her1 head.

It had triggered something in Cami and made me regret ever painting it in the first place.

It was good that Cami and Grey were painting over it. It was good that they were reclaiming it as their own.

She sprayed and slashed arcing strokes across the cavernous walls overlain with the dark brown base.

There was a smile on her face that I hadn't seen in the entire time that I'd ever known her.

Grey's hands tightened on her, and I felt a pinching sensation overcome my chest. This was too much to watch, to bear. Their happiness, though well deserved and earned, was slamming into my heart and forcing me to bear witness was almost torturous.

I slipped out of the cave unnoticed, following the sounds of Alec throwing rocks at the outside entrance.

"Hey," I started, not sure where I was going with this but wanting to get it out nonetheless.

"Hey."

For a moment, we just stared at each other.

There was nothing we could do in the gravity that kept us suspended in a realm of limbo, a sea of 'what if's' and could've been's. Maybe if things had been different from the start. Maybe if I'd actually seen things for what they were and not for what the world would do to me if I decided to be true to myself...

"I don't really know how to do this," I began, stuttering on every other word because the words felt like lead bullets in my mouth and I was cocking the proverbial gun by starting down this path, this dangerous, treacherous path.

"How to do what?"

It was like I was under water for so long, and finally staring at him was like parting the surface and watching as the sun came out for the first time in a decades long stretch of ever present darkness. It was like having him here with me in this life was everything I could ever want, even despite the fact that I'd denied it to myself for so long.

I didn't want to admit it; that there was something wrong, some-thing different, something that would have others look at me differently.

But standing before him, I realized it.

There was nothing wrong with me. There was nothing wrong with who I was in love with, and I was going to make sure he knew that too.

"I thought I was bi for a while, you know? I appreciated a beau-tiful girl. I still can, but I'm not attracted to them. Not really. So I guess that makes me...gay. I've never said it out loud before, but we've texted about you before, so I started going over important moments in my life. How I lost my virginity and felt nothing. How I was just going through the motions of a life I wasn't even sure I wanted as my own anymore.

"It was when you started trying to hurt yourself for how you felt inside that I realized how much I could sympathize with you. Because I wasn't just hiding this thing from the rest of the world; I was hiding it from myself. I wasn't about to admit it to myself, ever. I was positive it would never come out, that *I* would never come out. But after everything with Grey and him almost dying, three times so far at only eighteen, I realized that it was time I stopped worrying about the what-if's and actually decided that it was time to stop being scared. I know you've been going through a lot, Alec, but I want you to know that you don't have to go through it alone."

He didn't look my way. His eyes faced the horizon in the distance, wistful temptation crossing his star flecked features.

"I've known about you for a while. We used to tease each other all the time on the phone, and we've flirted with pictures and texts for a long time now, but it was never in person. You'd never been this direct with me. I was convinced you were going to live in the closet forever. I...I told my parents yesterday. Everything I was worried about—them kicking me out of the house and disowning me—it was all in my head. They were so happy for me. They knew all along."

"Alec, that's—"

"But I still wasn't happy. Because the one person I wanted to be out with, to be happy with, was still in denial. How long have you known this and waited to tell me?"

"I've known it all along, but I didn't want to admit it to myself. I've known I was going to tell you since Grey's surgery complications, but I was just waiting for the right time."

"And you think this is the right time?"

"Yes? No? Why does it feel like you're mad at me right now?"

He stepped closer, hair glinting in the spray of sunlight beams coating his body.

He was so tall—he towered right over me, but I didn't back down. I stared right up into his gilded eyes.

"I'm not mad. I'm overwhelmed...I've waited for this moment for a whole hell of a lot longer than you'd think. Fuck, Parker. Do you know how long I've been in love with you?"

I didn't waste a moment. I was going to make this happen.

My first *real* kiss.

It was warm and strong, his lips slipping between mine like they were always made to be there. His arms wrapped around my sides and pulled me tighter to him as the breath left my lungs in one large whoosh of air.

I was tasting colors and sifting stars through my fingertips.

I was floating through galaxies and spinning in interstellar webs of sunlight and cosmic dust.

I was everything and nothing all at once, pulled apart and stitched back together by this man holding me like I was the world to him.

He pulled away suddenly, breathless, flushed, beautiful. Perfect. *Mine.*

"You're in love with me?"

A wolfish grin pulled at his features.

"I thought that was obvious."

"I love you too."

Another grin, cocky and the hottest thing I'd ever seen.

"I know."

He pulled me by the arm back into the cave and wrapped it around my waist, but I didn't pull away even as Cami and Grey turned to view us walking in together.

"Hey, I think she finally got this right!"

"Let's see what you painted, then," I said to cami as we ambled over to the spot of cave that they'd claimed for themselves.

I stopped dead in my tracks.

I'd been expecting paint splatters, not an actual outline of a painting that, once fully fleshed out, would be breathtaking.

They were silhouettes, and for some reason I could discern which person they represented.

There was Cami in the middle, her silhouette purposefully smaller than the rest while the rest of the figures spread out on either side of her. Grey was to her immediate left, tall and imposing, and I was there on her right, steady and strong.

Fanning out, I could pinpoint her best friend Mori, my mother, even Alec and Victoria as the two of them had grown close in the aftermath of the attack.

More and more figures panned out as she began explaining the meaning behind the painting.

"It's supposed to be everyone in my life, and everyone who's ever been in it. I used to think I was alone in the world, but I was wrong. I have people that are there for me. I have you guys, my old foster siblings, my new friends, and I still have my mom, somewhere out there."

Grey turned her toward him and she tipped her head up and laughed when he brushed a thumb beneath her wet lashes.

"You're right. You're not alone—none of us are. We've got each other."

"Alright, no more waterworks, let's get back to painting."

Cami sniffled once more and Alec caught my eye with a gleam sparkling in it.

"Nah, you have one assignment left before that."

"What?"

I didn't give her or Grey a chance to back up before I stumbled forward with Alec on my arm as we pulled them into a crushing bear hug.

"Group hug? Really?"

Grey's voice was dry and sarcastic, but the smile on his face told me that he was secretly happy for it.

The sun crested over the lip of the cave at the opening directly above us, and for a moment the entire cave was awash in pale yellow sunlight—every painting I'd ever painstakingly brushed and sprayed and sketched bathed in brightness that it normally never received.

Reds and blacks glimmered harshly in the light; pinks and whites glittering beautifully with the new bright treatment the paint was receiving.

Scenes of pain and beauty glowed for a few moments as I clasped the people I loved around me, and for that one moment together, the entire world gleamed bright and pure and vivid, shining with all the pigments of a kaleidoscopic rainbow stretching over a dreary horizon.

I picked up the nearest spray paint bottle and held it out with a flourish to my family beside me.

"So, who's next?"